The Unpleasant Poet

The Unpleasant Poet

C.D. Payne

Aivia Press

ISBN-13: 978-1882647088

ISBN-10: 1-882647084

Thanks to Philip Larken
for the inspiration

Warm thanks again to Till Hack for his editorial assistance.

OFFHAND I can think of four reasons why I drink:

First, I'm a creative person, and what I create always falls disturbingly short of my expectations. Alcohol helps neutralize the disappointment.

Second is my appearance. I'm tall and bald and wear thick glasses. In photos I look like a serial killer on the lam. Or Dr. Mengele's lab assistant. I used to say I was prematurely bald, but now at age 38 it's fairly unexceptional to be bald. My bare dome is one of those polished cabochons that looks like it never was capable of sustaining hair. Since my eyeglass lenses are so thick, I don't bother with designer frames. I buy the generic black plastic like Clark Kent wears.

Third is my name. I go by my middle name Daniel. Danny Nixon is what they call me. I'll give you one guess what my first name is. My dad, a rock-rib Republican, thought his hero was robbed when he had to abdicate. Nah, we're not related. And yes, I have looked into changing my name. Too much work. Anyway, I'm kind of used to it now. It suits me.

And finally, I drink to cope with stress. I refer you to an incident a couple of weeks before Christmas in 2016. A guy and I are driving down an empty highway late at night in a distant suburb of San Francisco. In the trunk of my car is a dead body. At least I hope it's dead. I have my doubts. The fellow driving looks remarkably calm. Nerves of steel. I, on the other hand, am a wreck. Cold sweat, the shakes, heartbeat up there in hummingbird territory. My life had become one fiasco after another. Clearly what I desperately needed was a stiff drink.

SEPTEMBER, 2016

Vacation! On the road to Tahoe in my new car: a 1978 Chrysler Cordoba. You may remember that model. Mine has cloth seats though, not the fine "Corinthian leather" that pitchman Ricardo Montalban flogged on TV. (My previous car, a 1978 AMC

Concord, needed a part that has disappeared from this planet.)
I liked the Cordoba's color (Diaper Tan) and the fact that the
vinyl roof was peeling on top. If you're going for the bald look,
I say why not be consistent? I talked the seller down to $1,200
cash. The oversized chrome spinner wheels were worth at least
that much. It was like I was getting the car for free.

I only drive cars from 1978, the year of my birth. Same for
stereos and other appliances, though I had to make an excep-
tion for my TV after my old Trinitron died.

A guy I know who's trying to be a poet wrote this about my
new car:

Danny's Cordoba

A cool chrysalis from Chrysler:
The Cordoba of the disco years.
Gleaming glamour on a budget.
Detroit styling with an amigo flair.
A Mopar 318 throbs within;
Bigger than a six, yet easy on gas.

Four decades down the road
The transformation is complete:
Aspiration rusts, glamour fades,
Petroleum smells intrude as
Wings of chrome bear aloft
The resplendent tackiness.

Uh-oh, bad news. The Cordoba's cigarette lighter doesn't
work. This is a very serious flaw in a Danny Nixon car. I can't believe I forgot to check that when I was inspecting the car. Sure,
I can use my pocket lighter, but that maneuver is so much less
cool than flaming your Chesterfield with the red-hot glowing
coil. Definitely something my mechanic will have to jump on
when I return. Hell, it almost merits an emergency call to A.A.A.
right now.

It was raining when I got to Tahoe City. I don't mind rain.
It's like a free wax job for your car. Shines the metal right up.
A tan Cordoba glistening in the rain: it doesn't get much bet-

ter than that. I booked a room at the Durango Motel. I stayed here once before and found a Harrah's $100 poker chip stuck in the Gideon Bible. It's as close as I've ever come to a religious experience. Too bad they've filled in the kidney-shaped pool. It used to be a place where you could chat up chicks while closely inspecting the goods. I expect a pool wouldn't be getting much action anyway since it's presently 49 degrees and still drizzling. The radio says we may get some snow tonight. Is it still mid-September, or did I hurtle through a time warp?

I like this motel because it's right next door to a liquor store. And no view of the lake to jack up the price. Lots of history has gone down in these decrepit cowboy-themed rooms. You know the mattress itself has witnessed 10,000 acts of sexual intercourse. You're definitely reclining on hallowed ground here. The bedspread smells a bit rank though.

Three days later. Haven't made it to a casino yet. Been holed up in the Durango swigging Jack Daniels, smoking Chesterfields, and watching daytime TV. A whole world of entertainment I'm missing daily while at work. In my next life I'm coming back as a bored housewife. Just me, the TV, the gin bottle, the neglected vacuum cleaner, and baby comatose in his crib. You know I'd have my hand in my panties all the time, keeping that button raw and feverishly aglow. I'd make the paperboy collect in person and seduce the lad in between game shows.

Finally got it together to shower and shave and hit a few of my favorite bars. I avoid the places with shiny arrays of Harleys lined up out front. You could be chatting up some likely prospect and find out too late she's somebody's biker chick. Fortunately, many of those ladies are now heavily tattooed and therefore easier to spot. There's always a trade-off for patrons of dive bars: attractively priced liquor vs. the risk of needing expensive dental work after being laid flat by some brawler.

At Sierra Stumpy's there was one unaccompanied gal down at the end of the bar. She let me buy her a cream sherry.

"Where's your hat?" she asked as we clicked glasses. I was sticking with bourbon.

"Don't wear one. I don't mind the rain."

"You smell like my ex-husband."

"How's that?"

"He smoked Chesterfields too."

"Wow, you can tell a person's brand just from their smell?"

"Only Chesterfields. I'm surprised you're not over in Nevada. You can smoke in the bars there."

"True. But then I'd have to drive back on treacherous mountain roads in the dark. I wouldn't want to wreck my vintage Chrysler Cordoba."

"Are you by any chance Ricardo Montalban in disguise?"

That confirmed it. She was older than I first thought. Evidently a TV-watcher back in the 1970s. Damn these dingy bars and their dim lighting.

"I wish. My name's Danny."

"That's odd. You look more like a Richard."

Kind of unnerving. "Really? You think so?"

"I almost would have sworn it. My name's Barbara."

"Nice to meet you, Barb. What do you do?"

"I teach third grade."

"Really? You spend your waking hours cramming long division into eight-year-olds?"

"Pretty much. Also how to spell big new words like exciting and interesting."

"Is that exciting and interesting?"

"What do you think, Dick?"

"It's Danny."

"So you say."

"Any chance of advancement in your profession? Do you aspire to be teaching fourth grade someday?"

"Not if I can help it. What do you do, Ricardo?"

"Computer work. Glued to a screen for the man. My life only gets thrilling in my off hours."

"Oh? You a fire-eater in your spare time? A handler of venomous snakes? One of those idiots jumping off high cliffs in squirrel suits?"

I laughed. "You interest me, Barb. You really do."

"I wish I could say the same about you, Tricky Dick."

She surprised me by singing, "How are things in San Clemente?" to the tune of that Glocca Morra song.

"Damn! have we met before?" I asked.

"What do you think?"

"I really don't know. You tell me, Barb."

"Three years ago. Same bar. Different stools. You were drinking vodka tonics like a worldwide shortage was threatening."

"I was in my vodka phase back then. I don't touch the stuff now."

"Still camping out at the Durango, Mr. Nixon?"

"You got it. Did we by any chance, uh, you know?"

"Can't remember, huh? Not very flattering. A girl likes to think she's at least slightly memorable."

"I'm sorry, sweetheart. I must have blacked out the whole incident. How far did we go?"

"Wouldn't you like to know."

"Let me make it up to you, Barb. I'm fairly sober now. Mr. Moderate in all matters. How about we go back to my motel and rewrite history starting on page one?"

"I expect you mean starting on the bed. Sorry, Mr. President, been there, done that. Still having performance issues, are we?"

"Hey, I must have been seriously wasted not to recall a fox like you. I can assure you, darling, that wouldn't be a problem tonight."

"Darn. Too bad, Dicky boy. I guess neither of us will ever know."

With that, she drained her drink in one gulp and strolled out. Damn, she didn't look half bad from the back. Probably no older than late-forties. With a nice matronly bust too. And perhaps a lingering aroma of chalk and waxed classroom floors once you got her clothes off.

Teacher, teacher, teach me to love!

I wish.

I had breakfast the next afternoon across the street at the Lazy Lasso diner. Since I derive 90 percent of my calories from alcohol and nicotine, I don't eat that many meals. A fairly economical lifestyle (if you stick to budget brands) and easy on the teeth. I gave the waitress my most entrancing smile, but she wasn't having any. No wedding ring either, but then everyone is shacking now. The only folks who get married before the first kid arrives these days are gays and the Royal Family of England.

The guy I know trying to be a poet has explored this theme:

Modern Marriage

Marriage is in a parlous state;
No one wants to tie the knot.
Virgins rarely think it's great
To hang real tight on what they've got.

Ministers preach to empty churches;
Teens are playing mom and dad.
Consciences are free of searches;
Fornicators are seldom sad.

Boyfriends now sire all the tots;
Wives are simply not their thing.
Very few rank as touch-me-nots,
Even kiddies do some incesting.

Two/AWAY SHE FLEW

That evening an older woman and I converged on the motel ice machine at the same time. I gallantly let her go first.

"Do you mind if I ask you a question?" she said, filling her plastic bucket.

"I guess not."

"Are you a pimp?"

"Jesus, why do you ask that?"

"I saw you driving that old car with the obscene wheels."

"Those are called spinners. People die every day in the ghetto for such primo wheels. Sorry, I'm not a pimp."

"That's too bad. I was hoping to inquire how you get a girl to stand on a street corner, sell her body to anyone who stops by, and hand over all the money to you."

"I think it has to do with charisma."

"Harrumph," she snorted.

"I'm having a party for one in my room," I said. "Care to join me?"

"I've had a very trying day, young man. But I don't like to drink alone. What are you serving?"

"Bourbon."

"Yuck. I'll bring my own bottle. Give me a minute to freshen up."

She arrived at my door looking pretty much the same. She was dressed in a white blouse and plaid skirt like some vintage Catholic schoolgirl. She was carrying a brand of scotch I'd never seen before.

"I'll stay only if you turn off that damn television," she said.

"Not a problem," I replied, grabbing the remote and switching it off. "Is that an expensive single malt?"

"Hardly. It's Walgreen's house brand. I'm not normally a

boozer, but this day has been a disaster. My husband left me."

"I'm sorry."

"That wasn't the disaster. He left me two years ago. Where are you sitting?"

"On the bed."

"OK, I'll take the chair. I'm not here for any hanky-panky. You can put that out of your mind. I'm old enough to be your mother."

"Right. My name's Danny."

"You can call me Margot. My actual name is similar."

"Want to tell me about your disaster, Margot?" I said, offering her a clean glass.

She helped herself to ice and poured a tall one from her bottle. "My husband left me for a younger woman. Men do that. For this they should be tortured creatively and then shot, but I've adjusted. Moved on. I've been corresponding with a fellow up here. I live in Redding. He persuaded me to come here and join him on a bird-watching hike."

"Like a date?"

"Of course like a date. I didn't drive over 200 miles just to observe some drab mountain birds. He seemed very nice online. Similar interests, progressive politics, and all that."

"You'd seen his photo?"

"Yes. Nothing objectionable in his appearance. Or so I thought."

"What happened?"

"I got here and the man made my skin crawl. I had the most visceral reaction to him. I couldn't get away fast enough. I tried to be civil, but I said a hike with him was out of the question. I drove away as quickly as possible. Fortunately, I hadn't given him the name of my motel."

"What about him turned you off?"

"Just a feeling. But immediate and very powerful. He made my skin crawl! I shudder to think of it."

"Yeah, I know what you mean. I have that effect on people sometimes. Mostly chicks."

"So far, Danny, I'm not getting that vibe from you. You have extraordinarily thick glasses. You must be blind as a bat."

"I got my first pair when I was nine. I was amazed to discover that trees had individual leaves. I thought they were big fuzzy balls like green cotton candy."

"Your neglectful parents should have had your eyes checked before that. What brings you to this dreary budget motel?"

"Vacation. I thought I'd do some gambling, but mostly I watch TV and drink."

"I expect you're a depressed alcoholic with an inappropriate car. Are you married?"

"No, and not likely to be."

"Just as well. I'm sure you're saving some poor girl from a miserable life."

"Yeah, and then down the road I'd dump her for someone younger."

"The male of our species leaves much to be desired. Have you ever been in love?"

"Not really. How about you?"

"Of course. I loved my husband passionately. The rat."

"Well, at least you can say that. Any kids?"

"The usual assortment, scattered to the far winds. What do you do besides drink and watch TV? Any hobbies?"

"I try to pick up women."

This amused her. She laughed heartily, spilling her drink.

"What about that statement strikes you as funny?" I asked.

"Just the incongruity, Danny. I'm sure that hobby is just as valid as any. And do you find it rewarding?"

"I get my share. You'd be surprised how many desperate women there are these days."

"No, I don't think I would be surprised. Not in the least. You get these women to sleep with you?"

"Sometimes. I turn on the charm and down they plop."

"Amazing. And this happens on your first date?"

"It's been known to. That's certainly my goal."

"You enjoy doing it with total strangers?"

"Sure. Why not? Variety is the spice of life."

"No awkwardness after the passion is spent?"

"Not usually."

"She's clutching the sheet to her breasts as she hunts for her brassiere, while you cover up your sticky and now flaccid manhood."

"Is that a question, Margot?"

"That situation doesn't bother you?"

"Not really. I find sex to be a real ice breaker."

"And how do you meet these girls? Do you go on-line and discuss your mutual interests?"

"No. I encounter them in the real world. They have to know right away what they're getting in the looks department. Paul Newman I'm not."

"You could be fairly presentable, Danny, if you cut down on your drinking, ditched the cigarettes, and cleaned yourself up."

"God almighty! Why would I want to do that?"

"Why indeed? You can strike that last remark."

"So, Margot, have you had any dates besides the disaster with the creepy bird watcher?"

"One other in Redding. Set up by a friend. A sincere fellow, but not my type. Sorry, I don't do square dancing at the senior center."

"It might not be that bad. You could give it a try."

"Right. And you could go to AA and turn your life around."

"Touché. Need some more ice in your drink?"

"No, I'm going now before I pass out and become another victim of your hobby. Thanks for the conversation. If you're ever up in Redding, please don't stop and visit."

"I'll be sure not to, Margot. I hope you meet some nice guy. They're out there."

"Right. Mostly buried in our local cemeteries. You take care, Danny."

"Will do. And thanks for the pimp suggestion. Since I've got the requisite flashy car, I'll look into it."

"You do that, Danny dear. I'm sure it beats working for a living."

She was nice enough to leave behind her half-empty bottle. I usually stick to bourbon at higher elevations, but I tried a swallow of her off-brand scotch. I've had worse. I may be stopping in at Walgreens now for more than just jock-itch cream and condoms.

After the bourbon was gone and most of the scotch, I made my 18th call to my girlfriend Kimberly. I think she may have given up on me at last. She hasn't responded to my last 17 calls, including the message I left last week begging her to go to Tahoe with me. She wasn't expecting much for her birthday last month, but the used blender (a thrift store find) may have missed the mark. OK, the base was rusty and the glass was chipped. It's just that I hate a girl without a blender. How can it be party time if she's not equipped to whip me up a stiff margarita?

There was a time when Kimberly was hinting around for a ring. Doesn't that girl realize marriage is supposed to be forever? OK, I'm stuck with myself, but I don't know why anyone else would want to be. The rusty blender probably was a wise move after all.

As usual I got Kimberly's machine. I said I was up in Tahoe City with my new girlfriend Margot. I said I hoped she was enjoying her blender, which was the final model made in the USA and would be whirling up cocktails long after she's deceased. Then I turned out the lights and crawled into bed.

* * *

Two inches of slushy snow on the streets this a.m. and me with no snow chains. A good excuse to stay inside and watch TV. I keep missing the free donuts and coffee grudgingly provided in the Durango's lobby. Nothing but crumbs and an empty urn by the time I get there. I bought a frozen pizza at the liquor store to go with my Jack Daniels. Nuked it in the microwave, which the neon sign out front advertises as a "kitchenette." I've unplugged its companion mini refrigerator that quivers like a poodle needing to pee. I'd forgotten how much I love pepperoni. I peel off each cheesy slice, dip it in bourbon, then savor it on my tongue. A real vacation treat. Like a communion wafer for my own private religion.

News bulletin: I have a new neighbor next door. An unaccompanied female, not excessively old or fat, driving a Prius.

She immediately switched on the TV, then headed over to the liquor store. Possible soul mate sighting? Probably not, considering her automotive choice. Still, she bears watching.

After the snow melted, I took an anti-constipation stroll down to the lake, shimmering a brilliant tourist-blue in the late afternoon sun. It's the state's largest natural lake, although most of the shoreline is hogged by Nevada. I sat on a bench and soaked up some restorative vitamin D, while taking a few tipples from my flask. This one is disguised as a large cellphone. It really is a Golden Age for us closet drinkers. Alas, I missed out on smoking's Golden Age. It ended the day they banned tobacco ads from TV in contravention of the Bill of Rights.

Feeling no pain, I nodded off, slumbering peacefully until a pigeon pecked at my toes, bare in my sandals. Why are these urban slum birds loitering beside an alpine lake? And why aren't vast swarms of eagles feeding on such easy prey?

When I returned, my new neighbor was outside in the parking lot inspecting my Cordoba.

"It's a 1978," I informed her, smiling. "The outer wheel sections spin on their own as you drive, producing many fascinating optical effects."

"Cost you a mint to get that vinyl top fixed," she replied, neutrally. Up this close, she was frighteningly attractive. Incandescent topaz eyes. Skin like dew-freshened rose petals. Very clearly out of my league.

"I've scheduled a complete overhaul as soon as I get back," I lied. "Going to cherry her out. Are you on vacation too?"

"Business. I work for the Water Resources Board."

"Well, there are millions of gallons in that lake."

"Over 120 million acre-feet," she said. "It's the second deepest lake in the U.S."

"That's impressive," I replied. I didn't want to put her on the spot to name the deepest. Instead I said, "Got any plans for dinner? I hate dining alone."

She gave me one of those long evaluative looks that only chicks display. I hoped I wasn't making her flawless skin crawl.

To tell you the truth, I've never gotten used to that sudden look of alarm/panic that results when I ask a girl out. The best I can hope for is indecision mixed with mild revulsion. I remind myself that hall-of-famer Mickey Mantle, a guy who never married Marilyn Monroe, but might have if she hadn't burnt out on ballplayers, struck out at the plate over 1,700 times. It could be years before I rack up that many rejections from chicks.

"Are you buying?" she asked.

"Of course," I replied.

A gold-digger with a possible drinking problem. I could work with that.

"Want to come in and have a drink first?" I asked.

"I need to take a shower. How about we meet out here at seven? My name's Abby."

"Nice to meet you, Abby. I'm Danny. OK, seven it is. Where do you want to go for dinner?"

"I don't care, Danny. Someplace expensive usually suits me."

"Great. I feel exactly the same."

I didn't, but I knew cheap bastards didn't have a prayer with this girl.

I got cleaned up: coordinating brown wool slacks with my Harris Tweed sport coat. It's that classic collegiate style with leather elbow patches and cigarette burns. No tie, but my shirt was relatively unwrinkled and free of vomit stains. My black socks looked semi-formal under my sandals. To add a note of hopeful optimism I pinned on a vintage WOMEN FOR NIXON button. A $25 gold Rolex knock-off completed the dress-for-success look. I found a toothbrush at the bottom of my suitcase and gave my nicotined teeth a buffing. The Durango was too cheap to provide any free toothpaste samples, so I dipped my brush in the little shampoo bottle instead. Rather nasty, but good for freshening the breath.

Abby had opted for the tourist-destination evening sportswear look. Very fetching and nothing too complicated to remove when grappling in the throes of passion. Her figure I'd rank in the 99th percentile for libido inflaming. She examined the interior of my Cordoba and declined to enter it.

"Let's walk, Danny," she said, taking my arm. "I know a good place just a few blocks away. And no possible DUIs on the way back."

A gal who intended to do some serious drinking on my tab. A mixed blessing to be sure.

As it turned out, she made do with an $85 cabernet, most of which I drank. My liver doesn't mind wine as an occasional light tonic. Abby ordered the Seared Bay Scallops appetizer ($8.00) and the Elk Sausage with Black Lentils ($35). I ordered the Meat-less Burger and Fries ($9.00) from the child's menu.

"Had a big lunch did you?" asked our waitress.

"Saving room for dessert," I explained. "My sweet tooth goes on a rampage when I'm on vacation."

We began with the usual exchange of personal details. She said she had been married once, but was now divorced. I said I was the same. (At my age it looks suspicious if you haven't been dragged to the altar at least once.)

"I wanted kids, but Todd didn't, so that was that," she said.

"Same for me, Abby," I lied. "I wanted at least two, but Kim-berly said no way."

"Did she give you a reason, Danny?"

"She'd been attacked and bitten severely by an infant in Safeway, and therefore was gun shy."

"Really? How did that happen?"

"It escaped from its stroller and was terrorizing the store. It made the evening news in the Bay Area. How do you like the wine?"

"I think it's a bit corked, but it's drinkable. I hate to make a fuss by sending wine back."

I interpreted that to mean she'd drink $1.89 wine out of a gallon jug if that was all she could get. She persuaded me to eat one of her $2 scallops. I do like a gal who likes to share. Her elk sausage smelled like a recent zoo escapee, but she tucked in without complaint. My meatless burger was authentically veg-etarian, as was the child's portion of fries.

"You have a hearty appetite," I observed.

"I got up at four today and ran twelve miles."

"Why? Were you being chased?"

"I had meetings scheduled all morning. I work out to clear my mind."

"Same here," I lied. In truth I drink to draw a curtain on my troubled id.

"Are you a runner, Danny?"

"Not lately. Mostly I lift weights."

Lugging in those boxes after a trip to Bottle Chalet is no job for wimps.

"I went out with a guy once who had eyeglass frames like yours. Turns out it contained a miniature camera that was snapping a photo every ten seconds. He was taking photos of me naked and sharing them with his dirtball pals."

"That's criminal! What did you do, Abby?"

"I knocked the glasses off his face with my purse, extracted the micro SD card, and shoved it as far as I could up his nose. He had to make a trip to emergency to have it dug out of his sinuses. He could have had me charged with assault, but he didn't dare."

"Wow, that was, uh, rather forceful. Would you care to check out my glasses?"

"That's OK. I trust you. I've already inspected them closely. A girl can't be too careful these days. Plus, I'm fully dressed. Gee, I'm still hungry. What should we have for dessert?"

Abby had the chocolate bread pudding with brandy sauce ($13) and a cappuccino ($6). I had a scoop of vanilla ice cream ($3) from the kiddy menu.

Over dessert we talked mostly about my life–all details fudged, obscured, or buffed to enhance my appeal. Abby ordered a refill on her cappuccino, then excused herself to go to the restroom. She was gone quite a long time. I ate the rest of her pudding and sneaked a swig or two of her cappuccino. The minutes ticked by. I hoped the long delay didn't imply that she was incapacitated by periodic female trouble. That could put a definite crimp in my evening plans.

Eventually, the waitress dropped by with the check.

"Are you waiting for your wife?" she asked.

"Uh, yes I am."

"I saw her leave quite a while ago by the patio. No rush on the check, sir. You can pay me anytime you're ready."

I paid and hurried back to the Durango. No Prius parked in front of Abby's room. I asked the desk clerk if he knew where the gal in room 17 had gone.

"I guess she left. She said she only wanted the room for the afternoon to rest up before driving back to Frisco. I charged her a full day's rate anyway. We're not running a hot-sheets passion pit here. She a friend of yours?"

"Uh, no. I was just wondering. Say, what time do the donuts show up?"

"Seven a.m."

"And how late can you still get one?"

"On slow mornings they sometimes last until eight."

"Damn! Aren't these people on vacation? Why aren't they sleeping in?"

"I couldn't tell you. Maybe it's the brisk mountain air."

"Could you put a couple aside for me?"

"Sorry, bub. It's first come, first served. And the maid informs me you're violating our no-smoking rule. All our rooms are smoke-free as is clearly stated by our numerous signs."

Who reads signs? I just thought the management was too cheap to provide ashtrays. And that Mata Hari of a maid won't be getting any tips from me.

"Right," I said. "I'll try to remember that."

I walked forlornly back to my room, which had always smelled like untold generations of heavy smokers with unclean socks had been fornicating in it. I lit a Chesterfield and reflected on my evening.

So lovely Abby cut out on me. Frankly, that left me feeling somewhat used. But I guess I always knew she was out of my league. I should have suspected there'd be a catch. Still, I did have the pleasure of dining with the most stunning gal in the joint. I guess that's something. And now I'll never have to face that future day of reckoning when I piss her off and she sticks something dreadful up my nose.

That unpublished poet I know is seldom at a loss for words:

32 Gigabytes Up Your Nose

Beautiful girls favored by nature,
Winners in the game of looks.
Exalted above their plainer sisters:
Leading lives out of storybooks.

Eyes that captivate with a glance.
Princesses of regal pulchritude.
No truck have they with lesser sods;
Away you peons is their attitude.

Peering down their sublime noses,
Ascending life on a golden path,
Their dazzling aura sweeps all before.
Just pray you never incur their wrath.

Three/CAREFREE TO BEASTLY

That alien wine must have goosed my dormant dreamer. Last night I dreamed I was starting grad school. At age 38! The 22-year-olds were looking at me like I had wandered into the building by mistake. Lady professors, many years my junior, were informing me of their office hours and assigning lengthy reading lists. Hard to believe I was once accepted into the graduate programs of several semi-distinguished universities. At the time it seemed like a potential alternative to working for a living. No dice for Danny though. I have as much chance of writing an academic thesis as I have of inching my way up Half Dome by my fingernails. Or exploring Abby's pants.

I was never a striver, so it was find a government job or starve. I tried the post office when I got out of college, but sorting mail made me even more suicidal than usual. Letters were going wildly astray; I couldn't cope with the deluge. The overflow I was having to deep-six in assorted dumpsters. Then it was grunt work in a county hospital, but I'm not a helping person. Nobody liked my attitude. When you're around that much sickness, it's hard to get worked up that someone is dying. Like I'm supposed to care? And sneaking smokes around those oxygen tents was a short route to self-immolation.

Now I work in the basement of the courthouse in the Documents Department. Me and a coworker Tim Chapben produce most of the county documents. Our stuff looks printed, but it's all done on a fancy photocopier. I do the desktop publishing jobs. My latest brochure was "You and Your Probation Officer," a handout for new parolees telling them what they need to do to avoid that return trip. One side in English, the other in Spanish. The deputy in charge thanked me for cleaning up his prose. I had some room left over so I dropped in a stock photo of some clean-cut guys reveling in their ethnic diversity. They didn't look much like the types we get shuffling through.

I'm still pissed about Abby. I suspect ol' Todd may not have been entirely opposed to parenthood. He just didn't want to have kids with her. Hey, Todd, I'm joining your club! Kimberly once broached the subject of children with me. I told her I was mildly titillated by giggling lesbian schoolgirls, but otherwise that age group left me cold. Not the reply she was looking for.

Now that my vacation is ending and it's time to depart, Tahoe City's brief fling with winter is over and summer has returned. The TV is forecasting temps of 105 degrees in the Central Valley today. Not a pleasant prospect since the Cordoba's cooling Freon has long since winged skyward to deplete the ozone layer.

And so we bid a reluctant farewell to scenic Lake Tahoe and the Durango Motel. I never did make it over to the Nevada side to try my luck at a casino. Just as well. I'm still waiting to win nickel one in those joints.

The drive was pleasantly cool until I hit Auburn. Farther on, Sacramento was broiling in the heat like an overdone pork chop. I pulled off the freeway and headed for a neighborhood dive that my dad used to frequent when he had business in that burg. A giant swamp cooler on the roof was trying to recreate the humidity of Ho Chi Minh City. Over the bar a big new TV was tuned to a college football game. I hate it when perfectly adequate dive bars aspire to sports bar status. If they must have a TV, it should be smallish and showing: A) boxing or B) wrestling. Sweaty pummeling and grappling are the only appropriate programming choices.

I sat at the bar and requested a tall glass of their coldest draft beer.

"That would be Bud Light," said the bartender.

"Make it your second coldest," I said.

He poured my drink and brought me change from my twenty. "You going to buy a drink for Smitty there?" he asked, nodding toward an old guy a few stools away. "He's turning 70 today."

"Sure. Give him what he's drinking."

Smitty, a serious drinker, was downing boilermakers.

"Thanks," he said, hoisting his beer glass. "You know what I hate about getting old?"

"No, what?" I said.

"Not only do you get shorter all the time, but your dick shrinks too. That's news you won't read in the *A.A.R.P. Magazine*."

"Wow. Sorry to hear that," I chuckled.

Some people get happy when they drink, some get mean. Evidently, Smitty was the type that got candid.

"It gets worse," he continued. "Your sensitivity goes to hell too. Next time you have sex slap on four or five condoms. That's what it feels like getting laid when you're 70–assuming you can still get it up."

"Have you had things checked out?" I asked. "You might have some kind of nerve problem."

"No. I've got an age problem. I've discussed it with other guys my age. Same story for all of us. Of course, it doesn't help that after five kids my old lady is wider down there than a Greyhound bus. I might as well be waving it in the breeze for all the stimulation I get."

More information than I really wanted; I decided to concentrate on the football game. Smitty swallowed his shot in one gulp.

"Here's my advice," he went on. "Get as much of it as you can now while you can still enjoy it. You married, buddy?"

"Uh, no," I said. "Not me."

"That's smart. A different girl every night of the week and two on Sunday. That's what you need. That's where I'd be if I was 40 years younger. I'd be milkin' every damn drop out of that thing."

"Right," I said, finishing my beer and heading for the door. "You have a nice birthday."

"Thanks for the drink," he called. "And don't forget. Keep that thing workin' overtime. These are your prime years!"

Gee, I hope not, I thought as I lit a cigarette in the oppressive heat and headed toward my car. Still, having a steady girlfriend at my age might be worth considering. Someone willing to put out on a semi-regular basis with a minimum of fuss. Hell, that should be doable. It's not like my standards are all that high.

When I got home, my landlady informed me that: 1. A man had been here looking for me. 2. I needed to get rid of my dead AMC Rambler.

"What man?" I asked. "What did he want?"

"I don't know. He didn't say. I only allotted you one parking space, not two."

"I know, Mrs. Goodsolm. I'll move it right away. Let me get unpacked first. I just got back from my vacation."

I rent the attic in an old house from an even older lady. Chilly in winter, stifling in summer, but the modest rent doesn't overtax my budget.

"Where did you go, Danny?" she asked.

"Tahoe."

"You didn't get very tanned."

"Not the greatest weather. It snowed one day."

"Snow in September! I could never live up there. Don't forget to move your car."

"Right away, Mrs. Goodsolm."

I decided to remove its license plates and push it out to the street. With any luck the city will tow it away for free. A fellow came along just in time to help. He pushed and I steered.

"Hey, thanks for your help," I said, now parked at the curb in a bus zone.

"Are you Richard Daniel Nixon?" he asked.

"That's me," I replied.

"You've been served," he said, handing me a legal document.

"What the fuck is this?"

"A temporary restraining order. You'll find the date of your court hearing noted inside. Are you related to Tricky Dick of Watergate fame?"

"No, I'm not. Who the fuck wants me restrained?"

"Your domestic partner, I expect. Have a nice day!"

I took the TRO upstairs, put on my thickest glasses, and looked it over. Damn! Kimberly had signed a complaint against me, alleging I was making "harassing phone calls" and had "threatened her life."

What the fuck!

I poured myself a stiff drink and called Kimberly's friend Denise.

"Oooh-ee, she done dropped yo' ass. You history, dude!"

Denise is a middle-aged white gal from Oakland, who for some reason adopts the persona of a black party girl when talking to me.

"What's with this damn restraining order?"

"You a menace, Danny baby. You be enjoined to stay 100 yards back from that chick 24/7. You gotta go to Home Depot. Get yo'self one of those *lo-o-ong* tape measures."

"If she didn't want me to phone her, she could have answered my call and told me so."

"That girl figure you smart enough to deduce that shit yo'self. I say prob'ly not knowin' him."

"And what's this bullshit about my threatening her life?"

"She savin' that tape. Gonna play it back for da judge. You sayin' she gonna be dead before that cheapo blender you give her. She got the goods on you now, dude!"

"That's ridiculous, Denise. I was just making the point that my gift was better than she assumed."

"Judge gonna make that restrainin' order permanent, Danny. Gonna be on yo' record ev'ry time a cop pulls you over. They gonna be approachin' you wit' they guns drawn. Kimberly done fixed yo' ass, dude."

"Tell Kimberly I'm sorry about the misunderstanding. Tell her if she cancels the order, I'll leave her alone for good. I'll never have anything to do with her. Ever again! I don't want to cause her any trouble or worry."

"Too late, Tricky Dick. That train already done leff da station. You goin' down big time, convict Danny!"

"Just tell her what I said, Denise. And lay off the fake ghetto talk. That's racist and offensive."

"You in big trouble, bald guy. You treated her bad. I tol' her you weren't no marriage material. Now she puttin' a big crimp in yo' flabby butt!"

"Good-bye, Denise. Just tell her what I said, OK?"

"Sho' 'nough, honey. You have yo'self a super nice day!"

Personally, I think Denise is some sort of racially confused closet lesbian who wants to get into Kimberly's pants even more than I did–not that I ever brought much enthusiasm to that task.

* * *

Next morning the Rambler was still there, but now a ticket was gracing its windshield. Probably none of the parties involved had much hope of that being paid. I phoned Sid, my graying auto mechanic. He was willing to make an emergency house call on Sunday to deal with my inoperative cigarette lighter for $100 cash plus parts. I said that sounded fair.

Sid arrived with his toolbox and a bag of donuts. He sold me two custard-filled bars for the full retail price. In less than two minutes he replaced a faulty fuse and fixed my problem. He charged me an additional $10 for the fuse, which may have been excessive even for him. I forked over the ten spot and asked his age.

"Be 69 next March. Still rebuilding carburetors with the best of them."

"I encountered a contemporary of yours in a bar this week. He said having sex when you're 70 is like doing it while wearing four or five condoms."

"Your point being?"

"That sensitivity declines radically with age. Plus, your dick shrinks. Is that true?"

Sid flashed me a long hard look. "Yeah, that's about the size of it. Sucks doesn't it?"

"Big time!" I gasped. "How come we're not warned about this when we're younger?"

"Why do you think? Guys my age don't want to admit we're not studs any more. I hear it's even worse for you smokers. Just make sure you develop some side interests. Me, I like to read hot rod magazines. My old lady plays bingo and dotes on the grandkids."

Discouraged, I asked Sid what it would cost to resurrect the Cordoba's dead A/C.

"Be at least a grand, Danny. Probably quite a bit more. The warm weather's winding down. Bring it by the shop next spring if it's still running and I'll have a look at it."

"What do you mean if it's still running? You said the 318 was a great motor!"

"It's an OK motor. But this heap is nearly 40 years old. That's a lot of miles under the bridge. God knows how many times your odometer has turned over."

"It's no older than I am, Sid. And I'm still running strong."

Sid looked at me skeptically. "Right. I meant to say bring it by the shop if *you're* still around."

All this was so unsettling I bought three more donuts off him, which I paired with a quart of brandy. Working together, they eventually restored my equanimity.

Another versification effort by that unknown poet:

The Male in Decline

Three times a day
Is what you crave
When you're 17.
No fluids do you save.

Three times a week
You're regularly bedded,
When you're 25
And newly wedded.

Three times a month
Is what you're allotted,
When you're 40
And no longer besotted.

Three times a year
You may cop a tingle,
When you're 70,
If still able to mingle.

Four/SORE ON THE OFFICE FLOOR

What compares to the horror of returning to work after a week's vacation? Truly a blow to one's newly restored mental health. The spirit rebels, plus one is confronted by that stack of backed-up work. And where the fuck was my coworker Tim? He didn't show up and he didn't call in sick. I was left to cope with running this entire department by myself. No wonder I spent most of the day chain-smoking outside by the back entrance. I also had to take mucho grief from sheriff's deputies who heard about my TRO. No, these are not kept confidential, but are widely circulated among police jurisdictions. What an invasion of my privacy! I said it was all a big misunderstanding, but they were getting more than a few chuckles at my expense. Just wait until the next time they need me to clean up their kindergarten-level prose.

Tim pilfers supplies like toner that he sells on eBay. I look the other way, so he's cool with my drinking. Major crisis a few years back when they put guards and metal detectors at all the entrances. I found a flask that looks like a camera. Now all the guards think I'm an avid shutterbug. One asked me to photograph his wedding, but I said my style wasn't conducive to romantic celebrations. I like to mix it up: one day tequila, another day gin, sometimes a cheap scotch. If I can stick it out here for 26 more years, I'll get a pension. Right in time for my pustulating lungs and liver to give out.

Tim finally called as I was about to leave for the day.

"Where were you?" I asked. "This place is a mad house."

"Don't exaggerate, Danny. You work for the government, dude."

"Gladys was on my ass all day!"

Gladys is our efficiency-crazed supervisor.

"You may be on your own for a while, Danny. I'm in a bit of a pickle."

"What happened?"

"Got arrested. They nailed me in a motel with an underage girl."

"Really? How underage?"

"Hey, I thought she was at least 25!"

"Still looking forward to her 18th birthday, huh?" I asked.

"More like her 17th, but who's counting?"

"You obviously weren't. How did you get caught?"

"Her damn ex-boyfriend followed us, waited 15 minutes for the preliminaries to be over, then dialed 9-1-1. He claimed it was a kidnapping and possible sexual assault. Four cops burst in with guns drawn."

"Damn, that's a tough break, Tim."

."That's not the worst of it, Danny. Her dad is threatening to kill me."

"You could take out a Temporary Restraining Order. I understand they're easy to get."

"Won't do me much good. Her dad works in law enforcement. You know him in fact: Deputy Fred Grizzoffski."

"They caught you banging Deputy Grizzoffski's daughter? Are you insane? That guy was a Marine combat sniper. Kill shots to the head was his daily routine. He liked to bag at least three before he broke for lunch. I'm scared just to pass him in the hallway."

"I didn't know he was her father. We never got around to last names."

"Where did you meet her?"

"At the county employees picnic last month. She was the looker in the short shorts and skimpy shirt with no bra. Kind of hard to miss. I thought she was a newly hired secretary or welfare case worker."

"Are you in jail?"

"I made bail, but I'm in hiding at an undisclosed location. I don't dare come to work. Her dad would shoot me down like a dog. So don't tell anyone you talked to me."

"OK, I'll stay mum."

"It's not fair, Danny. Here I am fearing for my life and I wasn't even her first. Far from it. You could hint around on that point to Grizzoffski if you see him."

"I will if I'm feeling especially suicidal. You be careful, Tim."

"Always. You know me. And don't spill about my eBay thing."

"Not a problem. You can trust me."

Damn, he clicked off before I could ask him how she was in the sack. Probably far removed from the "utility lay" category as jail bait usually is. But likely still not worth dying for. I think I remember that girl. Lips like Angela Jolie's and curled into a perpetual pout. Bearing absolutely no resemblance at all to Deputy Grizzoffski. None whatsoever. Could she be his sexy stepdaughter?

Tim and I are both mining for sex at the bottom of the gene pool. He's better-looking (except for his beer belly) and truly has no standards at all. A quantity-not-quality kind of guy. Still, he generally does better at the game than I do.

The English poet Philip Larkin wrote a poem on that theme titled "Letter to a Friend about Girls." You could look it up. The friend he was referring to was the novelist Kingsley Amis. Handsome and outgoing, Kingsley was the more successful ladies man of the two. Both dead now, of course. Both are regarded (by some) as unpleasant fellows. (Their published letters are a bit raw in spots, appalling several generations of female grad students.)

* * *

The phone rang that evening as I was medicating my nerves.

"Danny Nixon please," said a businesslike female voice.

"This is Danny."

"Hi, Danny. This is Monica."

"Monica who?" I asked, drawing a blank.

"Monica Mickleheim. We used to go out."

A name from the darkest recesses of my past. During my high-school years I had countless wrestling matches with Monica, all of which ended in a scoreless tie. The sexual revolution had reached Modesto's Sierra High, but it had missed unyielding Monica.

"Oh, hi, Monica. This is a surprise."

"Danny, I notice you haven't registered to attend the 20th reunion party this Saturday. The deadline for paying is coming right up."

"Yeah, I think I'm busy that night. Plus, it's all the way down in Modesto."

"Danny, you can't miss your 20th high-school reunion! It and the 50th are the two big ones."

"I might be free for the 50th. Let me check my calendar."

"I'm going to pay for you, Danny. You can be my date. It will be fun. I'm meet you at the door at seven o'clock sharp. Don't be late."

"Why don't you go with your husband, Monica?"

I had heard from somewhere that some guy had wrestled her into submission.

"I'm divorced, Danny. It didn't work out with Elroy. All he cared about was martial arts, kickboxing on TV, video games, lesbian porn, and his stupid car. I'll see you Saturday. And try to dress nice. All the guys will be wearing ties."

"I don't think I can make it, Monica."

"Be there, Danny. I'm counting on you. I'm paying 45 bucks for your ticket. That includes dinner, dancing to a live band, and a no-host bar. I've talked to a bunch of girls from our class. They're all looking forward to seeing you. Remember, I'll be waiting by the door at seven. Bye, honey!"

She hung up.

Wow, could it be true that all those stuck-up girls who rebuffed my advances in high school were now anxious to see me? It seemed at best improbable.

I suppose my parents would put me up for the night. They're always agitating for a visit, having forgotten how overjoyed they were when I finally left home. As I recall the feeling was mutual.

The phone rang five minutes later. It was Monica again.

"I forgot to ask, Danny. Do you want the swordfish or the steak?"

"Uh, steak I guess."

"That's what I put down, dear. I can see you haven't changed a bit."

* * *

Another hellish day at work. I may have to reconsider my career trajectory. I was still on my first cup of coffee (doctored from my camera flask) when Gladys roared in and chewed my ass. She says with Tim gone I now had to get serious and "step up to the plate."

"I mean it this time, Danny," she insisted. "Mr. Petersen is on my case about you."

Darnel Petersen is Facilities Manager and the big cheese El Supremo boss of our department.

"What's Dandy Darnel's problem this time?" I asked.

"He checked with the door guards. You took seven smoking breaks yesterday totaling two hours and 18 minutes. You have to do better, Danny."

"I didn't realize we were living in a police state."

"Mr. Petersen is threatening to out-source all documents work. He says the office expenses are out of control. We spent over $10,000 last year just on toner supplies."

"Right. Uh, that should be going down in the future."

"Why's that, Danny?"

"I'm trying to introduce more white space in my layouts. He doesn't realize I'm doing the work of a high-priced graphic designer. Not to mention the skilled copy editing I do."

"Your job is hanging by a thread, Danny. The sheriff would like this space for another holding cell. And he has Mr. Petersen's ear. I'm limiting you to one five-minute smoking break in the morning and one in the afternoon. You really should try to quit."

"Smoking has been a defining masculine activity for centuries, Gladys. It's not as bad as they say."

"I'm sure it's far worse. And that restraining order your girlfriend filed against you hasn't improved your image with Mr. Petersen. He doesn't think the union will go to bat for you if you're discharged."

"I'm sure they'd fight for me tooth and nail."

"I suspect not, Danny. So let's go to work and get that printing machine humming!"

After she left, I naturally felt a fierce need for a cigarette. So I retired to the men's room for a recuperative smoke. And who should waltz in for a pee, take one sniff, and pitch a total fit? You guessed it: the main man himself, Darnel Petersen. I can't catch a break.

When I slunk back to my office, ever-menacing Deputy Grizzoffski was occupying Tim's chair. Did he wake up screaming in the middle of the night from guilt over all those guys he wasted? Probably not.

"Good morning, Deputy," I said, feigning nonchalance. "May I help you?"

"I need the location of that dirtbag Tim Chapben."

"I think he's home sick. Have you checked there?"

"He ain't home. The whole day shift is out looking for him."

"I'm sure they'll find him," I smiled. "They're all professionals. Do you intend to detain him?"

"I intend to kill him."

"Is it really wise to mention that to people? It could be incriminating if something happens to him."

"I'm not worried about that, Nixon. After I snuff that worm, nobody's ever going to find his body—what's left of it. No corpse, no crime. It's not like anyone will be missing the bum."

"Uh, right. I understand the initial 9-1-1 call was placed by your daughter's former boyfriend. Were you aware of that youth's relationship with your daughter?"

"I quizzed her about that. Just a few after-school dates and some minor hand-holding. And what's it to you?"

"I'm totally on your side, Deputy Grizzoffski," I assured him. "It's just that kids grow up fast these days."

"Not in my family, Nixon. My kids go to church and go to confession. They walk the straight and narrow."

"Right. I'm sure they do."

I wouldn't mind being the priest in the confessional when his daughter flounces in to confide her sins. Naturally, I'd want to get *all* the details.

Somehow I made it through the day and even made a slight dent in the towering jobs pile. I left all the spell corrections up to the computer, never cleaned the photocopier drum, and printed a major job on pink paper instead of the specified white. Fuck 'em. Pink is more festive anyway.

I did get one piece of good news when I returned to my attic hovel. My old Rambler had been towed away.

After a few cocktails to relax, I made that always-dreaded phone call home. Not having perished from dementia, my parents were pleased to host me on the weekend. My mother was inclined to chat further, but I rang off as fast as I could. One really doesn't want to arrive home with nothing further to say.

To round out my evening I watched a porno film and drank some rum that I found in the back of a cupboard. Time to make another run to Bottle Chalet. And I really need to do something to revive my love life, which is lying prostrate on the floor.

Too late I looked up the forecast for Modesto on Saturday: Sunny and 109 degrees. That's appropriate: going home should be like reentering the flaming gates of hell.

Another poem from that hapless striver I know:

Work Sucks

Work is what you do
For the privilege of eating.
Not wanting to starve
You trade your life for a seating

At the table of commerce,
And all those tasks that consume
Your hours until that distant
Day when time may resume.

But by then the vitality
That you traded
Buys you only a few years
Of idleness degraded.

Five/A DRIVE TO JIVE

The consensus around the vending machines this morning was that Tim has fled the state and possibly the country. He's probably not dead and buried yet because Deputy Grizzoffski is still stomping around looking pissed. He's been giving me very dirty looks like I'm withholding vital information. I've only been able to function because a gal up in accounting sold me some of her prescription nicotine gum. It tastes like spearmint-flavored rubbery death, but makes it possible for me to survive until my next cigarette break.

I had a paper jam in the photocopy machine today that nearly pushed me over the edge into complete nervous collapse. We artistic types are prone to those and often spend a few of our best years salted away in mental institutions. Like the poet Robert Lowell, I'm sure I'd benefit from a few months in a quiet refuge learning to crochet doilies or weave baskets. A coed facility with some attractive inmates struggling to cope with their sexual addictions.

To my surprise the fugitive himself phoned after lunch.

"Hi, Danny," said Tim. "How's the climate there? Is it safe for me to come back to work?"

"Jesus, Tim, I hope you're phoning from somewhere in Patagonia. Grizzoffski is very serious about wanting you dead. He's got the whole department out looking for you."

"How can I abandon ship, Danny? I got an ex-wife and a kid in Hayward. I just bought a condo. Plus, I got six listings closing this week on eBay."

"Grizzoffski told me he's going to dispose of your body so that it's never found. And he's not planning on your death being either quick or painless."

"Damn! He said that?"

"His very words. You need to be running. And running hard."

The deputy in question, his uniform bristling with weaponry, sauntered past my office door.

"Yes, we've been running that machine really hard," I continued. "And I've started getting some bad paper jams."

"He's there now, Danny?" asked Tim.

"Yes, I think they made this machine in Brazil. I understand many U.S. manufacturers are moving there now. It's the smart thing to do."

"Fuck, I gotta go," Tim said.

"Wait! He's gone now. Pardon me for asking, but I need to know. How was it that night in the motel?"

"Fabulous, Danny. When the cops burst in, my whole system shot up to some supreme tantric level. It was the greatest orgasm of my life. I was still having lingering spasms when they were fingerprinting me a half-hour later."

"Wow, that's amazing."

"It's the element of surprise, Danny. It's that extra jolt that kicks you up to the sexual stratosphere. Of course, you have to be doing at the time with a true sex kitten."

"It sounds fantastic."

"Yeah, I definitely recommend it. OK, I'm outta here. Bye, Danny."

"Hasta la vista, big guy."

* * *

When you're slogging through job hell, you must have faith that eventually Saturday will dawn. It did finally and I got on the road. My 318 V-8 was purring, my renewed cigarette lighter was sizzling into my Chesterfields, traffic was flowing smoothly over the Altamont Pass, my spinners were dazzling my fellow motorists, my skinny "band-aid" tires were thumping rhythmically. The only fly in the ointment was my destination: Modesto, California. Aptly named, as its attractions are certainly modest.

Born in Modesto, named Richard D. Nixon, and balding by the age of 12, it's hardly surprising I didn't turn out to be an All-American Boy.

When I was a lad, Modesto was just an overgrown Central Valley farm town. Now over 200,000 people had crammed into this wide place on the road between Stockton and Fresno. Sweltering in the summer and often disappearing under a dense tule ground fog in winter. (Beware the multi-car pile-ups on fog-shrouded Highway 99.) Lots of good restaurants if you enjoy Mexican food. And be sure to stop in at the local bookstore: it stocks all the popular Christian titles.

My parents' house hadn't burned down, snuffing out two elderly victims. The towering pine outside their bedroom hadn't topped over, crushing them as they slept. Both came out to greet me when I pulled into the driveway.

"What the hell do you call that?" asked Dad, nodding toward my car.

"Another classic from 1978, the year of my birth," I replied, gingerly hugging my mother.

"Chrysler never produced a car with nigger wheels like that," he said, not shaking my hand.

"Very true," I replied. "I forget. How many times have they gone bankrupt?"

Don't ask me what that point was trying to prove.

"Some duct tape on your vinyl roof might prevent it from shedding further," suggested Mom.

"Be better to drive it out to the country and set the whole damn thing on fire," said Dad. "You missed lunch. And you smell like a distillery."

"Come inside, Danny," said Mom. "I'll fix you a nice fried baloney sandwich. I made some of that macaroni salad you like so much."

We all gathered around the dinette and drank ice tea while I ate. This was a house that floated on an ocean of ice tea. It was hot inside; Dad hadn't switched on the air yet. He was czar of the thermostat and the TV remote control. He also held the only key to the liquor cabinet. He paid for it all, as he reminded me many times in the past. He had paid for it by selling roofing supplies from behind a desk in a prefab metal building in an industrial park. On the telephone eight hours a day for decades. Now he plays golf, hunts ducks in season, and watches golf on TV. His well-oiled shotguns were always a temptation, but they're locked away too. He drives the cleanest Buick in town; his lawn is the definition of immaculate.

As usual I got updated on my aunts, uncles, cousins, the neighbors, the neighbors' kids, Dad's former coworkers, their kids, and assorted people from my high-school class who had registered a blip on my mother's news radar. She said Monica Mickleheim got laid off from Radio Shack when it closed down, has been divorced for two years, and has a little girl that for some reason was currently residing with Monica's mother.

"Who's this Elroy guy?" I asked.

"Some fellow she met at Fresno State. Well, she was attending Fresno State. He was changing the oil in her car. At least that's the story I heard. She looked so pretty in her nice strapless dress when you two went to the prom."

Another teenage disappointment for Danny. Monica had ignored the hallowed tradition of putting out after the prom. Even while swathed in evanescent lemon chiffon, she managed to keep most of her charms off-limits when grappling with me in my mother's minivan. (Rare was the night when Dad let me borrow his Buick.)

By then I was way overdue for a smoke, so I excused myself and retreated to my usual spot behind the garage. I puffed away, took a few well-earned toots from my cellphone flask, and drained out many hours of accumulated liquids. Not that private back there, but I'm sure all the neighbors had seen one before.

The reunion party was being held at a posh country club where my dad sometimes golfs. The only reason I felt motivated to go was the alternative: staying home with my parents. Plus, Monica had bought me a ticket. And in a warming pan somewhere an overcooked steak was waiting with my name on it. And sexually experienced women–now allegedly eager to see me–would be massed there for my delectation. So at 6:45, as dressed up as I'll be until my parents' funerals, I headed off in the newly duct-taped Cordoba. Egged on by my mother, my father had undertaken the repair with his usual ruthlessness. The many layers of industrial tape would hold secure, even if my car was strapped to a Saturn V rocket and launched into space.

A big homemade sign, lettered in orange and green (our school colors) proclaimed: WELCOME CLASS OF '96!!! 20 YEARS BETTER!!!

Better than what? I wondered as I spotted Monica waiting in front of the main building. She waved as I drove in and parked. She was dressed in a slinky silver gown, sparkling with sequins, and was made up like a bride on her wedding day. She was more than twice as old as when I'd last seen her, but didn't look that bad.

"Hi, Danny," she called, as I approached. "I knew you'd be bald!"

"Hi, Monica," I replied, receiving a bosomy hug, a peck on the cheek, and a powerful whiff of her perfume. "I knew you'd be 30 pounds heavier."

"Only 12 teensy pounds since graduation, you stinker," she laughed. "I love that you rented a gag car for the reunion, Danny. You were always so creative! Still writing those cute little poems?"

"Who me? Never."

My busy nose told me it was the same come-hither scent she had tormented me with back in high school.

"That's a funny-looking camera, honey. Are you going to take my picture?"

"Maybe later, Monica. Let's go find the bar."

Three gals, unknown to me, squealed in unison when we entered. Apparently they were thrilled both to see us and to collect our tickets. I stared appropriately at their chests upon which were adhered name tags. Patti, Suzanne, and Jennifer. Nope, still didn't ring any bells.

"You know those girls, Monica?" I whispered as we applied our tags.

"Of course, silly. I'll know everyone here. I didn't spend my high-school years zoned out on reefer."

Was that a dig already? My only real friend back then grew amazing weed in a remote corner of his dad's walnut orchard. I wondered if Owen would show up tonight.

The noisy bar area was jammed with at least 100 couples.

Loud rock hits from the '90s, blasting from ceiling speakers, added to the din. Here and there I spotted a few familiar faces. I was the baldest guy there, but at least I hadn't gained 200 pounds like some of the aging jocks. Most of the girls looked fine, but quite a few of us guys appeared way older than our 38 years. Clearly, we were on a faster trip to the grave than the chicks.

Drinks at the no-host bar were five bucks a pop (no host = no fun), but the fruit punch was free. I bought Monica her requested white wine and poured myself a glass of punch, which I doctored from my camera flask. I took a sip. The artificial cherry flavors clashed for supremacy with the gin. Next time I'll bring rum.

"I bet that thing doesn't take photos at all," said Monica.

"You'd win that bet."

She dragged me around to hobnob with our classmates. That's another reason I hung out with Monica way back when. In social situations she did most of the talking. While she chatted away, I looked around.

"My God, it's Danny Nixon," said a gal I recognized as Lizzie Harger, one of those brainy girls who went back east for college. "I see you're still with Monica."

"Yes, and have been except for the intervening 20 years. Why do people come to these things?"

"Out of curiosity, I suppose. High school is the most socially intense experience most of us have in our lives. We operate those four years in a closed and finite group sized like what our ancestors knew: a clan or tribal unit. Then we go on to live an essentially splintered and rootless existence amid thousands or millions of strangers."

"Good lord, Lizzie. Did you come up with that off the top of your head?"

"No, I was thinking about it on the drive down. It was how I was persuading myself not to turn around."

"Turn around and go back to where?"

"Portland. I teach up there at Reed College."

"Steve Jobs went there."

"Briefly, until he dropped out. Teaching college is a bit like high school. It provides you with something of a tribal unit. Not very harmonious, of course, with all those Ph.D.s on the payroll."

"What do you teach?"

"International relations."

"What's that? Sex with foreigners?"

"Something like that."

Lizzie was looking much better than she did in high school. Her low-cut dress was providing a peek at actual breasts. A large diamond sparkled on her ring finger.

"Is your husband loitering about?" I asked.

"He refused to come, Danny. I can't say I blame him."

"How's your beautiful sister?"

"Delia's leading a charmed life as usual. She has a new baby."

Noticing I was chatting with an attractive female, Monica yanked me away. She often did that in the old days too. I was getting a strong feeling of déjà vu here. I noticed the popular kids were passing by and saying "hi," but didn't have much to say beyond that. Clearly, I was still outside of their orbit.

I was doctoring my third glass of punch when I saw a familiar face–or what was left of it. Owen was standing by himself near the hallway to the restrooms. The lower half of his face and his neck were badly scarred. He gave me a nod and sipped his beer as I walked over to him.

"I lose that bet," he said, shaking my hand. "I never thought I'd see you here."

"Same for you, dude. Is that a souvenir of Iraq or Afghanistan?"

"Not hardly, Danny. I was cooking up a batch of honey oil and a propane canister blew up on me. After I got out of the hospital, the state gave me a time out for 19 months at Soledad."

"Sorry to hear that. Are you still in the business?"

"Are you a narc?"

"I wish I had such a high-paying job."

"Me too, Danny. I help my dad now with the walnut crop. It pays OK, if the drought and pests don't kill you."

"Have any recent harvests to sample?"

"I might. Let's go out for some air."

We found a private spot behind dumpsters in back of the kitchen. In the distance some golfers were finishing up on the back nine. We lit up and silently sampled the merchandise. The sun was going down, but the valley heat lingered on. After a few puffs, I could feel my brain cells writhing in my skull.

"You found your calling, Owen. This is the best I ever had."

"It's OK. You could be out of practice, Danny. Getting much lately?"

"No on all counts."

"I was surprised to see you with Monica."

"A one-night stand, if that. She called me and insisted I show up. You married?"

"Divorced."

"God, everyone's divorced, and I'm still looking for wife Number One."

"How seriously are you looking?"

"Not very. How long were you married?"

"Nine years. She didn't want to wake up every morning in bed next to the Phantom of the Opera."

"It's not that bad. I bet a plastic surgeon could clean that right up."

"He already has. You should have seen my before pictures. No mouth to speak of. I was eating out of a tube."

"Damn, that's a tough break."

"I'm used to it. Did you notice that exactly three-fifths of the cheerleading squad are now fat?"

"You always were statistically minded, Owen. That Lizzie Harger's looking pretty sharp."

"Yeah, I noticed her. I'm surprised you never asked her out. One brainiac communing with another."

"Monica always had me in a headlock. No touching below the neck though."

"Oh, there you are, Danny!" she called, suddenly materializing. "I've been looking for you. They're starting to serve dinner."

I handed Owen what was left of my joint as I got dragged away. We sat at one of the fringe tables with some of Monica's friends. She proudly told them I had a good government job up in San Francisco.

"Actually, I'm out in the burbs," I corrected her. "The distant burbs."

"What do you do, Danny?" asked a gal named Jeanie.

"I manage our publications division," I said, carving into my overcooked steak.

After that Monica did most of the talking as I was still adrift on a high astral plane from Owen's potent homegrown. During dessert some student-council types stood up and gave a few speeches. Then our old gym teacher was honored for some reason. For being the Idi Amin of the teaching staff? Then the lights were dimmed and the live band went to work. I do recall being dragged out to the dance floor a few times, once possibly by Lizzie Harger herself. Or I may have imagined that. By then both of my flasks were empty, and I was reduced to purchasing intoxicants on the open market. I visited the men's room, where–two decades later–the same guys were hunkered down sneaking smokes (myself included).

And then the band was packing up and people were saying good-bye. A few were in tears for some reason. As we exited Monica rudely grabbed my car keys.

"You're not driving anywhere, Danny," she said. "I'm taking you home."

"Don't be riducble, ricicu–. Don't be absurd. I'm perfectly capable of driving myself."

"Hardly, Danny. You can come retrieve your car tomorrow."

"Are we going to your place? Am I at last going to collect that elusive prize? To boldly go where hardly any guys have gone before?"

"I don't think so. You're kind of a mess, Danny. I hate to say it, but you've gone to seed. In a big way."

She opened the passenger door of her anonymous Toyota

and pushed me in. She got in on the other side and made me buckle my seatbelt, which fought back like a tiger. Eventually, we got underway.

"Hey, Monica!" I said, feeling suddenly feisty. "How come you never had sex with me?"

"Why? Because I didn't want to go past the point of no return with you."

"Why the hell not?"

"You had too many demons, Danny. You were too messed up."

"Yeah, well one of my major demons was my sex life to nowhere with you."

"I was just as frustrated as you were."

"I very much doubt that."

"Do you ever wonder where we'd be, Danny, if we'd stayed together and gotten married?"

"I don't recall ever proposing to you."

"Right. And probably never would have either. For years every time I watched a movie with a wedding scene I'd fantasize that it was you and me exchanging vows."

"Really?"

"Yes, really. But now I'm glad it never happened. You're lost, Danny darling. I'll be amazed if you make it to 50. And that's only 12 years away."

"You don't have to be so mean, Monica."

"I say that with love in my heart, dear. With love in my heart!"

My mother was still up when I stumbled in through the side door.

"Did you have a good time, Danny?" she asked.

"The best, Mom. It was so great seeing the old gang again. Now I'm off to bed."

"I bet now you wish you'd never left Modesto," she said brightly.

"So true!" I lied. "So true indeed!"

That poet who shall go nameless excreted another one:

Reunions

All those grads you miss so much
Whose names you can't recall;
Gathered in awkward celebration:
A golden memories free-for-all.

Faces lined with layers of time
Like moss upon a tree.
Coupled now to strangers,
Who must fake their bonhomie.

Behold those sporty types
With muscles turned to flab;
And erstwhile curvy coeds
Now as shapely as a crab.

And over there is that one
Who vulcanized your soul.
Still so damn indifferent about
The heart that they once stole.

This day we come together
To reverse the outward spin
That sweeps us all so far away,
And glimpse again what might have been.

Six/MIX OF TRICKS & KICKS

Morning in Modesto. Sorry I missed it. Mom made me waffles (much to my father's annoyance) when I emerged from my old bedroom at one-fifteen.

"You look like a wreck," he observed, watching me eat. "And where's your damn car?"

"It was getting so many compliments at the golf club I left it there overnight. Any more bacon, Mom?"

"Here you go, honey," she replied, sliding another generous portion onto my plate.

"You didn't tell me about Owen's accident," I said.

"It was in the paper," she replied. "You shouldn't associate with such hoodlums."

"He's hardly that, Mom."

"He certainly did his best to fry your brain," added Dad. "He got what was coming to him."

I sighed. Mom sighed. Dad looked out the window at his busy bird feeder.

"What did Monica say about her daughter?" asked Mom, changing the subject.

"Not a thing, Mom. The topic didn't come up."

"You should have asked her, Danny. You should have shown an interest."

"I'm not getting back with Monica, Mom. That ship has sailed, struck a mine and several icebergs, and sank with all hands on board."

"He doesn't need somebody else's discarded goods," said Dad.

"I'd like to see him happily married before I die," she replied.

Good luck with that!

I expect that thought crossed all of our minds.

After I packed, the three of us rode to the country club in Dad's latest Buick. He said it was likely to be his last one. They were now importing a model from China and trying to pass it off as the real thing. My father would vote for a Democrat or marry a black woman before he'd buy a Chinese-made car.

There was a rude note on the windshield of my Cordoba from the management stating that it would be towed unless "moved immediately." Those philistines should be gratified to have such a distinctive classic gracing their parking lot. This time I had to hug both of my parents, always an ordeal. Soon though I was safely beyond the city limits of Modesto, a geographical progression that never failed to lift my spirits.

I was still annoyed at Monica. How dare she say I had "gone to seed." She was divorced and doing temp work for an agency. I doubt that paid much more than the minimum wage. At least I had a real job. Did she drag me down to that reunion just so she could cast aspersions on my lifestyle? I don't need her to judge me. I despise myself well enough on my own.

I stopped at a Walgreens in Livermore and bought some of their groovy house-brand scotch. I also loaded up on some over-the-counter nicotine gum for work. I was hoping it didn't taste as rotten as the prescription stuff. I don't need it to put hair on my chest and get my pecker hard, I just need it to keep me sane until my next smoking break.

* * *

Got a padded envelope with no return address in the mail at work today. Inside was a key and a short note from the fugitive. The key was to Tim's condo. He said I should go there, sell all his stuff in a big garage sale, and keep the proceeds until he alerts me where to send them. He added that I was free to use the condo until such time as he returned.

Of course, I had to go there as soon as I got off work. The neighborhood wasn't bad, but the building was one of those stucco eyesores built to enrich the developer at the expense of the planet. For being a sexual libertine, Tim kept a fairly neat house. He had a combo living-dining room, adjoining kitchenette, two smallish bedrooms, and 1-1/2 baths–all in about 600 square feet. I was amazed he could afford even that on our salaries, plus the guy was paying child support. Only one beer in the refrigerator and no booze anywhere. I guess you can stretch a budget farther when you're not an alcoholic. Not much of value to be seen except his extensive porno collection. Can you peddle that at a garage sale I wonder?

I was drinking the beer when someone knocked on the door. I expected it to be Deputy Grizzoffski with guns drawn, but it was an attractive gal who identified herself as a neighbor from across the hall.

"I was wondering where Tim is," she said, peering at me doubtfully. "The cops have been here looking for him. Is there some kind of trouble?"

"Tim had to leave rather suddenly," I replied. "He's asked me to liquidate his possessions."

"Oh, dear. That's terrible."

"I know. Bad break for Tim. Do you see anything here you like? I can make you a good deal on it."

"Tim doesn't allow smoking in here. What sort of trouble is he in?"

I snuffed out my Chesterfield.

"I'm not at liberty to say. It involves a personal vendetta. The other party has expressed a desire to kill him. Can you use a sofa? How about this nice leather recliner?"

"It's vinyl, not leather. Do you have some sort of written authorization to be here?"

I showed her Tim's note, which I stressed must be kept confidential.

"Are you a friend of Tim's?" I asked.

"Sort of."

"I could use some help for the sale. Are you free this weekend?"

"I guess I'll be around."

"My name's Danny," I said, smiling and extending my hand.

"I'm Maeve," she replied, shaking it with ill-disguised distaste. Apparently she was one of those gals whose skin I caused to crawl.

I advertised the sale on Craigslist and in our local paper. I billed it as an "estate sale," which it very well may turn out to be. Lovely Maeve helped by putting up signs around the neighborhood. She's one of those willowy blondes on the wrong side of 35, but still ringing the gong for me. She probably had a thing for Tim, never suspecting she was well outside his target age bracket.

I advertised the sale as starting at 10 a.m. When I arrived there at 9:30 on Saturday, Maeve already had collected over $900 from premature buyers.

"A very disgusting man in pants cut off way too short paid me $500 for those boxes of DVDs," she said, handing me a thick wad of bills. "I also sold quite a bit of kitchen stuff and some linens. I hope that was OK."

"You're doing great, Maeve. Keep up the good work."

Damn. The porno collection was gone before I'd had a chance to sort through it. And probably sold way too cheap. No time to think about that as the bargain-hunters descended *en masse*. One woman offered me ten dollars for the TV, which I had marked at $200. Where do these people get off? I told her to drop dead, which brought a look of reproach from Maeve. I also caught a kid trying to walk out with Tim's autographed Spice Girls poster. I made him pay me a buck for that.

Some time after noon Owen showed up with a large boxed pizza and a six-pack of beer. I had emailed him an invitation, but hadn't expected him to come. I introduced him to Maeve, then the two guys retired to Tim's micro balcony for a smoke break. Owen does grow a potent product.

"Who's Maeve?" he asked. "Your girlfriend?"

"I wish. She's a neighbor. Lives across the hall. Very pretty, but I make her skin crawl. You probably do too."

"No doubt. Did you go home with Monica after the reunion?"

"Struck out again. I'm beginning to think I'll never part those milk-white thighs."

"I've got a confession you may not like, Danny."

"What? You banged her?"

"Did she tell you that?"

"No, but at the reunion I saw a glance pass between you two that I gauged to be suspicious."

"I ran into her at a bar once a few years after high school. I guess we both had an itch we needed to scratch."

"Great. I can't get past second base for three solid years and you nail her at the first go. How was it?"

"If you really want to know, she was pretty hot. Of course, I was drunk at the time."

"Fuck! That is so sick!"

"I shouldn't have told you."

"I'm glad you did, Owen. It added the final cherry on top to my high-school years."

Maeve opened the sliding door a crack and said she had heated up the pizza in the oven. We gathered around the mini breakfast bar for a beer and pizza break. Owen related his medical/criminal history in a few terse sentences, then it was on to other topics. Maeve, it turns out, designs women's sportswear for a local catalog company that is quite well known. Not by me, but that's no surprise. She was wearing some of her designs, for which both men expressed much appreciation. I couldn't help thinking she'd look even better out of them.

By the time we closed the door at 4:30 only a few big items were left: the sofa, recliner, coffee table and bed, plus clothes and that miscellaneous stuff that no one wants. The total take came to a bit over $2,700. That should pay for a few grilled llama tacos in Peru.

"Where should we go to dinner?" I asked. "Tim's buying."

The other two looked at me uncomfortably.

"Uh, Danny," said Owen. "Maeve and I already made plans for dinner."

"Fine," I said. "I guess I'll see you back at my place later."

"Mind if I borrow the key? I was thinking of crashing here tonight."

I handed him Tim's key and wished them a pleasant evening. I added that he should be alert for a deputy sheriff who might break in and shoot him. But not to worry, it would be a mistake.

Rather uncomplimentary to me I thought as I drove back to my attic hovel. I make her skin crawl, but she's eager to go out with a guy with half his face burned off. And an alumnus of Soledad State Prison to boot.

* * *

On Sunday I did my laundry and mowed Mrs. Goodsolm's patch of grass. I'm on call for such chores in exchange for my below-market rent.

I took a break from yard work when Owen dropped off the key on his way back to Modesto.

"Did you have a good time?" I asked, offering him a swig of brandy from my cellphone flask. He declined.

"I did, Danny. She's very nice. I like her a lot."

"Better than Monica?"

"Let's not go there."

"Are you planning to see her again?"

"Yeah, I'm coming back next weekend."

"She's not likely to be willing to move to Modesto," I pointed out. "And you can't harvest walnuts in her condo."

"It's too soon to think about such things."

"I'm told long-distance romances are hard on your wallet, your car, and your heart. Did she say anything about me?"

"She thinks you're OK. She's impressed that you're helping Tim."

"But you're the one she wanted to go out with."

"Here's the thing, Danny. You might have more appeal with the ladies if you cut back some on your boozing."

"Hah! That's funny coming from you. How many Friday nights did we spend trying desperately to scrounge up some liquid refreshments? How many dark alleys did you splatter with your drunken vomit?"

"Well that was then, Danny. This is now. Gals our age aren't looking to party. They're looking for security. They're looking for husbands. Their biological clocks are ticking."

"Then God help us all."

"I'm just saying, Danny, you might want to think about cutting back a bit."

"Lots of heavy drinkers score well with chicks, Owen. Richard Burton drank like a fish and married Elizabeth Taylor–twice. Richard Widmark and William Holden were boozers and had two girls on each arm. Mickey Rooney had eight wives and died at 93 with unpaid bar bills all over town."

"I guess that's the secret, Danny. All you have to do is become a big-time movie star."

"Will you be wanting to borrow the key next weekend?" I asked.

"No, I'm staying with Maeve."

And probably not on her couch. Damn!

"Right. Well, maybe I'll see you around."

"We'll get together, Danny. Thanks for inviting me."

"No problem."

I watched him drive off in his 15-year-old Honda. You'd think there'd be enough girls in Modesto to keep him occupied, but no he has to come poach on my territory. It's hard to compete with those hideous scars for winning sympathy from chicks. I'm too chicken to set myself on fire, but perhaps I should look into faking a few grotesque deformities.

"That grass isn't going to mow itself!" called Mrs. Goodsolm from her kitchen window.

"Getting right on it!" I yelled back.

Another poem from that unknown and unwashed poetaster:

A Boozer's Lament

My drinking curbs her libido,
Or so I've been informed.
My breath blasts off a torpedo
That leaves her chloroformed.

All that gin and scotch and rum
That soothe my inner fires
Signal hark! He's just a bum
Not worthy of your desires.

Where once I wowed 'em with my charm,
With my wit and patter winning,
Now my wink sparks only alarm
At the very thought of sinning

With such an oaf who'd fight
For primacy in the bar room,
But sneer at starving junior's plight:
Prostrate on his mommy's tomb.

Seven/FAR FROM HEAVEN

When I got to the office on Monday morning, two workmen were loading the photocopier machine onto a dolly.

"Are you taking that somewhere?" I asked, unwrapping the day's first stick of nicotine gum.

"Back to the warehouse," said the older of the two. "Your lease is up."

"Let me check on that," I said.

I phoned Gladys, who ambled down from her office. She told the workmen to proceed with the removal.

"What's up, Gladys?" I asked.

"There's been a reorganization, Danny," she said, avoiding eye contact even more than usual.

"Are we getting a different machine? Something new and improved?"

"Mr. Petersen has been meeting with the Graphic Arts department at the J.C. They do wonderful work over there."

"We do terrific work over here," I pointed out.

"Mr. Petersen has figured out we can save thousands of dollars by having their students handle our printing needs."

"What! You mean I'm fired?"

"Not at all, Danny. It's just that your position has been eliminated because of the reorganization. Your department is closing."

"So I'm still out the door. As of when?"

"As of today, Danny. But you'll be getting the standard severance package, which is one week's pay for every year of service. For you that comes to, uh. . ."

"Four lousy, stinking weeks of pay!"

"Right. And perhaps some accrued vacation hours. But just think: we'll be helping to train the next generation of artists and printers."

"Great, Gladys. And meanwhile the present generation is unemployed and starving."

"It's not entirely dire, Danny. You'll get to stay on the health plan for a year. Of course, now you'll have to pay the premiums yourself. As a single person in your age group that comes to $1,178 a month."

"Fantastic, Gladys. I can pay that out of my monthly income, which will be zero because county workers don't qualify for unemployment compensation."

"That's unfortunately correct, Danny. However, you are welcome to apply for any other county job openings for which you may be qualified. Although to be frank, it is unlikely Mr. Petersen would look favorably on your application."

I spat out my gum and lit up a Chesterfield.

"Smoking is not permitted anywhere in the building, Danny."

"So call a cop, Gladys. I'll be out of here in five minutes. I just need to pack up my stuff."

"They'll want to see you up in H.R., Danny. There are some forms you need to fill out."

"I know about those forms, Gladys. I produced them."

I tried looking on the bright side on the drive home. Sure I'm unemployed, but now I'm a free man. No more slaving away in that windowless room doing that boring work. Breathing toner dust and my own farts while sneaking toots from my camera flask. And no more chewing that ghastly gum. I can light up a Chesterfield anytime I feel like it. Except now I might be buying those no-name, tax-free discount smokes they peddle at Indian casinos. How bad could they be? Hell, didn't Indians invent smoking? As for booze, I might have to scavenge for discarded fruit in dumpsters behind Safeway and distill my own moonshine. I wonder how Mrs. Goodsolm would react if I set up a still in my living room.

And how am I going to pay my rent? The Cordoba is a finely crafted automobile, but I'd rather not take up residence in it. I'm a white male college graduate with computer skills and a proven job history. Employers are clamoring for guys just like me. There is absolutely no cause for panic. Feeling reassured, I steered into Safeway and bought their largest plastic jug of off-brand bourbon (aged in Kentucky for several days) and three large frozen pepperoni pizzas. Since my ready cash was running low, I put that purchase on plastic. Fuck, if worse came to worse, I could run up all my credit cards and then declare bankruptcy. Except I only have one credit card and it's pretty close to being maxed out.

Mrs. Goodsolm was surprised to see me back so soon. I told her I got furloughed (with full pay) while contractors cleared the courthouse of hazardous asbestos. Your landlady should be the last person to suspect you're without a job.

The rest of the day was devoted to TV watching and cheesy pepperoni dipping. Soaked in bourbon and held on the tongue while the tangy vapors tantalized the sinuses. Not better than sex, but close. And oblivion achieved this way lasts so much longer than the fleeting nirvana of an orgasm.

* * *

Owen stopped by my place on Friday on his way to Maeve's. He found me somewhat the worse for wear.

"Jesus, Danny. What happened to you? You're a mess."

"I'm really tired of people telling me that. I need someone to tell me I'm a handsome, clean-cut, prosperous-looking, debonair fellow."

"Probably not going to happen anytime soon. So what's the story?"

"I'm moving on to the next exciting chapter in my distinguished career."

"You got fired, huh?"

"Certainly not, Owen. They loved my work. My position was eliminated."

"Same difference. So what are you going to do?"

"I'm weighing my options."

"Looks like you're weighing them at the bottom of a bottle."

"I'm ready for a change of stimulants. How about a sample of your Modesto Gold?"

"Didn't bring any, Danny. Maeve hinted strongly that she doesn't go out with dopers."

"Fuck! Is there no end to the tyranny of the female sex?"

"Get cleaned up, guy. You can come have dinner with us."

"And why would I want to do that?"

"Because you need a decent meal. And some time away from this hole. So get moving. Hit the shower. I don't want to be late."

Maeve in her small but artistically furnished condo was even lovelier than I remembered. She greeted Owen with a heartfelt kiss and me with no outward displays of revulsion.

"Danny lost his job," announced Owen. "They closed down his department."

"Oh, no," she gasped. "That means Tim lost his job too."

"Yes," I said, "but I may be feeling it more acutely, since I'm not currently on the run in Bolivia."

"I hope he's not that far away," she said. "This is terrible, Danny. What are you going to do?"

Why do people keep asking me that? It's like asking people who just received a diagnosis of cancer if they've selected a mortician to handle their funeral.

"I have several irons in the fire," I replied. "I smell rosemary and oregano."

"I'm making spaghetti," said Maeve. "Have a seat while Owen opens the wine."

She and the ex-doper met in the kitchenette for a clandestine conference. Then she announced that she had "forgotten" to buy wine and hoped I wouldn't mind having lemonade instead. As I never went anywhere without my cellphone flask, I said that sounded fine.

The joke was on them, since I spiked my drink openly while they got stuck swigging the sugary stuff plain. The dinner, I'm sorry to report, was excellent. I hate it when a long-time friend lands a sexy girlfriend who also can cook. That seems so unfair. Maeve whipped up some tasty zabaglione for dessert–no doubt to impair further my brittle arteries.

Over coffee they discussed Danny's job prospects.

"The catalog is gearing up for the holiday rush," said Maeve. "They usually hire some temps to help out in the warehouse. Can you drive a forklift, Danny?"

"Probably straight into a wall and skewering the boss in the process," I replied.

"Couldn't he work the phones?" said Owen. "You know, taking orders. He's good on a computer."

"The order-takers have to advise customers on styles, colors, and sizing," she replied. "Naturally, they're all gals or gay guys."

They looked at me. I didn't appear to qualify under either category.

"I'm thinking of putting in my application at Bottle Chalet," I said. "I understand they give their employees a hefty discount." I took out my pack of Chesterfields. "Mind if I smoke?"

"Out on the balcony," said Maeve. "But the neighbors won't like it."

"Not to worry," I said. "We smokers are inured to criticism and complaints. The sensitive types have either all quit or died off."

They insisted I spend the night next door in Tim's condo. In the same bed where God knows what had been done to whom. I prayed some of that good fortune would rub off on me.

The next day I stopped in at Bottle Chalet to make some inquiries. The manager gave me a short verbal quiz on wine. I flunked. Apparently, the store only hires wine snobs. How you become a connoisseur on the wages they pay is anybody's guess.

Later, I was in our neighborhood mini mart buying some smokes when I spotted this notice: WANTED: CLERK. MIDNIGHT TO 8 A.M. MINIMUM WAGE. SEE MR. PARK. Since Mr. Park was in his usual spot at the register, I introduced myself and said I was interested. He looked at me doubtfully.

"Very thick glasses," he said. "How good you see?"

"I see fine," I assured him.

"OK, Danny Nixon, we do a test."

He had me stand behind the counter while he went to the far end of the store.

"OK," he called. "What I just do?"

"You slipped a box under your shirt."

"What kind of box?"

"Uh, tampons, I think."

"So what you say, Danny Nixon?"

"Hey, you! Put that back or I'll call a cop! Right now! I mean it!"

"That pretty good," he conceded, returning to the register. "When customer in store, you no read magazine. You no pick nose. You watch customer! You watch in person and in big round mirrors on ceiling. You get that?"

"I understand, Mr. Park. The price of freedom is eternal vigilance."

"Here's the thing, Danny Nixon. You a good customer. Many years you come here. You buy many packs of cigarettes in my store. You and a skinny Chinese lady my only Chesterfields customers. But no smoking by my clerks."

"Not a problem. I'll just chew nicotine gum."

"You can't go outside to smoke. Leave customers inside to heist goods."

"I understand. I'm thinking of quitting smoking anyway."

Right. Just like I'm thinking of becoming a billionaire.

"Here's the thing, Danny Nixon. You also buy many pints of whiskeys in my store. But no drinking on the job."

"I buy those pints for my landlady. She has a bit of a hollow leg. I'm practically a teetotaler myself."

"Here's the thing, Danny Nixon. This store have total video security. I review the tapes. Also my wife. If you steal, you fired! If customers steal, you fired! If you smoke or drink, you fired! If coffee pots run out, you fired! If hotdogs on roller grill run out, you fired! If you not check I.D.s of kids, you fired! If you not polite, you fired! If you not show up, you fired! You get it?"

"Totally, Mr. Park."

Wow, who knew that this business was harboring its own little Hitler?

"OK, Danny Nixon. I give you trial. You come tomorrow night at 11, I train you. Bring your own lunch. You eat my store food or sneak my candy bars, you fired!"

"Right, Mr. Park. I'll be here. You can depend on me."

"One more thing, Danny Nixon. You get shot by holdup man with gun, you pay hospital bill, not me."

"Er, right. That sounds fair."

Of course, I can't live on his lowly minimum wage. The thing to do is make yourself indispensable and then demand a raise. Having shopped at countless mini-marts, I'm also familiar with the scams run by clerks to pad their paltry wage. Like cheating on the change when someone pays with a big bill. Or you palm a buck when you're handing over a bunch of singles. Most people stick the wad of bills into their wallets without checking. Every dollar you score is under the table and tax free.

I've always been a night owl, so the graveyard shift may suit me. And I'll be my own man. The captain of the ship–with no bosses breathing down my neck. Fortunately, ours is a relatively crime-free neighborhood. Most of the trigger-happy stickup artists are working over in Oakland.

By now this so-called poet needs no introduction:

Ode to a Mini-Mart

The mini-mart is where you shop
For smokes and booze and snacks.
Down the block, just one short hop,
Handy when a craving attacks.

All the essentials on the shelf
And in the glass-door coolers.
Arrayed right there, just help yourself,
Plus slushies for the parched high-schoolers.

Yes, the prices are a bit excessive,
But surely that's to be expected:
Mr. Park's hours are oppressive,
His wife and kids are oft neglected.

Need a condom in the wee small hours?
All the drugstores closed up tight?
Don't despair while she seethes and glowers.
See Danny tonight. He'll help you unite!

Eight/MAN'S FATE

Mr. Park was very thorough. He showed me how to work the cash register, the bar-code scanner, and the Lotto and slushy machines. Where to slip the big bills into the floor safe. How to check for counterfeit currency. What to say if credit cards are declined. He showed me the drill on the coffee pots and all the hot snacks. What to look for in fake I.D.s (as if I didn't know). What to put in which bags. Where the aluminum baseball bat was concealed under the counter, and where 9-1-1 was programmed on speed-dial on the phone. What to do when I need to pee (lock the door and hang up the BACK IN 2 MINUTES sign). And never, ever lock the door for more than four minutes. And never, ever switch off the neon OPEN sign.

"What you do, Danny Nixon, when two kids come in and one distracts you?"

"I watch the first kid, but I especially watch the second kid. If there's any monkey business, I come out swinging with the baseball bat."

"Mostly you menace them. They usually drop the goods. I don't want big lawsuits by angry parents. No tragedies in my store!"

"Right, Mr. Park."

"Any trouble, you call 9-1-1 and me. I have good friends with cops. They know this store. They come in for coffee and donut. You smile and say no charge. OK?"

"Right. We're paying off the cops."

"OK, Danny Nixon, I leave now. I trust you with my store. You do good job, OK?"

"Don't you worry, Mr. Park. You go home and get a good night's sleep."

"Hah! I wish!" he said, shaking his head.

For being a guy with no friends, I'm something of a chatty person. Clerking at the mini mart is a much more social job than slaving in the courthouse basement. One meets and interacts with fellow humans in all their diversity. At least you do until around two a.m. Then the traffic slows way down. The minutes crawl by. You sit there knowing that three video cameras overhead are recording your every twitch. You can't light up, you can't sneak a toot from your flask, you can't chat up that girl in tall boots and hot pants because she's gone to meet a client. You can only sit on your stool, chew your nicotine gum, hope the next car pulling into the lot isn't driven by a madman with a gun, and think about the missteps in your life that have landed you behind the counter of a mini mart in the middle of the night.

At three a.m. a guy with a big vacuum mounted to his pickup rumbled in and swept the lot. The neighbors must love that. He also emptied the outside trash bins. At 3:30 a Mexican fellow named Mongo arrived to mop the floor, clean the toilet, and restock the shelves. He does this seven days a week, and then he's off to his other two jobs. Not at all talkative when I tried to chat him up. Insuperable language barrier?

Traffic picks up again a little after four. People with long commutes start pulling in to load up on coffee and snacks for the drive. A truck drops off stacks of newspapers. A gal delivers big boxes of donuts. Insomniacs arrive to buy cigarettes and huge bottles of cola. Dog-walkers show up and also high-school athletes heading off to early practice. Then somehow it's eight o'clock and Mr. Park returns, pleasantly surprised that his store hasn't burned down or I haven't absconded with the till.

"Any problems, Danny Nixon?" he asked.

"No, sir, everything was fine. You can call me Danny, you know. Nixon's my last name."

"Like the president?"

"Yeah, but I'm not related."

"Too bad. He very famous man."

When Richard Nixon was my age, he was already a senator from California and being talked about as a running mate for Ike. It is unrecorded whether he shopped at mini marts.

* * *

Not surprisingly, Friday was a much busier night at the store. Beer and wine sales doubled, and bags of chips were flying off the racks. Sometime after one o'clock a girl sauntered in and looked at me in surprise.

"Where's Hwan?" she asked.

Hwan was the previous late-night occupant of my prestigious stool.

"Gone to Korea to get married," I replied.

"He told me he wasn't going. He said he didn't want to marry that girl."

"Sorry, I'm not up-to-date on the particulars of that amatory crisis. You look a bit young to be out this late."

"That is of no concern to you. Hey, I know you! You're the dude who drives that old car with the fancy spinning rims. We saw you driving by the other day. You know what my friend Clare said?"

"No doubt she expressed a fierce desire to date me."

"Hardly. She said, 'God! They're letting anybody be a pimp these days.' I about bust a gut."

"Adolescent humor is an acquired taste. Are you buying something?"

"Hold your horses, Mr. Clerk. What's your name?"

"Danny. What's yours?"

"Olivia, but that's too many syllables these days, so they call me Olive."

"You're rather pale and unswarthy for that name."

"I know. I've totally failed at trying to tan. How come you're working here? You got a heavy car payment to make? Is your girlfriend knocked up?"

"My doctor said I should spend more time under bright fluorescent lights, especially after midnight."

"I'm not believing a word you say, Danny boy."

"What do you do, Olivia?"

"I'm a senior in high school. Impressive, huh?"

"Very. How are things on the cheerleading squad?"

"I'm sure I wouldn't know. So do you sleep during the day like a bat?"

"I try to. My landlady likes to run her vacuum, hair dryer, blender, and other violent appliances."

"I have trouble falling asleep and trouble waking up. What does that mean?"

"I think it indicates you're a teenager. You might try keeping more regular hours."

"As if that's going to happen. What's with all the gum-chewing, Danny? Are you being paid by the stick?"

"Nicotine gun. I can't smoke in the store."

"My dad's trying to quit. It makes him even more deranged than usual."

"I expect you contribute your share to his mental wear and tear."

"I do my best. Well, Danny dear, I think you've figured out by now that I'm not a decoy. I'm not part of a police sting operation. My good buddy Hwan used to sell me the occasional wine cooler."

"Perhaps that's why he had to flee to Korea."

"Not at all, Danny. His family wanted him to marry a nice Korean girl. Can we agree that one measly wine cooler for me tonight is not going to be a problem?"

"Sorry, Olivia, I'm not going to lose this job to appease your need to party. Besides, wine coolers are very déclassé. I'd be more inclined to sell you a bottle of scotch."

"No one's going to know, Danny."

"Dream on, kid. This store is lousy with security cameras."

"I know, Danny. Except for the dead zone."

"The what?"

"Hwan discovered there's one small part of the store that the cameras don't cover. He called it the virgin video zone. That's where we conducted our business."

"And where is that?"

"I'll show you, if you sell me the wine cooler."

"Sorry. That's not happening."

"OK, I'll just shoplift one the next time you have a customer."

"I've been trained to deal with that, Olivia. I'll be obliged to bean you with a baseball bat. You'll be arrested and you can forget about getting into Stanford. Or, in your case, the J.C."

"That wasn't nice, Danny. How about I dial 9-1-1 and say you tried to rape me?"

"Not going to work, Lolita. The security tapes would exonerate me. You'd go to jail and be the victim of a brutal lesbian assault."

"I bet you'd like that too. You'd probably want to watch. OK, Danny, I'm leaving. I was trying to like you, but I find that's now impossible."

"Excuse me while I go slash my wrists."

She turned and flounced out. Not a beauty, but an interesting face. Pixieish I suppose, with an impish body to go with it. I'd have dated her in high school, although I expect it would be Owen who nailed her.

An hour or so later a patrol car pulled into the lot, and Deputy Grizzoffski came in and headed to the coffee station. He got a large cup of the extra-caffeinated and two custard-filled bars. He was surprised to see who was manning the register.

"Well, if it isn't Danny Nixon. How the lowly have fallen."

"Hello, deputy," I smiled. "Disposed of any bodies lately?"

"No, but I know a good place to stash yours. Your pal Tim is going to have to crawl out from under his rock eventually. And I'll be ready for him. He'll be begging me to put him out of his misery. Meanwhile, I'm going to keep my eye on this store. And you."

"Hang out all you want. I appreciate the police presence."

"I'm surprised they let you handle money, Nixon. I'd have thought you'd be out in the parking lot. Being paid a couple bucks to wave a sign."

"Anything else, deputy? Would you like your pastries gift-wrapped?"

"No thanks. And I'm sorry I missed your going-away party."

"They didn't have one for me."

"Sure, they did, Danny. It was a big blowout the next day to celebrate your firing."

Probably a lie, but Darnel Petersen may have hosted some small celebration. I'm sure it made his day to ax my butt. He'll be sorry though, when his primitive prose comes back unimproved by those students.

Twenty-four hours after her departure, Olivia returned to the store. She picked a fashion magazine off a nearby rack and pretended to read it.

"Hello, Olivia," I said.

She ignored me.

"I've been thinking about your problem, girl. Why aren't you dating some college guy who's old enough to buy you wine coolers? I'm sure getting you inebriated would fit right in with his plans."

"You're a very sick man, Mr. Clerk," she said, not looking up from her magazine. "You should be locked up, not flirting with underage girls in the middle of the night."

"That dead zone of yours: I wouldn't mind knowing where it is. If such a thing exists, which I doubt."

"It exists all right. A very cute Korean guy may have felt me up in that exact spot."

"You found Hwan to be attractive?"

"Way more attractive than you," she replied, still leafing through the magazine.

I gave it some thought. An occasional recourse to my cell-phone flask in this alleged video-free zone did offer a certain appeal.

"OK, Olivia, go get one. And show me where to meet you."

"You're the best, Danny!" she exclaimed, dumping the magazine and heading toward the cooler.

The $2.35 changed hands right between the canned vegetables and the motor oil. Olivia slipped the bottle into her purse and gave me a peck on the cheek. I liked her perfume. She surprised me by lingering at the counter.

"So do you have a boyfriend, Olivia?" I asked.

"Would I be hanging out with you if I did?"

"I'm sure there are guys asking you out."

"Nobody I'd want jumping these sexy bones. I take it you're not married."

"No, although I am beseeched constantly by attractive women."

"Is that why you work the night shift? To dodge those pestering babes?"

"Yes, but I fear they may track me down anyway. Your parents don't mind you roaming the streets this late?"

"They're asleep in bed. I live right around the corner."

"I live three blocks south. I can walk to work."

"That's convenient, Danny. I'm sure it beats commuting to Sunnyvale as a high-paid Apple executive. I should come check out your place sometime."

"I doubt your parents would approve of that."

"Don't you worry about them, Danny. I don't."

"You're not the guy they'd be sending up-river to jail-bait jail."

"I'll be 18 in two months. Can you wait that long?"

"I'll try, dear one. But I can't make any promises."

Sunday and Monday are my days off. Who mans my shift those nights? The ever-formidable Mrs. Park. She also does all the office work and somehow has found the time to have three children. Just watching her makes me tired.

Speaking of which, my circadian clock has adjusted at last to my new schedule. So it was shocked that Sunday afternoon found me lunching with Owen and Maeve in a Thai restaurant instead of sleeping in my cozy bed. They didn't tell me they were bringing along a friend of Maeve's for me. A gal named Pucia. Very artistically dressed. Exuberant eyeglass frames intended to disguise the thickness of her lenses and the size of her nose. She must be as blind as me. Not bald though. Short red hair of a boldly artificial hue, looking like it had been combed with a rake. Making an effort to display an interest, although I could tell she was put off by my constant stifled yawns. And I may have nodded off during dessert, letting my mango ice cream melt. Pucia probably concluded ol' Danny was a very dull fellow. Or a possible narcolepsy victim. People wishing to fix me up with dates should restrict their selections to night owls, insomniacs, and graveyard shift workers. Or the very rich who desire to support an idle BF.

Maeve was taking a few days off work; the two of them were heading down to tour the walnut farm. Believe it or not, she has never been to Modesto. Will she love it? Some people do! Ask my

mother. Owen was manifesting that look of deep sexual fulfill-
ment that's so alarming to the celibate. I may have to strike him
off my (short) list of friends.

At least I've been flirting avidly with the gal who delivers
the donuts. Her name is Wenda Coleman. I feared it was her
husband who fries them, but it turns out that's her brother's
job. She's pretty in a roughhewn sort of way, with one of those
little-girl voices so popular these days. Rather like conversing
with a shapely six-year-old. She delivers donuts to mini marts
and restaurants all over the region. There's a job that makes
people happy—as opposed to, for example, designing the next
generation of H-bombs at Livermore. She may have a boyfriend,
but no mention of one yet. Usually gals trot him out right away if
they suspect I'm coming on to them. The last time I saw Wenda
we met in the dead zone and shared a swig from my cellphone
flask. Her lips touched where my lips had slobbered. That must
mean something!

Another word stampede from that deranged poet:

Fishing for Love

Love is elusive in this cold world.
That grim sea is so over-fished.
Hooks cast out are warily twirled,
Snaring nothing or the unwished.

My boat has sunk a thousand times,
Gone down with a glance or a sneer.
I sail on again, though sometimes
I wonder why I persevere.

The odds seem set against us
For anything more than fleeting.
A connection misses and thus
We cast out another greeting

That wings off to reach the ear
Of someone with strong emotions
About their ideal, although it's clear
I conform not at all to their notions.

Nine/SHE'S SO FINE

A Prius pulled into the lot. I went back to reading my news-paper. Alabama was getting ready to execute a guy who had pis-tol-whipped and shot a convenience-store clerk. They need to fry that felon fast. And make a big poster of the deed we can post in our window. The Prius driver entered and headed for the cooler. I'd seen that shopper before.

"Hello, Abby," I said, when she brought her six-pack to the counter.

That startled her.

"If that's really your name," I added.

"It's not, as it happens," she said. "But it's the one I use most often. You're uh, Donny?"

"Danny. I thought you said you lived in San Francisco."

"Did I say that?"

"I don't suppose you work for the Water Resources Board either."

"Jesus, Danny, do I look like a bureaucrat?"

"Not really."

"I thought you said you worked for the county."

"I lied," I lied.

"I guess we're a couple of chiselers, Danny. Would you like me to pay for my share of the meal?"

"Nah, I enjoyed your company."

"Yeah, I liked you too. You're kind of a fun guy."

"I try. Are you off to a party?"

"You probably shouldn't ask, Danny. I'm rarely that can-did."

"I like that in a person, Abby. Untrustworthiness is a quality to be valued. I bet you get a lot of free meals."

"A girl has to play the cards she's dealt, Danny."

"Well, stop in any time, Abby. It's always a pleasure to see you."

"I'll keep that in mind. How much for the beers?"

"They're on me this time. You can get the next round."

"I'll be sure to do that," she lied, flashing me a beautiful smile.

A gorgeous creature and deeply flawed. What more could you ask?

Inspired by her example a few minutes later I made $80 off a guy who had paid for a bottle of tequila with a $100 bill. He was driving a Lexus and already had a few drinks under his belt.

"Hey, didn't I give you a hundred?" he asked, swaying on his feet.

"No, sir. It was a twenty. If it had been a hundred, I would have put it in the floor safe, but see: I have your twenty right here." I showed him a $20 bill that I palmed from my pocket.

"But I remember having a hundred in my wallet."

"I'd talk to your wife, sir. It might have been her turn to buy lunch for the girls."

"Yeah, I'll do that. Damn!"

A good grifter always knows where to deflect the blame.

Olivia's been dropping in every night to keep me company. I do like that girl. She tells me what's happening at school and I tell her about my non-life. She's something of a reader. We talk about books, and I've suggested a few authors for her to check out. Not being a complete dirtbag, I refuse to sell her wine coolers on school nights. She claims they help her sleep. I suggested masturbation as an alternative.

"Yeah, Danny, I bet you're a real pro at that."

"I'm available as a consultant, if you need any pointers."

"I sure won't be thinking of *you* when I do it."

"As long as it's not your lady gym teacher."

"It won't be, Danny. Don't you worry about that. Clare and I are going to a movie at the mall on Sunday. If you come and sit in our vicinity, we won't scream."

"It would have to be a show after six. I sleep during the day."

"I know. Like this poky hamster I used to have."

I got my first paycheck from Mrs. Park. What a joke. After Uncle Sam's deductions, I'm left with a few kopeks over $300. For a week's work! I had to dip into Tim's garage sale stash to pay my October rent. I need to be looking for another government job. You can starve in the Darwinian private sector. But will Gladys give me a decent reference? I wasn't very nice to her there at the end. Blowing smoke in her face from my illicit cigarette was probably a mistake.

I found out Wenda, my donut queen, is only 29. I thought she was older. I guess working in the middle of the night does take its toll. It's not from excessive donut consumption because she got sick of those years ago. The good news: she recently dumped her boyfriend. From her description, he sounds like a real cad. She could hardly do worse with me.

We shared some swallows of gin in the dead zone and I gave her a bit of a nuzzle and grope. The problem is she works seven days a week. The city-wide demand for donuts is insatiable. Most of her off-hours she spends sleeping or volunteering at the local cat shelter. Unfortunately, she's bonkers about felines. One strike against her ex-BF was that rude dude owned two big cat-loathing dogs. She's weaseled it out of me that I'm presently cat-less (and have been for the past 38 years). Now Wenda is agitating for me to adopt one of their surplus strays. I'm willing to do almost anything to get laid, but I draw the line at that.

* * *

A city cop woke me up today to tell me I had missed Kimberly's court hearing. Damn, it had totally slipped my mind. Anyway, the busybody judge made her restraining order permanent. If I try to contact her, it will mean jail for Danny. I told the cop I was over her anyway and could barely remember what the chick looked like. I said I was sorry for causing them any trouble. I told him to come by the mini mart any time after midnight for a free coffee or hotdog.

Of course, my landlady wanted to know why a policeman was visiting her tenant.

"I've been temping at the mini mart while they work on the

courthouse, Mrs. Goodsolm. There was a shoplifting incident. The cop wanted a more detailed description of the perpetrator."

"What did they steal, Danny?"

"An entire rack of birthday cards."

"Probably some pensioner my age with too many grandchildren. If you don't send them a card and a gift, the little bastards really pitch a fit."

"Kids feel so entitled these days," I yawned. It was the middle of the night for us day sleepers.

"I think abortion is not only a right, in most cases it should be compulsory."

"Right on, Mrs. G."

"I tell you, Danny, I don't want to live on a planet where every bushman and goatherd has a cellphone, a big-screen TV, and an SUV."

Probably not. Although I feel strongly that these lifestyle staples should be within reach of your average mini-mart employee. Right now, I'm only scoring one for three. I think people who sacrifice their sleep and normal life to work all night should be paid like surgeons and CEOs.

I suppose people-watching is one of the (few) perks of the job. A woman ran in the other night at three a.m. to buy a can of ant spray. You wonder why it couldn't have waited until morning. Were army ants invading from the tropics? Were they carrying off her cat? She took the time to pause and tell me I reminded her of her ex-husband. I've heard this comment before. No matter the age of the chick, I always reply that she reminds me of my grandmother. That usually settles the score.

There are definite sex differences in post-midnight purchasing. For example, at least 95% of the people buying beef jerky are men. Who knew that dried cow was a male food? Nor are women inclined to gulp down a hotdog or burrito at two in the morning. Men are also the predominant purchasers of candy. When chicks have a sugar craving, they go for the plain Hershey bars. They want their chocolate straight. Nougat, caramel, and nuts do not excite them. This is possibly useful information.

Startling fact: I sell more tampons to men than women. I assume this is because chicks send in boyfriends or husbands for the goods. When gals buy such items, it's always in conjunction with other stuff such as mints, gum, etc. The message to the clerk being, "Yeah, I'm a chick so I might need this someday, but I'm not presently menstruating, so get your mind off that." They don't want some stranger thinking about their private parts. Hah! I'm usually thinking about that anyway just to stay awake. And boobs: I check out every pair that comes through the door. Most, alas, are a complete waste of my time.

I've also observed ethnic differences. White people buy chocolate and vanilla ice cream. Black people buy strawberry ice cream. You could make money betting on this. Asians go for the triple combos like coffee-almond-fudge. Fruit sherbets appeal only to Latinos and the occasional lactose-intolerant Asian.

Cigarettes, beer, and booze are the biggest sellers, of course. Their appeal is universal. They'll be paying the tuition bills when Mr. Park's kids go to Stanford and U.C. Berkeley. I also sell truckloads of aspirin and other pain meds. Numbing reality: that's our stock in trade. Some items are just there for show; they never move off the shelf. I've yet to sell a single can of corn, although grizzled old guys shuffle in sometimes for a tin of beef stew. Are the people working in beef-stew canneries depressed by their jobs? Having to add exactly four soggy peas to each can. Something I think about as the minutes drag by in the dead of the night.

* * *

On Sunday at the mall Olivia showed up for the movie without her friend Clare. She had daubed on lipstick and eye shadow, and immersed herself in a bold floral scent. Was I now dating high-school girls? I suspected as much, though I made her buy her own ticket and popcorn.

"What happened to your pal?" I asked, while we waited for the lights to dim.

"I hate going to the movies with Clare," she replied.

"How come? Does she hog the armrest? Does she crack her gum during love scenes?"

"She never wants to talk about the movie afterwards. And gets mad if I try to. She thinks movies should just be absorbed like baby spit-up on a paper towel."

"Some people are like that, Olivia. It's a valid point of view. They think you lose the complexity of the experience by putting it into words."

"I think she's just lazy, Danny. She doesn't want to make the effort. Anyway, most of the movies we see aren't that deep. They're not life-altering experiences."

"Yet they stick in your mind, Olivia. Twenty years later, you'll be watching TV and thinking, hey, I've seen this flick before. Thousands of Hollywood tales are swimming around in our brains, affecting our thoughts and conduct in subtle ways."

"I guess that explains you, Danny Nixon."

"I guess it does, darling."

"Are you going to share what you're drinking out of that fake cellphone?"

"Not hardly, dear one. You be a good girl and eat your popcorn."

The movie was a frothy comedy about a bride who instantly falls in love with a hunky priest called in at the last moment to perform the ceremony after their usual priest got sick. All during the honeymoon she's obsessing about the sexy padre and her seemingly insurmountable problem that he's unavailable for dating by Papal edict. She's fantasizing non-stop about ways of seducing him, while the new hubby is stewing over his lack of marital relations. (Had I written the script, I would have complicated matters further by having the priest in a committed relationship with an altar boy.) Everything works out when it is revealed that the "priest" was in reality an actor hired by her wise old grandmother to invalidate the marriage because she knew it was a mistake. Not surprisingly, the pretend priest also falls for the bride. All ends happily except for the balding ex-bridegroom who gets it big-time in the neck. His pain and distress add to the fun as the credits roll.

Exiting the theater, we adjourned to the mall's food court, where my date was free to buy her own pizza slices. I visited the

Chinese stand for a plate of egg rolls and a beer.

"How did you like the movie?" I asked.

"It was OK. Kinda lame though. I mean why would a hot chick like her want to marry that turkey in the first place? The guy was such a lump, of course she's going to fall for the first cute guy she sees."

Olivia helped herself to a swallow from my beer.

"Sometimes hot chicks go for inappropriate guys, Olivia. There was this girl I knew in college: beautiful, smart, body like a Victoria Secrets model. A real stunner. She hooked up with this loser and went out with him for a couple of years. The guy was no prize in the looks department and had the personality of a slug. Her friends couldn't figure out what she saw in him."

"So what happened to them?"

"Eventually, she wised up and dumped him. She went on to have a brilliant career in the tech industry. Married some brainy M.I.T. grad, and they have a fancy estate up in the wine country."

"And the guy? Do you know what happened to him?"

"Last I heard he was clerking in a mini mart. Working the graveyard shift."

"She should have married you, Danny. It might have worked out."

"Not likely, Olivia. Nature prefers a better balance in matters of the heart."

I had embellished the story only slightly. I knew such a girl, but she had been going out with my roommate at the time. She never had much to say to me.

"I think marriage is weird anyway," said Olivia.

"Why's that?"

"Being shackled to the same person all those years? Getting on each other's nerves? I think marriage should have term limits like politicians. Every year you have to sign on for another term or you're automatically divorced."

"And what happens to the kiddies under your scheme?"

"They go off to the orphanage, where they get to hang with their peers and party all the time."

"Sounds good to me."

"So you loved that girl, huh?"

"I forget. It was a long time ago. So what's the plan for getting you home?"

"The plan was I was going to call my mom to come get me, but instead I could ride home with you. Or we could go back to your place." That last part she said with a seductive smile.

"I think we better stick with the original plan, Olivia. We'll call that the Jail Bait Avoidance Plan."

"Gee, Danny, you're kinda paranoid about that. Elvis met Priscilla when she was only 14. He didn't go to jail."

"It helps to be an international superstar, darling. You get to live in a golden dream world. Call your mother. And please don't mention my name."

* * *

When Mr. Park showed up for work Tuesday morning, I hit him up for a raise.

"After three months! After three months! You on probation now."

I pointed out that after three months I will have starved to death on my present wage.

"You got plenty of flab to lose, Danny. How long you wear that shirt? I need my employees to look sharp and smell good."

"I could afford to do laundry, Mr. Park, if I made more money."

"After three months! That's the American way. You do good job so far. Now go home and do your wash. And iron too. We want to make good impression on customers!"

What a cheap bastard skinflint. He leaves me no choice but to run more grifter scams on his customers. Too bad the restroom doesn't have a window. I could retire to the toilet, don a disguise, exit out the back, run in the front door, rob the till, then be back inside 30 seconds later. I could steal the place blind and tell the cops I forgot to lock the door when I went to take a leak. The perfect plan. Except there's no window in the crapper. There is a back door, but it has a video camera trained on it.

Instead of doing my laundry, after I woke up that afternoon I went to visit the donut queen at the cat shelter. Wenda was manning the cash register in the adjoining thrift store. That's how they keep all their homeless cats in eats and rubber mice.

"Hi, Danny!" she piped brightly in her little-girl voice. "Come to adopt a kitty?"

"I told you already, darling. My landlady doesn't permit pets."

"What's her number? I'll call her up and vouch for our cats. They're cleaner and neater than humans!"

"Forget it, Wenda. She's allergic."

"Not a problem. We can supply anti-allergy drugs too."

"Not happening, love. Not everyone on this planet is capable of coping with a cat. I think I was eaten by a lion in a previous life as an early Christian. Got any dinner plans?"

"You could take me out after I lock up. Go look around, Danny. I'm sure we've got something you need to buy."

I helped myself to a glazed donut from a box of day-olds on the counter, then checked out the store. The prices seemed kind of high for secondhand castoffs. I found a shirt in my size that Mr. Park might have approved of, but the price was six bucks. Too rich for me. I settled on a 25-cent potholder for which Wenda charged me $1.25.

"How come so much?" I asked, shocked.

"A quarter for the potholder, Danny, and a buck for the donut."

"Nowhere on that box does it say those stale donuts are one dollar," I pointed out.

"We used to write the price, but we found we sell way more donuts if we don't."

"Damn, you cat lovers are ruthless. And unscrupulous."

"It's for a good cause, Danny. Fork it over."

Naturally, she had to drag me through the back to see the cats before we left. Yeah, cats are cute, but those boys come equipped with teeth and razor-sharp claws. They like to shed hair and are known to be rapid transit for fleas. Plus, they prefer to eat dainty food out of those pricey little cans. Which they then barf into your lap. Their dream is to enter your home and shred all your furniture. You can see videos on YouTube of swaggering cats knocking big TVs off their stands. Some have been known to gnaw on your extremities while you sleep. And I haven't even touched on fur balls and the sex needs of the cat. Keeping all that in mind, I successfully resisted the impulse to walk out with one.

All of Wenda's people are from southern Oklahoma, which is practically Texas. We went to a favorite restaurant of hers, where she had the breaded and fried calves brains. You'd think eating like that she'd have a voice like Kathleen Turner's. I played it safe and went with the chicken-fried steak. Those Oakies do love their gravy. Wenda told me more about her job. Her brother Floyd fries while she dips, pumps, and boxes. She dips into sprinkles and frosting, and pumps in the jelly and custard. Then boxes up the goods for delivery. Her early-morning delivery route encompasses 46 stops over 115 total miles.

"Wow, that's a lot of donuts," I said.

"You bet your sweet patooti, Danny. Care for a bite of brains?"

"Er, no thanks. I've got plenty here."

I proposed splitting the check, but she replied, "I believe the gentleman invited the lady."

Did I? That doesn't sound like me. Next time I'll record the conversation on my cellphone. My credit card proved elastic enough to handle the charge–always a pleasant surprise. We went back to her place, where I got introduced to her four cats and the litter of kittens she's fostering. Those dudes will be moving on to new homes when they get old enough to shred sofas on their own. After all the cats got fed, the litter boxes cleaned, and hugs administered, there was no time left for fooling around with Danny. I was due at work in 15 minutes. Yet another reason to exclude cats from one's life. I did get a semi-passionate kiss and a bit of a feel up. She has an extremely palpable body. Her upper torso I'd rank right up there with Abby's.

I left with an erection and a fine dusting of cat hair.

This poem I found stuck under my windshield wiper:

Cat Caveats

Cats like to claw
And dally with vermin.
They eat 'em raw
While they're still squirmin'.

They saunter in for a lap,
And languidly start a bath:
Tonguing off the blood and crap
Like a furry psychopath.

They demand a pet
And a gentle caress.
Whisper only lest they fret
You're invoking cat duress.

"What a sweet kitty!"
You simper and coo.
In fact it's a pity
You don't flush 'em down the loo.

Or dice 'em in a stew,
And feed 'em to your crew;
Not that vile to chew.
Hell, it beats kangaroo!

Ten/NO WISE MEN

I got a nasty shock when I went to work. Young, handsome, and possibly virile Hwan was back.

"I thought you were in Korea getting married," I said.

"I was in Korea. Everyone in that country wanted me to marry that girl, except me. I refused."

"Good news, Danny," said Mr. Park. "Hwan is back, so now you work Mrs. Park's shifts on Sunday and Monday night."

That sounded like good news for his overworked wife, but bad news for Danny.

"You mean you're cutting me back to two nights?" I said. "How am I supposed to live on that?"

"You experienced now, Danny. You apply at mini marts for other days. I give you good recommendation. That look like same shirt from yesterday!"

"No, I've got two of them," I lied.

"I have Mrs. Park phone around," he said. "Maybe she find you other work. You go home now and do laundry. Come back on Sunday. Look at Hwan's shirt! It very clean and neat!"

True enough, but I wasn't hanging out with marriage-minded females in Korea for the past month.

I went back to my attic hovel and counted my cash reserves: a little over $800. That was all that was left from Tim's $2,700. The rest I had spent on rent, bills, gas for the Cordoba, Chesterfields, endless packs of nicotine gum, and excursions to Bottle Chalet. I had to do something fast or I'd be living in my car by Christmas.

Frankly, I was surprised I hadn't heard from the fugitive demanding his money. At this point I was kind of hoping that Tim had gone to Mexico and been decapitated by bandits.

Since it was still the middle of the day for me, I retired to my local dive bar. The bartender seemed pleased to see me.

"Hi, Danny," he said, pouring me a double tequila. "Where you been keeping yourself? I was beginning to think you were dead or married."

"No such luck, Sam. I've been working nights over at the mini mart."

"How's that pay?"

"Like hacking coal out of a Chinese mine. Know anybody who's hiring?"

"Can't say I do, Danny. We don't get many patrons from the employer class. Most of my customers are selling their blood for cash."

I was on my fourth double tequila when my cellphone rang. It was Olivia checking up on me.

"Danny, where are you? Hwan says you're only working weekends now."

"I'm at my men's support group. It's a school night, girl. Why aren't you in bed?"

"What kind of men's support group meets at one-thirty in the morning?"

"The best kind. Did Hwan sell you a wine cooler? Did that bastard feel you up?"

"The answer is yes to one of your questions. Gee, Danny, are you jealous?"

"You go home, darling. Right now. Don't become a teenage statistic."

"You sound like you've been drinking, Danny."

"I should certainly hope so. Take your wine cooler and go home."

"Are we having a date this weekend?"

"Certainly. Unless you get a better offer from Hwan."

"It's tough, Danny, because I like you both."

"Apparently, Olivia dear, you have a thing for mini-mart clerks. When you make up your mind, let me know."

"OK, Danny dear, you take care."

"Always, love. Always."

How to avoid getting a DUI on the drive home late at night

from a bar: Don't drive too slow or fast. Don't weave. And don't have your window rolled down. I learned that from a friendly deputy sheriff. The not weaving part is the hardest if you're really smashed. Oh, and try not to kill anyone.

Mrs. Park herself called me the next morning. That enterprising gal had found me a job at another mini mart. This one was in a neighborhood where convenience-store clerks have the same life expectancy as helicopter gunship pilots in Vietnam in 1968. Not wishing to die for the minimum wage, I declined the opportunity. She sounded a bit pissed when she rang off.

When I finally crawled out of bed, I felt exceptionally rotten even for me. I looked like something laid out on a slab for dissection by anatomy students. My hands shook as I lit my Chesterfield. I decided that what I needed to do was go to Tim's condo and see if there was anything left that I could sell or pawn for cash.

The condo was just as we had left it. Too bad we had sold off most of the furniture. I could have listed it on Airbnb and been renting it out for big bucks to well-heeled tourists from Scandinavia. I'm sure such visitors are dying to experience far distant suburbs of San Francisco.

The kitchen appliances were bottom-of-the-line builders' grade. I doubt I could get a hundred bucks for the lot of them. Too bad I'm not addicted to heroin. I might consider ripping the wiring and plumbing out of the walls and selling the copper. Way too much work for Danny. I did find $1.73 in loose change under the sofa cushions. I sat back in Tim's recliner and pondered my options. I could wait until all my money ran out and commit suicide. Not an uncompelling prospect. Be a nasty Christmas gift for my mother though. I could leave a note asking to be cremated in my Cordoba. Monica and other high-school chums could gather around and toss Molotov cocktails at it. With my corpse propped up behind the wheel and a cigarette in my lips waiting for a light. Dad probably would go for that.

Here I was a college graduate, but somehow I had missed that express bus to the Good Life. Prosperity was not happening for Danny Nixon. I had no job prospects. Nor was I particularly employable. Jewel-draped women were not giving me the eye. No wealthy relatives were about to drop dead and leave me a generous legacy. Well-connected friends were not reaching out to offer their assistance. Influential magazines were not snooping around to herald my unsung genius. No help was on its way from the Richard Nixon Fan Club or his well-appointed presidential library. (Does anyone visit there, I wonder? I expect they have some very slow days. Might they need a writer in residence? For example, I could write a biography for middle-school readers of Checkers the dog.)

Not likely, I suppose. All was now perfectly clear. I was at the bottom of a very deep pit.

I lit a cigarette and took a swig from my cellphone flask. Today's flavor was discount rum. Damn, was this it? Had all my dreams (such as they were) come to naught? Was this the end of the line for R. Daniel Nixon?

* * *

A faint glimmer of a ghost of a plan may be emerging. Not a great plan, but slightly more enticing than leaping off the Golden Gate bridge. Anyway, Good Samaritans are always dragging depressives off the bridge railing, and then the courts slap you with a big fine. The more practical types jump off the Bay Bridge. No pedestrians to dodge on that bridge. You just stop your car and leap. Not a glamorous way to go, but it gets the job done.

I spent the next few days doing some research and putting my desktop publishing skills to work. Bought some upscale frames at Wenda's rip-off cat store. I was finishing up the project when a woman knocked on my door. She looked vaguely familiar.

"Can I help you?" I asked.

"I'm Anne Chapben, Tim's ex-wife. He told me to come by and pick up the $2,700 you're holding for him."

"Where is Tim?" I asked, stalling for time.

"I'm not at liberty to say."

"Is he outside of the country?"

"I'm not at liberty to say."

"Uh, right, I suppose not. Would you mind showing me some I.D.?"

"OK," she said, opening her purse and displaying her driver's license. Unfortunately, she appeared to be Tim's ex-wife.

"Gee, that's the weirdest thing," I said.

"What is?"

"Do you know if Tim was married before? Or even after you?"

"No. I'm his only marital victim so far."

"The thing is, Anne. Right after the garage sale, another gal came to collect the money. She also claimed to be Tim's ex-wife."

"What!"

"That's right. I had no reason to suspect she was not who she claimed to be. So, of course, I gave her the full $2,700. In cash. I made her sign a receipt if you'd care to look at it."

"That won't be necessary. No doubt it's some scam of Tim's to get out of paying his child support. What a goddam chiseler. I'm gonna talk to my lawyer. He won't get away with this!"

"I can offer you my sincerest apologies for the mix-up," I said.

"What a goddam rat. How am I supposed to deal with this? I have bills to pay!"

"I know, dear. We're living in hard times."

Eventually, she left. Not a bad looker. I'd have invited her in for a drink, but she appeared too distraught to be interested in getting better acquainted with me. I did feel bad about stiffing her on the funds. But then I'm the last person I'd entrust with any significant wad of cash.

Step two of my plan: I wrote out my ad and posted it on Craigslist. Then I invited Wenda over for a cat-free dinner and seduction at my place. As usual I served fried shrimp. Here's the recipe: melt butter in skillet, dump in shrimp, fry until done. If you're really putting on the dog, you can squeeze on some lemon. Serve with boil-in-a-bag rice and a fine $2.89 Chardonnay.

Later, the sofa-based nuzzling was proceeding apace when Wenda dropped some disturbing news. Still reeling from her last breakup, she has revitalized her Catholic faith. She goes to church, she goes to confession, and she asks herself what would Jesus do. Apparently, Jesus would not go for petting below the waist or intercourse outside of marriage.

"Jesus, Wenda," I said, sliding my hand down her bra, "We're both adults here. Adults go out a few times and then have sex. That's standard operating procedure. You have very lovely breasts, darling."

"I'm glad you like them, Danny. But I think the tried-and-true old ways are the best. I feel it would be disloyal to my future husband to have sex with you."

"But what if I turned out to be your future husband?"

"Even more reason to dedicate ourselves now to the sanctity of marriage. Was that a proposal?"

"Not in so many words, no. But I do like you, Wenda dear."

"And I like you, Danny. That's why I'm kissing you and permitting myself to be groped within reason."

Groped within reason: leave it to the Catholics to cook up such a monstrous concept.

We were interrupted by vigorous pounding on the door.

"Who's there?" I called as Wenda extracted my hand and tucked things back in.

"It's me," replied a voice. "Owen."

I unlocked the door and Owen barged in, looking agitated.

"Wenda, this is Owen," I said. "Owen, Wenda. What's up, guy? We're kind of busy here."

"I'm here about the money, Danny. What's this bullshit you told Tim's wife?"

"Ex-wife, Owen. As I explained to her, it appears he has two of them."

"That's bullshit and you know it! You intend to keep the money yourself!"

"I hardly think so. And what's it to you, anyway?"

"We paid her the money! Maeve and I scraped up $2,700 and gave it to her. So she could pay her rent! So she could buy food for her daughter!"

"A noble gesture, I'm sure. If I ever see the gal who collected the funds, I'll ask her to pay you back."

"I'm not falling for that bogus story, Danny. You really are a case. You really are a complete failure as a human being."

"Hey, I'm a failure, huh? At least I wasn't so stupid and careless as to disfigure myself for life."

Here's another factoid in the Case Against Owen: once in downtown Modesto we passed a couple pushing a baby carriage. Owen said to the fellow: "That's one ugly baby, sir. It looks just like your wife." He was lucky he didn't get punched out. Admittedly, he was 15 at the time, but I ask you, was that the remark of a caring human being?

"I'm not claiming I'm any great shakes as a person, Danny, but you're about the lowest snake I know. Miss, if I were you, I'd steer clear of this deadbeat."

"I really don't know what you're talking about," Wenda replied coldly in her juvenile voice.

She looked at her watch.

"I need to go feed my babies, Danny. Thank you for the nice dinner."

"You don't have to go, Wenda. Owen's leaving right now."

"No, I'm not," he said. "I'm going to collect some of that $2,700 you owe us. Hand over your wallet, asshole."

"Get your phone, Wenda, and dial 9-1-1. Some intruder is trying to rob me in my own home."

"Don't bother," sighed Owen. "I'm leaving. But I'll be back. You better have the money ready too!"

"Dream on, fool. And try not to set yourself on fire again on your way out."

"Who was that?" asked Wenda when he was gone.

"Some guy I knew back in high school. I foolishly befriended him at our reunion last month. He's been bugging me for money ever since. Kind of a sorry mental case. Would you like to check out my bedroom?"

"I've got to go, Danny. I need to feed my cats and get ready for work. Ask yourself what would Jesus do, Danny. He'd probably want you to pay back the money."

I need Jesus to butt out of my personal life. I need that in a very big way.

* * *

On Saturday I didn't go to the movies with Olivia. Instead, we hopped on BART (Bay Area Rapid Transit), had lunch in Oakland's Chinatown, and toured the Oakland Museum. Kind of fun and all her idea. She insisted on holding my hand on the train, possibly grossing out our fellow passengers. I was hoping we were passing as divorced dad and affectionate daughter on a court-sanctioned visitation outing.

At the restaurant she said her friend Clare was advocating that she drop me.

"Why's that?" I asked, fishing a chicken foot out of my soup.

"She thinks you may be a pimp trying to recruit me for your stable of hos."

"Do a Google search for mug shots of convicted pimps. I don't really fit the profile."

"I know you don't, Danny. I'm sure you would have blackened at least one of my eyes by now and forced me to submit to your deranged lust."

Smiling saucily, she took a big swig of my Tsingtao.

"Please get your mind out of the gutter, girl. What else does Clare say about me?"

"She's pointed out the Christmas dance dilemma."

"What's that?"

"She claims if you take me to the Christmas dance, I'll be laughed out of our school."

"No doubt a valid point, dear one. I'm sure I'd be arrested on the spot. Your lovely corsage would be confiscated as evidence of my depravity."

"It's too bad, Danny, you don't look like a young Ben Affleck. We might get away with it then."

"Yes, that thought often occurs to me. Resembling a handsome movie star would solve so many of my problems."

"I like you just the way you are, Danny. You look very distinguished."

"You exhibit rather peculiar taste in men, darling."

"I know. I'm considered one of the weirder girls in my senior class. People are always amazed I haven't dyed my hair blue or had a teardrop tattooed on my cheek. You know: normal stuff that weird people do."

"Instead you go out with fellows twice your age."

"Charlie Chaplin and Woody Allen both married girls barely out of high school. And then there was that school teacher who had a baby by one of her elementary school boys."

"We're not getting married and we're not having any babies, Olivia."

"I know that, Danny. That's all in the future."

"The very distant future. For you, girl, only for you."

"Well, we'll just have to see about that," she said, leaning over and helping herself to another swallow of my beer, while flashing another alluring glimpse of an impish breast.

I refused to let my mind go there; I'm not the sort of person who would thrive in prison. Better to battle the Pope for Wenda's elusive prize.

A gallery at the museum was displaying some Diane Arbus prints.

"Danny, all these people look like your relatives," commented Olivia.

"Thanks. This deranged fellow bears a strong resemblance to your future husband."

Olivia inspected the photo with interest. "Not likely, Danny. Unless I marry you. How come she killed herself?"

"Crippling depression. Why else? Her brother was the poet and novelist Howard Nemerov."

"Do you like his stuff?"

"Some of his poetry is OK. I could never warm up to his novels. As dry as overdone toast. Apparently, he used to get it on with his sister."

"You mean like incest?"

"The very thing."

"Is that why she was depressed?"

"I'm sure I wouldn't know. As I recall her mother was similarly afflicted. Do you like her photographs?"

"Yeah. A lot."

"Me too. She grew up in the shadow of her famous brother. And now hardly anyone remembers him."

"I think it would be fun to be famous," said Olivia.

"Right. I think Charles Manson and Donald Trump had the same idea. Didn't turn out so well for either of them."

A rummage through the discard drawer of that alleged poet uncovered this zircon:

The Perks of Fame

You say you aspire
To the glories of fame:
Where all will conspire
To jubilate your name.

Any notoriety will do
No matter how niggling:
To bump you from the queue.
(Though some may be sniggling.)

Avid throngs will acclaim
You from their knees;
Their souls set aflame
By your every sneeze,

And twitch and yawn.
So cool to be the cynosure
Upon whom they fawn.
But tiring of the exposure,

You face the masses in dark glasses.
Mixing only with the elite
And the pedigreed classes.
So tiresome to have the rabble at your feet!

Eleven/MANNA FROM HEAVEN

When I showed up for work Sunday night, Mr. Park inspected my shirt and said it was "OK." He also informed me that Hwan sold twice as many lottery tickets as I did.

"It's my face," I explained. "It does not conduce optimism about sudden financial windfalls."

"No, Danny, you just lazy! You must say to customer: 'You want change back in lottery tickets?'"

"You've been asking me that for years and I always refuse."

"You cheap guy, Danny. Many other peoples say 'OK.' You sell more tickets, Danny, I think about raise for you sometime!"

"OK," I sighed. "Whatever you say."

The government expects us to walk the straight and narrow, but meanwhile it runs a lottery scam on its most gullible citizens. Someone will win the mega-millions jackpot, but it won't be you or me—no matter how many tickets we buy. You can count on that.

An hour or so into my shift Abby breezed in looking beautiful. This time she was buying a pint of Johnny Walker.

"You want your change in lottery tickets?" I asked.

"I hardly think so, Danny. I don't play those sucker games. How come you never call me?"

"You haven't given me your phone number, darling. And if you did, it would probably ring a tollbooth on the Golden Gate Bridge."

"They got rid of those. It's all automated now. They fired all the toll-takers. I don't suppose you own a decent suit."

"Why? Do you want to run off to Reno and get married? I'm free at eight."

"I'm looking for someone to impersonate a lawyer for an hour or two."

"I've got a respectable dark suit, Abby. Genuine wool blend. I plan to wear it to my parents' funerals. I keep it neatly pressed in anticipation. How much are you paying for this acting job?"

"I was thinking $500."

"Kinda puny compensation for felony work. I'll do it for $2,700."

"That's a rather specific and exorbitant figure."

"It's my firm price."

"OK, I'll think about it, Danny."

"I'd need 27 Benjamins laid on my palm before I'd commence the deception."

"Jesus, Danny, don't you trust me?"

"I wouldn't insult your intelligence by suggesting that I did, sweetheart. Are you giving me your phone number?"

"I'm running kind of late. I'll get back to you on that."

"Always a thrill to see you, Abby dear."

I could marry that woman. Naturally, I'd say the vows with all fingers crossed behind my back. And I'd look into getting some martial arts training before the honeymoon.

Not much of a nuzzle with Wenda this a.m. She was in a hurry to finish her donut deliveries so she could make it to mass. She tries to go at least every other day. Even worse, she invited me to go with her.

"I'm not a Catholic, darling," I pointed out.

"That's OK, they don't check for rosaries at the door."

"I also feel strongly that churches should confine their services to Sunday morning. For heavens sake, give it a rest."

"Jesus, Danny, don't you want to nourish your spiritual side?"

I'd rather nourish my sexual side, I thought but didn't say.

"Some other time, honey. I'm bushed. The boss had me flogging lottery tickets all night long."

"We had a really cute cat come in this week, Danny. A shorthair tabby, already neutered and chipped. He'd be perfect for you."

"I won't keep you, honey. I know you're anxious to get to church."

It appears the only sort of pussy I can extract from that girl is the kind that purrs.

* * *

No replies yet to my Craigslist ad. That's discouraging. I may have to try a different medium. Should I don a sandwich board and march about in Union Square?

Olivia showed up the next night looking for a wine cooler and/or me. She had to settle for me. She had a confession to make.

"You know where I was last night, Danny?"

"In bed with your foxy lady gym teacher?"

"Get over that, dude. I'm not a lesbian. I went to the movies with Hwan."

"I'm very much annoyed to hear that, dearest one. You need to stay away from that guy!"

"I don't see why I should. Are we a couple?"

"We're a couple of kindred spirits. We're a couple of cool cats."

"OK, but am I your *girlfriend*?"

"You're certainly a friend. And I have reason to suspect you're a girl."

"If that's your attitude, Danny, then I'm going out with Hwan too."

"Remember: it's jail if either of us touches you. And juvenile hall for you."

"You're just being paranoid, Danny. No one's going to know."

"Parents always find out, Olivia. Then the shit hits the fan. The entire legal system frowns on older men preying on young girls. Judges are not inclined to be lenient."

"Hwan's only 24. I told my parents he was 20."

"And what did you tell them about me?"

"Nothing, Danny. I'm not stupid. I can't tell them about you because of your age. And Hwan can't tell his parents about me because I'm not Korean. It's all screwed up. So are you jealous of Hwan?"

"Of course."

"I do like you more, Danny. Hwan can be a bit boring. All he talks about are the new apps he's trying out on his cellphone."

"The guy's been joined at the hip to that phone for years."

"But he does solve my Christmas dance dilemma. I could go with him and nobody would raise a stink."

"What's with this obsession with Christmas functions? It's not even Halloween yet."

"Hello, dude! Halloween was last week."

"You're kidding. How did I miss it?"

"Don't ask me, Danny. Maybe you slept a few days straight in your hamster cage. How about a wine cooler, so I can go to sleep and dream about you instead of Hwan?"

"Forget it, girl. It's a school night."

"Damn. Dating you is like going out with my grandpa."

"That's who should take you to the Christmas dance. People would find it charming."

"Your generation maybe. My generation would find it totally sick–and not in a good way. Want to make out in the dead zone?"

"Not tonight, honey. You run along now and get your beauty sleep."

Damn, we're already into November and I haven't paid my rent yet. No wonder Mrs. Goodsolm was flashing me the hairy eyeball. Thanks to Tim's garage sale I have the cash for this month's rent. God knows where next month's is coming from.

The next night I was back in the mini mart buying an emergency pack of Chesterfields from Hwan.

"You want your change in lottery tickets?" he asked.

"Drop dead, Hwan. I want my change in cash money, preferably with an extra dollar or two because of your incompetence. By the way, if I find out you're messing with Olivia, I'm calling the cops on you. She's only 17."

"That goes double for me, Danny. I'll drop the dime on you so fast it will make your head spin. And she's not 17, she's 16."

"No way, dude. She's a senior in high school. That makes her 17 at least."

"Guess you never heard she skipped a grade in elementary school."

"What!"

"Yeah, I just found that out from her pal Clare. So she's radioactive for 13 more months. Anyway, dude, you should go out with grannies your own age. That reminds me, some lady was in here looking for you last night."

"Really? What did she look like?"

"Like a solid ten. Like totally scorching. Like way, way too hot for you. She left you a note."

"So hand it over."

"I will if I can remember what I did with it."

A frantic search by me at last turned up a business card stuck under the hotdog grill. On one side was a printed phone number. On the other side was this handwritten note:

Danny,
I need you in your suit on Friday. Call me.
–A

Was I surprised that Abby's handwriting was like exquisite calligraphy?

Not really.

The phone number rang her answering service, not Abby herself. That didn't surprise me either. I left a message saying I was ready and eager to perform on Friday.

She called me back the next morning.

"I need you clean shaven and sober, Danny. That means no alcohol on your breath."

"Not a problem, darling. You will have the Benjamins lined up and ready?"

"You want to round things off to an even $2,500?"

"I only round up, Abby dear. I'm fine making it $3,000."

"No, we'll stick with your original amount. I'll pick you up. Please, don't disappoint me, Danny."

"I wouldn't dream of it, dearest."

I extracted my suit from the deepest recesses of the closet. It still fit OK, but I discovered I lacked a shirt that projected attorney-client prosperity. I had to go to Wenda's thrift store and fork over eight bucks for a used Hathaway broadcloth. A classy shirt, but why did it have to be pink? The monogram embroidered on the cuffs and breast pocket did not match my initials.

"Very nice shirt," commented Wenda, ringing up the sale. "This is nice enough to wear to a wedding–even your own."

"Very true, darling. Of course, I could never think of asking someone to marry me unless I was sure we were sexually compatible."

Wenda made a face and charged me ten cents extra for a bag.

"I could never get seriously involved with a fellow who wasn't a cat lover, Danny. Shall we go visit Trevor?"

"Who?"

"That's the kitty I was telling you about."

Yeah, Trevor was cute. The little bastard had figured out he needed to appear adorably playful to facilitate his adoption by some sucker.

"A great little cat," I lied. "If it weren't for my allergies and my landlady, I'd take him home right this minute."

"We need to find you another apartment," sighed Wenda.

"Good luck on that, dear. I've got the cheapest rent in the Bay Area. I can't afford to move anywhere else."

I put ol' Trevor back in his cage and wished him a speedy adoption. Not surprisingly, he tried to bite my finger.

* * *

Abby picked me up in her Prius at the designated hour.

"How do you like my suit?" I asked.

"It's OK. Breathe on me."

I leaned over and breathed on her swanlike neck.

"OK, you'll do, Danny. And no guzzling from any flasks you may have concealed on your person."

"So lovely and so hard. I like that."

"What's the monogram on your shirt?"

"J.M. I'm thinking of changing my name to Jesus Marigold."

"I'll introduce you as John Mitchell."

"Richard Nixon's dicey Attorney General. That's a nice touch. Did you know Halloween was last week?"

"Of course, Danny. They're not keeping it a secret."

"Did you go to a party?"

"Naturally."

"Who with?"

"That's none of your business."

"If you went to a party, you must have worn a costume. Now let me guess. What could that have been? Did you go as the Disney princess from 'Frozen'?"

"You're ice cold, Danny."

"Little Bo Peep? Queen Elizabeth II? Ivanka Trump? Zazu Pitts? Cher? Angela Merkel? Princess Leia? Ethel Mertz? Golda Meir? The Easter Bunny?"

"You were slightly warm at Cher. Give up?"

"OK, tell me."

"I went as Billie Holiday."

"A black jazz singer. Cool. How did you accomplish that?"

"Some theatrical make-up. A gardenia in a dark wig. A slinky 1940s dress."

"I know what you are, Abby. You're an artist. You're an artist through and through. You do everything most artfully."

"And what are you, Danny?"

"I'm a drunk. And today I'm impersonating a lawyer."

"You could be more than a drunk if you put your mind to it."

"I used to think so too. Now I'm just trying to stave off sleeping in my car."

We parked in the lot of one of those big assisted-living facilities for old folks.

"OK, Danny. You remember what we discussed? You're to let me do most of the talking."

"Right, chief. And did you remember my Benjamins?"

She opened her purse, took out an envelope, and handed it to me. I gave the Benjamins a fast count.

"I'm only counting 26, darling," I said.

"Sorry, my mistake," she said, handing me another hundred.

The woman is such an artist.

She tossed me a briefcase and said, "OK, let's do this."

We passed many inmates inching down hallways on walkers. If a worldwide aluminum shortage strikes, the cause likely will be all those decrepit Baby Boomers hobbling on walkers. Quite a few of the oldsters we passed smiled at Abby and greeted her by name.

Our appointment was in Room 312 on the third floor. The door was opened by an ancient woman who had shrunk and shriveled like some humanoid prune. She was wearing a chunky bead necklace over polyester workout togs. One of the matching earrings was attached to an ear and the other was clipped to her sparse hair, dyed a fierce shade of gold.

Abby made the introductions. The gal sported a name as exotic as her appearance: Mrs. Valverta Bizal.

"Nice to meet you, Mr. Mitchell," she said, giving my hand a weak squeeze. "Is your wife named Martha?"

"It used to be, but we got divorced."

"Oh, right. I think I read about that. How are my roots, Abby?"

"Looking fine, Valvie. I think we can go several weeks more."

"Abby is the best hairdresser I ever had. And she makes house calls!"

"You're too sweet, Valvie. Mr. Mitchell brought the papers you requested."

"I don't want my rotten daughter to get a cent! I want all that money to go to my grandson!"

I put my briefcase down on the bed and snapped open its latches with lawyerly élan.

"I can assure you, Mrs. Bizal, that none of the proceeds from your life insurance policy will be going to your daughter."

"Good. That's what I want. Trixie turned defiant at age four and got worse every year since. Can you believe the latest low-life she married?"

"I'm told he's quite an unacceptable lout," I replied, removing some documents.

"That's putting it mildly! They went on their honeymoon on his motorcycle! Would you want to consummate a marriage while scraping bugs off your face?"

"Not my idea of a romantic union," I said, clicking open the gold pen that Abby had provided in the case. "Just sign here where indicated."

Valverta took my offered pen and paused. "Do you think I ought to read through this first?"

"Of course, Mrs. Bizal. I recommend my clients read through every document they sign."

"Ah, I trust you. Abby says you're the best legal eagle around. When did you move out from D.C.?"

"Quite some time ago, Mrs. Bizal. Just sign where I've indicated with the Post-It notes."

"Abby says you're doing this as a favor, Mr. Mitchell, but I think I should pay you for your time."

"That's OK, Valvie," said Abby. "Mr. Mitchell is obliged by his firm to do a certain amount of pro bono work. Besides, he owes me a favor."

"Quite an attractive girl, isn't she, Mr. Mitchell? Not married either. And so talented! You could do a lot worse."

"I'm afraid we have to maintain strictly a business relationship," I replied. "Professional ethics you know."

"In that case, would you like to meet my daughter the next time she gets divorced?"

"I'd certainly consider it, Mrs. Bizal. Please sign where indicated."

At last, she got to work scrawling her signature, which Abby then notarized–being licensed by the state to perform that task.

We chatted for a few more minutes and then left. Riding down in the elevator, I took a tipple from my cellphone flask and asked Abby if we were fleecing that old lady.

"Only her grandson Stewart. He's a dentist in Orinda. He doesn't need her money. Besides, the creep rarely visits her. He even charges her his standard rate when he cleans her few remaining teeth. How about sharing that flask?"

"Be my guest. So you're a hairdresser by trade?"

"Not licensed. But I can make a 90-year-old pass for 82. It's a good way to meet elderly people of means."

"She might live ten more years."

"Not likely, Danny. I've seen her medical records."

"Are we going someplace nice for lunch?"

"Not that nice if I'm paying."

"You're paying, Abby. It's your way of congratulating me for a job well done."

"OK, Danny. I admit you were semi-believable as a shyster."

She drove to a hotdog place in a marginal neighborhood. We got our dogs and chips, and sat in a molded plastic booth that looked out on the litter-strewn parking lot.

"I'm amazed this place is still here," I said. "I haven't dined here in years."

"Only the best for you, Danny."

"I wish. So how much are you making off this deal?"

"I'm working with associates. The take is being split several ways."

"I forgot to look. Are you named as beneficiary on that policy?"

"Certainly not. That would be suspicious. The money is going to a registered charity."

"And what does your charity do?"

"We take care of orphans in foreign lands."

"Let me guess. Those lands are very far away."

"Very far indeed, Danny."

"I thought so. And are you going after any more of her estate?"

"All things in moderation, Danny. If you try to grab the whole pile, that pisses off the family. One insurance policy paying off to a charity they likely won't fight."

"I like the way you think, Abby. Need any more associates on your team?"

"We'll keep you in mind for other jobs, Danny. You understand that absolute secrecy must be maintained."

"Always, Abby dear. My lips are nailed shut. Were you really married to a guy named Todd?"

"No personal questions, Danny. You know me. I can't be trusted to answer truthfully."

"I know, dear. That's one of your more sterling qualities. You don't have to do this, you know. You could marry one of those venture capitalists or hedge fund titans and live the life of the one percent."

"Be kept by some boring stiff who expects a blow job every Friday night? No thank you."

"How many times a week do guys fall in love with you?"

"I get my share of nuisance attention."

"I'll bet. And mostly from those aggressive types. Shy guys lack the nerve to approach beautiful women. So it's mostly the jerks who hit on you."

"Yeah. Kind of a selection process at work. Aggressive guys breed more, which is why there are so many assholes in the world."

"If I were a handsome non-alcoholic, would you go out with me?"

Abby chewed her hotdog and swallowed. "Hard to say, Danny. I might. And I might not."

Even hypothetically, she was a difficult gal to pin down.

After Abby dropped me off, I phoned Maeve, who greeted me with icy reserve.

"What do you want, Danny?"

"I've tracked down that first gal who came here to collect for Tim. I got the money back from her. If you want it, you've got to get here right away or bill collectors may beat you to it."

"I'm at work, Danny."

"I'm not kidding, Maeve. I'm not sure how long my resolve to fork over the cash may last."

"OK. I'll come there right now. Don't go anywhere."

"I'll be here wistfully fondling the Benjamins."

Maeve showed up 20 minutes later. I'd forgotten how shockingly lovely she was. Certainly the most attractive woman ever to grace my shabby living room. I handed her the envelope in question.

"It's very nice of you to return the money, Danny."

"Tell Owen I'm expecting a full apology from him."

"I'm sure he's sorry for what he said. How are you, Danny?"

"Great. Couldn't be better. Feeling a bit poorer though. How goes it with you two?"

"OK. We're having to confront our situational dilemma. We live 92 miles apart. I love my job here. Sorry, I could never live in the Central Valley."

"Not wowed by Modesto, huh?"

"Unfortunately, I wasn't. Owen's farm is kind of pretty, if you like nature strictly regimented. They line up those trees like German soldiers. It's all your fault, you know."

"How's that?"

"You introduced us."

"You could have gone out with me instead. I'm practically the boy next door."

"I want to have a baby before I get too old."

"Is Owen up for the job?"

"He says he is. We just have to figure out the logistics."

That unpublishable poet has churned out some verbiage on this theme:

Love vs. Geography

The heart being fickle
It clamps on willy nilly
And lands us in a pickle
When we go and get silly

On someone drop dead
Fine, but here's the vex:
You in your perfumed bed
Lie far from your suitor's sex.

Feverish and prone,
You coo as lovers do,
Your moans sent by telephone:
You're wired to talk, not screw.

Technology has shrunk
The world in many ways,
But so far it has stunk
At dissolving the maze

Of frustration when he
Prefers his rural home:
Where she can foresee
Only death-by-boredom syndrome.

So time accumulates
And the miles add up,
Until love at last terminates
'Cause, hell, you're both so fed up.

Twelve/DIG AND DELVE

Wenda called me Saturday afternoon.

"I've got something alarming to tell you, Danny," she said.

Hey, if she's pregnant, it wasn't by me.

"What's that, Wenda dear?"

"Some people are here. They want to adopt Trevor. Shall I tell them he's already taken?"

"No, I'm willing to let him go."

"Are you sure? I thought you two were really bonding."

"No. Let them take him, if you think they'll give him a good home."

"They seem quite sincere. OK, Danny. I'll call you back when they're gone. I have something else on my mind."

I hoped against hope it involved sex, booze, or petting below the waist.

She rang me again a half-hour later.

"Hi, Danny. Trevor's gone."

"How did he take it?"

"Like most of us when we're commencing a new phase in life, he seemed fearful but exhilarated. I went to confession this morning."

"I hope you didn't mention my name."

"We discussed you in general terms. The priest said something fairly shocking."

"Lay it on me, darling."

"He said he didn't think it was wise to marry someone without first making sure you were sexually compatible."

"Hah! A pragmatic priest. That's refreshing."

"I'm not sure that's official Vatican doctrine. He isn't our regular priest. He's substituting while Father Michael is away at a retreat. He sounded a bit shocked when I broached the subject of premarital sex. For some reason he assumed I was a child. We talk behind a screen, you know."

"Right. What else did he say?"

"He said I shouldn't derive all of my emotional satisfaction from God and cats."

"You told him about your cats?"

"No, he could tell I had some. He claimed–like you–to have cat allergies. He was certainly sneezing and sniffling. Are you taking me out to dinner when I close up here?"

"I could, I guess."

"We could go to your apartment afterwards–assuming you had some condoms."

"I'm well equipped in that department, darling. Also in what is inserted in them."

"Don't be gross, Danny. Should the sex go well, I'll assume that we are officially engaged."

"Uh, let me think about that, dear one."

"You can think about it over dinner. I'm in the mood again for some fried brains."

I thought about it on the drive to the restaurant. Hell, it might not be so bad being engaged. Lots more couples get engaged than ever get married. The attrition rate is fairly severe. If Wenda demanded a ring, I might be able to extract some heirloom bauble from my mother's jewelry box. I'd have to filch it on the sly though. I wouldn't want to get her hopes up that grandchildren were on the way.

I used to think of myself as an intellectual. Perhaps that's why the thought of devouring brains leaves me queasy. I wonder if Wenda was a zombie in a previous life? This time I ordered the buttermilk fried half-chicken with biscuits, which landed on my stomach like a 16-pound bowling ball. Forking in the brains, Wenda had more to say on the subject of marriage.

"None of the women in my family works after they're married, Danny. Though I might continue volunteering at the cat shelter until the baby comes."

"The baby?" I said, shuddering. "You know kids might be a stretch on my income."

"Oh, I expect you'll take over my job."

"Right. Delivering donuts seven days a week."

"You deliver after you dip, fill, and box. My brother Floyd is anxious to meet you."

"And I him," I lied. "You don't mind working seven days a week?"

"You get used to it. Most people have too much spare time anyway."

I hoped that wasn't a personal dig against me.

Once again Wenda expressed zero enthusiasm for splitting the check. I scraped up the cash after my credit card was declined.

"That's not a very generous tip," she commented.

I tossed another buck on the skimpy pile of singles.

Later, I had a spot of trouble in bed.

"It's not very complimentary to a girl when a guy can't get it up," observed my nude companion in her tiny voice.

"I don't usually have this trouble, Wenda dear. It's just the pressure of this being our first time. I shouldn't have eaten all that chicken."

"Or drank those four beers."

A girlfriend who counts your drinks. Never a good sign.

"You have a very sexy body, Wenda. We'll just wait a bit for the news to reach my lower extremities."

"Sorry, Danny, I can't wait," she said, retrieving her bra. "I have to go home and feed my cats, and get ready for work. Why don't you phone me when your anatomy is working again?"

"Will do, dear."

Well, I didn't get laid, but—on the other hand—I'm not officially engaged either.

* * *

I received two phone calls today. The first was from Owen, who said he was "amazed" that I had the "integrity" to return the $2,700.

"Thanks, Owen. I like you too. I hear you may be a father soon."

"I love her, Danny. She's the one for me. I have to find a job up here."

"What are you qualified to do besides grow walnuts and marijuana?"

"Drive a truck, maybe. I have my commercial license."

"That probably pays better than clerking at a mini mart."

"Not much better. Union jobs are hard to find these days. It's easier to get into Stanford than the Teamsters Union. I'm sorry for running you down like that. I was pissed and got a little carried away."

"Not a problem. I got a little overheated as well. Jack Kerouac worked as a brakeman for the S.P. You could check if they're hiring."

"Railroads are much more automated now, Danny. They're running lean and mean."

"Yeah, aren't we all?"

"We'll have you over for dinner again soon, Danny. Thanks again for returning the cash."

"My pleasure," I lied.

The second call was the first promising nibble from my Craigslist ad. I made an appointment to meet the guy at my office on Wednesday afternoon.

I didn't see Olivia again until my Monday night (technically Tuesday morning) shift at the mini mart. She strolled in at one-fifteen looking daisy fresh.

"I'm pissed at you, darling," I said.

"What the hell did I do, Danny?" she demanded, lounging on the counter.

"You lied about your age. You told me you were 17 going on 18."

"That Clare has a big mouth. Anyway, I didn't lie. I'm a very mature 16, Danny. That's the same as being 17."

"Not to the judge sentencing me for statutory rape."

"As if you have a hope of jumping this voluptuous bod."

"You need to look up the definition of voluptuous, dear one."

"Don't knock it if you haven't tried it, Danny. Anyway, I'm madder at you than you are at me."

"And why's that?"

"I heard the news from Hwan. You got yourself engaged to some donut pusher."

"What makes him think that?"

"He got it straight from the slag herself when she bounced in with her goods."

"She's not a slag. I've gone out with Wenda a few times. As far as I know, we're not engaged."

"It would be just like you, Danny, to hook up with some delusional chick."

"You mean like getting confused about her age?"

"I happen to believe you're as old as you feel. Guess what?"

"What?"

"A guy at school I've been saying hi to in the halls sent me a dick pic. It's my first."

"That's gross. What did you do?"

"I showed it to Clare. She was impressed."

"Let's see this atrocity."

Olivia flipped through her phone to the photo in question and held it up for viewing. Definitely an eyebrow-raiser.

"Yeah, I guess that's impressive, if that's really him. You should show that to the principal of your school. And get that degenerate expelled."

"Not likely, Danny. You think this means he likes me?"

"Who knows? I haven't a clue about the dating rituals of your generation."

"Want to go to the dead zone and neck?"

"OK. But we have to stop if a car pulls into the lot."

We had a bit of a nuzzle and grope. My dormant anatomy certainly revived with a 16-year-old in my arms. Extremely luscious lips, yielding invitingly to pressure. Girlish smells and the myriad of other jail-bait enticements. Eventually, I had to bring a halt to the steamy osculations.

"What time does that slag deliver the donuts?" asked Olivia, pulling down her jacket.

"Around six in the morning. Why?"

"I'll be back then."

"Don't be absurd, darling. You'll still be asleep."

"Nope. I'm setting my alarm. I need to check out the competition!"

Fortunately, Wenda arrived with her armful of pink boxes a little past five-thirty. So as to hasten her departure, I helped her arrange the goods in the pastry case.

"Wenda dear, could you clarify a matter for me?"

"I'll try, Danny."

"I was under the impression we weren't officially engaged unless the sex proved satisfactory."

"That was the original plan, Danny dear, but that deal may have been offering too much incentive to your little penis to slack off. Commitment issues can show up down there. I think being engaged now takes the pressure off of you to perform."

"Er, right. You know guys don't really appreciate their penises being linked with the adjective 'little.'"

"That was a term of endearment, Danny. Besides it really wasn't very large in its relaxed state—no criticism intended. I'm sure it will be all a girl could desire when erect. At least I hope so."

Olivia never showed. I wasn't surprised. No teenager in America could get up that early except at the point of a gun.

When I rose from my all-day snooze, a package was waiting for me. Inside was this note from Abby:

Danny,

Grateful for your help, Mrs. Bizal wanted to give you something. Enclosed is her late husband's toupee. She claims it was made by a famous "hairdresser to the stars" in Beverly Hills. She mentioned the names Frank Sinatra and Joey Bishop. You couldn't prove it by me. Feel free to toss it if you want.

–Abby

I unwrapped the tissue paper. Inside was the previously owned hairpiece, looking like a small dead animal. So much less welcome than a generous gratuity in cash. Nevertheless, I slapped it on my bare dome and checked out the effect in the bathroom mirror. Suddenly, I had hair–indeed a fuller crop than I possessed at age 11.

I decided to test out my suave new Rat Pack look on my landlady. I went downstairs and knocked on Mrs. Goodsolm's door.

"Hello, Danny. My goodness!" she gasped.

"Got it in the mail today. What do you think?"

"Damn! That's a very attractive rug. Quite sensational, in fact. It looks to be hand-tied human hair. And it's a perfect match to your hair color. It must have cost you a fortune!"

"Nah, it was a gift. From an admirer. You think I could sell it on eBay?"

"You'd be a fool to do that, Danny. You should wear it. That rug does wonders for your looks."

"Yeah, until it blows off in the first wind."

"You adhere it to your scalp with double-sided tape. They sell that by the roll in beauty supply stores."

"How come you know so much about toupees?"

"My brother Gus had one. He had to wear it for work."

"What was he? A gigolo?"

"He was a waiter. He worked at a bunch of those Dago joints at Fisherman's Wharf. He claimed he always made better tips when he wore his rug."

"You mean to say people are more generous to waiters with hair?"

"My brother proved that scientifically over a 40-year career. I bet it's true for other professions as well. Wear that rug, Danny, and you could be going places."

"You don't think it looks silly?"

"The cheap ones do. But, hell, you've got the Rolls Royce of toppers. It looks like it was custom made for you. Of course, you have to take care of it. Shampoo it regularly and comb it out. Nothing more unsightly than an ill-treated toupee. My brother always babied his."

"Thanks for the advice, Mrs. G. I'll think about it."

"You can think about it while raking up those leaves in the back yard."

"Oh, OK. I'll get right on it."

Later as I was passing a beauty supply store on the way to Bottle Chalet, I stopped in and bought a roll of that special tape. Kind of expensive stuff, but they always clip you for anything related to human vanity.

* * *

I was slightly late for my appointment on Wednesday. I had dressed for the occasion in my funeral suit and new rug. My prospective client was waiting by the entry to the condo when I pulled in and parked. He was a paunchy middle-aged man in a lightweight jacket over colorful golf attire.

"You Dr. Nixon?" he asked, when I hurried up.

"I am. You must be Eugene Crosley."

"Call me Gene. That's quite the car you're driving."

"I took it in trade from a client who was short of cash."

"What was he, a pimp?"

"I'm afraid that's confidential. My office is right down the hall."

I unlocked the door to Tim's condo and invited him in. He looked around.

"Kind of sparsely furnished," he said. "Did you just move in?"

"Recently, in fact. I moved here from Boston. The latest research has shown that office distractions should be kept to the barest minimum."

"I see you got a bunch of college diplomas and licenses," he said, examining my framed handiwork arranged on a wall. "You must like to study."

"It's a necessity to practice in my profession."

"Yale and Princeton. That's impressive. A Ph.D. too. I hear that stands for Piled Higher and Deeper. Do I take the sofa or the recliner?"

"You sit in the recliner. Make yourself comfortable. There are tissues on the coffee table if you need any."

"I'm not planning on doing any bawling, Doc."

"That's fine," I said, sitting on the sofa with my notebook and pen. "Now for a few preliminaries, Mr. Crosley. What is your occupation?"

"I own a towing company."

"You rescue people whose cars have broken down?"

"Yeah. And if they've run into a tree. Got to love all those distracted drivers texting on their phones. But the real money is in parking enforcement. The fools who park in tow-away zones are my bread and butter. What time you got, Doc?"

I looked at my watch. "Uh, ten after four."

"Lots of tow-away zones start at four. I expect my guys already snatched over a dozen vehicles. It all adds up, but probably not like your racket. Your ad said sliding scale. What are we looking at here for your fee?"

"My minimum is $125 per 50-minute session, payable by cash or check."

"You don't take insurance?"

"I did back east, but I haven't arranged for that yet. Is that a problem?"

"Nah, I'd rather not have my insurance agent thinking I'm a loony. I'm only here because my old lady is on my ass. She thinks I have a problem."

"And why is that?"

"I occasionally swipe things. No big deal."

"What sort of things do you steal?"

"Can I plead the Fifth Amendment on that?"

"Everything you say here is confidential, Mr. Crosley. You may speak freely."

"Mostly I swipe salt and pepper shakers from restaurants."

"And what do you do with them?"

"I store them in my garage."

"How many do you have?"

"I'd say over 500 sets. Could be a thousand. I doubt if I have 5,000."

"And why do you take them?"

"Isn't that your job to figure out? Anyway, it's not like I'm really stealing."

"How do you figure that?"

"Because I always leave more money than the bill. I'm a fairly generous tipper. I figure my tip buys me a souvenir of my choice."

"But your tip goes to the waiter and kitchen help. The restaurant is still out the price of the shakers."

"That's what my wife claims. I'm not interested in doing this if you're going to gang up on me."

"Not at all, Mr. Crosley. I think I can help you if you wish. I have extensive experience with these sorts of cases."

"I don't consider it a case, Doc. I consider it a hobby."

"Right. Well, we'll look into that. Shall we begin?"

"OK, Doc. You got me for one session. And then we'll see. I figure you must know what you're doing. The suit you probably got at J.C. Penney, your office seems kind of improvised, but that looks like one expensive toupee."

"You didn't think it was my real hair?"

"Why? Is that some sort of test you shrinks do? If I can't tell it's fake, that means I'm insane?"

"Not at all. I was just wondering. Why don't we start at the beginning? Tell me about your parents, Gene."

The 50 minutes zoomed by way faster than slaving at the mini mart. I even gave Gene a little extra time since we started late. He wrote out a check to R. Daniel Nixon that probably won't bounce since it was drawn on the Crosley Towing Service. He agreed to return the same time next week. An interesting case that should prove semi-fascinating to explore.

It's not like I'm totally unqualified to be a shrink. I've read some Freud and Jung. I watched the movies "The Snake Pit" and "One Flew Over the Cuckoo's Nest." Back in college I had a roommate who subscribed to *Psychology Today* that I used to read on the john. Besides, who wouldn't benefit from opening up to a compassionate stranger? Hell, the Catholic church has been mining that vein for millennia.

Not to mention that I'm giving him a great deal. Most pros in the Bay Area charge way more than my measly fee.

So far psychotherapy seems like an OK gig, except you have to wear a suit and listen to a bunch of whiners. The pay is way, way better than the minimum wage. If I got a few more neurotics on board, I might be able to pay my rent next month.

Another tedious time out to give that unknown poet his say:

Seeking Professional Help

Mother let you wail in your crib.
Dad got the sex instead of you.
Sister stole your bunny bib.
No wonder your id is a grisly stew.

Brother had a bigger member;
He used to wave it in your face.
Other traumas you can't remember,
Plus nasty stuff you can't efface.

All that's aboil in your brain;
Loved ones fear you're going nuts.
Your psyche oozes like a septic drain.
Now it's time to spill your guts.

Professional help is on its way:
Excavating the sick and smutty.
Putting your past on Instant Replay.
Hacking inward with Freud's machete.

Paying for each week's regression,
You gasp at every psychic blast.
And swiftly void each dark obsession,
'Cause at these rates you gotta get well fast.

Thirteen/CLIENTS PREEN

I decided to bone up by reading the Wikipedia article on kleptomania. A knotty problem related to pyromania with many possible causes and treatments. At least my patient isn't dining out and then setting the restaurant on fire. Interestingly, ol' Gene chose a profession where he (sort of) gets to steal people's cars. One possible cause is a "dread of castration." I can relate to that. And some of those salt shakers can be more than a bit phallic.

I could specialize in kleptos and start a side business fencing the hot goods. But that would be wrong, as Dick Nixon used to enunciate clearly into the Oval Office microphone recording his every word.

Business is looking up. I made appointments with two more possible therapines. (A word I just invented for people in therapy; our language needs to keep up with the times.)

I taped on my new hair and went to see Wenda at her cat emporium. She examined my altered hairline with interest.

"You look younger, Danny, but not as intelligent."

"Thanks, dear. I think."

"How much is this faux leopard-skin lampshade?" asked an artsy-looking shopper.

"Price is marked on the inside," replied Wenda. "What do you think of my boyfriend's new wig?"

The fellow checked me out. "I'd prefer it dyed a bright fluorescent orange. It's certainly better than Andy Warhol's. Did you find that thing here? Or did you skin some cat?"

"It's hand-tied human hair," I said. "From a shop in Beverly Hills."

"Very flattering," he said. "It's nice to know the toupee and the padded bra are here to stay. Can you do better than $18 on the lampshade?"

"Only if you also take a kitten," she replied.

"OK. Eighteen bucks it is."

After the fellow paid, I asked Wenda if she wished to return to my attic hovel for a bedroom rematch.

"Didn't I tell you, Danny? You're coming over to my place tonight for dinner with my brother."

"No, you didn't mention it. When should I show up?"

"At seven with a bottle of alcohol-free wine. And wear your new hair."

Naturally, I arrived with a bottle of real (albeit cheap) wine. Floyd was doing the heavy lifting in the kitchen. It appears he's the chef in the family. He's a bit roughhewn like his sister, except his features seem slightly askew. Like everything got jiggled out of place. He also walks with a limp.

"Care for a glass of vino?" I asked, after Wenda made the introductions.

"Not me," said Floyd. "This meal is like my breakfast. Wenda gets by on three or four hours sleep, but I have to snooze the full shift. Wenda says you have a drinking and smoking problem."

"I smoke and drink, Floyd. I function OK. Not a problem."

"I expect she'll be reforming all that. She does like her projects."

"Hardly a man around who can't stand some remodeling," said Wenda, pouring two cups of coffee and frowning when I said I was sticking with wine. Good thing I brought a screw-top bottle as no corkscrew was offered.

Dinner was pesto-stuffed chicken breasts over rice with grilled long beans on the side. Not bad for amateur work, as my father says to my mother after ingesting her meatloaf.

"Floyd got his limp in a motorcycle wreck," announced Wenda.

"Oh?" I said.

"Yeah," said Floyd. "I rode Harleys for years. An old guy pulled out right in front of me. I T-boned into the side of his Grand Marquis. Smashed my face all to pieces. I was in the hospital for two months. Wasn't making donut one. The business went all to hell. The doctors kept threatening to chop off my leg. Wenda wouldn't let them."

"You can't stand on your feet all night frying donuts if you've only got one leg," she said. "Now Floyd's into vans big time."

"I decided I needed more metal around me. I cherried out a vintage GMC, a '79. Did the whole interior in blue shag. Had the vibrating bed, the mini-fridge, mood lights, rotating mirror ball, glide-out porta-potty, and a stereo with 18 speakers. You could hear me coming from three blocks away."

"I'd like to see it," I said.

"Oh, I sold that one. Wouldn't pass the smog. And all that shag got a little funky over time. I hear you're driving a Cordoba."

"Right. A 1978. Same year as my birth."

"Good luck keeping that running. Not many cars from the 1970s left on the road. Engineers back then went wild with smog gizmos trying to clean up those carbureted motors. They really strangled the horsepower. Plus, your gas mileage sucked. I bought a brand new van last year. The extended model with seating for 12. Of course, I yanked out the three rear seats. I'm using them as sofas in my apartment."

"His living room looks like a bus-station waiting room," said Wenda.

"It gets the job done," he replied. "You like chicks in fuzzy sweaters, Danny?"

"Sure. Who doesn't? The tighter the better."

"I found some of that material. Feels real soft and plush like angora. Did the whole interior of my van in it. In shades of silver and baby blue. Makes you want to get naked and roll around in it."

"Right," I said, refilling my wine glass. "Do you have a girlfriend, Floyd?"

"Not yet. I haven't finished my van. I'm installing the flat-screen TV this weekend. When I get my van done, I'm going to find a chick and go cruising."

"You can't cruise very far if you have to work seven days a week," I pointed out.

"That's why I'm glad you're hooking up with Wenda, Danny. Once we get you trained, I figure you can take over some of my shifts. Then I can go out and get laid."

"You don't have to be so crude," said his sister.

"Everyone needs to get laid, Wenda," he said. "Probably even you."

That point is debatable, I thought but didn't say.

After dessert (pineapple parfait), Wenda volunteered me to do the dishes, while Floyd read his custom-van magazine and she fed her cats. Later, when I was ready for a roll in the hay, she informed me it was time for her to go to work.

Wenda has some peculiar ideas about marriage. Apparently, she thinks I'm going to give up smoking and drinking, and spend my nights frying donuts. I suspect ours will be a short engagement. And since when do you invite guests over for dinner and expect them to do the washing up?

* * *

My Friday appointment was with an attractive gal in her late twenties named Susan. After the preliminary chitchat, we got down to brass tacks.

"What brings you here today, Susan?" I asked, pen poised over notebook.

"I have something of a sexual problem," she confessed.

"Could you elaborate on that?"

"I think sex is disgusting," she blushed. "The act repels me."

"I see. Is this embarrassing for you, Susan? Perhaps you would feel more comfortable discussing this with a female therapist."

"I had one. I hated her. Not helpful at all. She treated me like there was something wrong with me."

"Right. So you don't find sex enjoyable?"

"How could I? It's *so-o-o* icky."

"Have you had many partners?"

"I've had seven boyfriends since I was 18. We always break up over sex. They pester me for it and get mad when I refuse. Why do guys want it so bad?"

"It's to perpetuate the species. To raise children to adult-hood, men have to stick around for at least 18 years. They have to deal constantly with obnoxious juveniles. It's like running your own day-care center. You have to read to them out of boring books and watch puerile videos until you're ready to scream. Plus, kids eat a lot and demand expensive athletic shoes and cellphones. Often they wreck your car and want you to pay for college. They play horrible music, have sex prematurely, and expect you to support the baby. Therefore, nature has to give the male a powerful incentive to hang around and put up with all that grief. Otherwise, the human race would die out."

"I get that, but why does it have to be so disgusting? Some guy lies on top of you and wiggles his thing around in you, then leaks out this yechhy fluid. How primitive is that? If that isn't the definition of gross, I don't know what is. And half the time he expects you to suck on the smelly thing. No thank you!"

"You don't have orgasms, Susan?"

"I have plenty of orgasms—with my trusty vibrator. Which I then wash thoroughly and put away until the next time. No odor, no fuss, and reliably sanitary. No diseases to catch either."

"But you don't climax during sex?"

"I hardly think so. Why would I? Penises don't vibrate."

"Uh, true. Let's start at the beginning, shall we? How do you feel about kissing?"

"Kissing is all right, as long as the lips stay dry and his breath is OK. I usually hand him a mint first. I could never kiss a smok-er. Yuck. And he can keep his tongue to himself. Double yuck. I always keep mine lodged firmly behind a molar. Do you have to chew that gum, Dr. Nixon?"

"It's nicotine gum. Would you rather I smoked?"

"Certainly not."

"OK. And how about touching?"

"I had a foot massage once that wasn't half bad. Scalp mas-sages can be OK too. But he can keep his hands off my breasts and my clitoris—assuming the oaf could locate it. And no tunnel-ing around down there for alleged G-spots."

"You don't find such touching pleasurable?"

"No, because by then he's got a bulge in his pants and I know where we're headed. Having a vagina myself, I admit they're disgusting. Nobody appreciates a stinky discharge. And the bleeding is an affront to all concerned. But penises are truly repulsive. Do guys know how ridiculous they look with a hard on? And all that unsightly pubic hair. Not to mention those grisly testicles. The droopy kind are the worst: saggy and lumpy like something out of a textbook on diseases of the sheep. I'm amazed guys are willing to take off their clothes. And please, whack off that cheesy foreskin! Plus the rest of it while you're at it."

"Perhaps you're over-intellectualizing here, Susan. Sex is more enjoyable if you can switch off your critical mind."

"That go-with-the-flow bullshit doesn't work with me, Dr. Nixon. Nor do alcohol, marijuana, soft music, slick Italian crooners, saunas, hot tubs, waterbeds, or porno flicks. And you can stick your tantric techniques where the sun don't shine."

"Perhaps your difficulty is with men. Have you ever tried making love with your own sex?"

"My previous therapist asked me that too. She may have been trying to come onto me. Dressed rather butch if you know what I mean. No, I'm not a lesbian. I'm a normal, healthy woman who doesn't want to be alone. I want to get married and have children. I want a family of my own."

"You have to have sex to have a baby."

"OK, I'm willing to do it a few times until I get pregnant. Or artificial insemination–that's even better. Are there guys out there who think like me?"

"Possibly. There are gay men who for whatever reason want a wife and family. Would that setup work for you?"

"Not if he's going to cheat on me with a bunch of guys. Marital fidelity is very important to me. Here's my ideal: me in my bedroom with my vibrator. My loving husband in his bedroom with his hand or whatever. And the kids asleep in their rooms. Is that too much to ask?"

"I don't think so, Susan. But you're not likely to encounter such men in the normal course of daily life. I think you would have better luck with a personals ad or by trying an online dating service. I think if you spelled out your needs and wants exactly as you expressed them to me, some candidates would be forthcoming."

"I'm not looking for a passive mama's boy, Dr. Nixon."

"Make that clear in your ad, Susan. Be specific."

"He's got to be aggressive in his career. He's got to earn at least six figures, and be tall and handsome."

"Right. Well, he's probably out there," I lied. "Would you like to set up a schedule of sessions to work on these issues?"

"I don't think so, Dr. Nixon. I think you've clarified my thinking. You've helped me immensely. How much do I owe you?"

"The fee for one consultation is $150."

"Not a problem," she said, extracting her checkbook from her purse.

"I'm happy I was of help to you, Susan. Let me know how your search goes."

"I certainly will," she said, handing me the check. "Say, I don't suppose you're unattached?"

"Uh, no. I'm engaged."

"Right. And anyway, I expect you're one of those types who'd want to have intercourse with me."

"I don't think we need to speculate on that."

"I just don't get it, Dr. Nixon. I just don't get the appeal of sex!"

"Well, different strokes for different folks."

"Or none as the case may be," she said with a shudder.

What a waste of a foxy body (hers not mine). Had she been willing to return for another session, I might have suggested working on her problem while reclining nude in the bedroom. I wonder how much extra I could charge for serving as a sexual surrogate?

My theory is she'd seen her father naked a few too many times. Or her toilet training started way too soon. Early bathroom trauma can put a person off sex for good. It's a shame we won't be diving into all that. I do have a headline for her personals ad: REPULSED BY SEX? I'M YOUR GAL.

My wannabe therapine on Saturday was a chick named Veronica. Not a beauty like Abby or Maeve, but certainly present-able in a Joan Cusack, girl-next-door sort of way. She said she was 33 and couldn't get a date.

"Guys want me as a friend," she said, "not as a girlfriend. It's been like that forever."

"So how long has it been since you had a date?" I asked.

"Can I just say multiple years?"

"OK. Do you find sex disgusting?"

"I think it's a beautiful and loving expression of human closeness. Why? Do I give off that vibe?"

"Not at all, Veronica. It's just a question we therapists have been trained to ask."

"You can call me Ronnie. That's what my friends call me."

"Have you had boyfriends in the past?"

"Three. They all cheated on me with other girls and then ditched me. I'm such a doormat."

"Never been married?"

"I should be so lucky to get a guy to think of me in that way. No, never been married. No proposals. No kids. No life."

"What have you done to try and get a date?"

"Everything. I've read the books and the magazine articles. I'm gregarious and upbeat. I dress nice. I smell good. I put my-self out there. I took up golf. I tried tennis. I even went to AA even though I don't drink. Three guys wanted to be my sponsor to keep me sober, but otherwise zip. The last thing I tried was joining a church."

"Are you religious?"

"Not at all, but it was a Unitarian church so that's OK. Met some nice guys there who are treating me like a favorite sis-ter. They take me aside to tell me about their love lives. I go to church potlucks with my blouse unbuttoned down to there and nobody looks twice. I feel like wearing a button that reads: GUYS, PLEASE FUCK ME. Do you think I come across as too des-perate?"

"I'm not getting that vibe, Veronica. I'm a bit concerned about the men you've chosen in the past. We could go into these issues if you like. My minimum sliding-scale fee is $125 per 50-minute session."

"I'd like that, Dr. Nixon. I have some money saved up. We could try it for a time."

"Good. Shall we do some role-playing?"

"What do you mean?"

"Let's pretend we're at a church supper and I've just sat down beside you."

"OK. I get it." She smiled and extended her hand. "Hi, I'm Ronnie."

"I'm Daniel," I said, shaking her hand and not smiling.

"I see you took some of the potato salad I brought. How do you like it?"

"It's not as good as my mother's."

"Really? Tell me about her."

"She's dead."

"Sorry to hear that. My condolences."

"That's OK. I didn't much care for her."

"Right. I know how that can be. Uh, what do you do, Daniel?"

"I'm unemployed."

"That's too bad. Were you laid off?"

"I was fired for sexual harassment. My secretary had to get a restraining order against me."

"Well, there are always two sides to every story. It sounds like you were in an executive position since you had a secretary. That's impressive."

"I only got hired because my dad owns the company."

"What sort of company is it?"

"We make land mines. We sell them through arms dealers around the world."

"That's fascinating, Daniel. I'd like to hear more about that."

"People step on them and get their legs blown off."

"Uh, I'm not getting the point of this conversation, Dr. Nixon."

"That's my point, dear. You don't have to be so upbeat and agreeable. Perky as a go-to mood can be distancing. Doris Day never had that great of a love life either. And isn't Ronnie a guy's name?"

"My parents named me Veronica. I can't help that."

"How about slicing out the middle and going by Vera?"

"Vera. I kind of like that. It's sort of exotic."

"It's also way more feminine than Ronnie."

"Yeah, I see what you mean."

"It's occurred to me I know a fellow around your age who's looking to meet someone."

"Really? What's he like?"

"I don't know him that well, but he seems like a nice guy. He's a hard worker. He owns his own business. He's an excellent cook. As a hobby, he likes to customize his van."

"He's not one of those seducers, is he? You know, one of those lowlifes who only wants to shag girls in his rolling passion pit."

"I don't think so. But it's good that you ask those sorts of questions. He has a bit of a limp. Do you mind that?"

"Not if he's otherwise intact."

"I believe he is. Shall I give him your number and see if he wants to call you?"

"Sure, Dr. Nixon. Please do."

* * *

That afternoon I called Wenda at the cat store to get her brother's number. She had some alarming news.

"I got mugged, Danny. This morning. While delivering."

"Really! What happened?"

"I was taking boxes out of the truck, when somebody pushed me from behind. They made me drop my load. I skinned up my knees. When I looked up, I saw some teenage girl running away."

"Oh, really. Did Hwan see who it was?"

"How did you know it happened there?"

"Uh, I don't know. I just assumed that, since that's where I know you from."

"Hwan claims he didn't see anything. But he has a clear view of the parking lot from the counter."

"He probably had his nose buried in his phone. Are you OK, darling?"

"I'll live. But we had to scrap nine-dozen mixed donuts. I dropped them off later at the homeless shelter. I told them to pick off the dirt and gravel."

"Right. Well, that's certainly shocking. Did your attacker say anything?"

"Yes, she did. She said: 'Keep your mitts off my boyfriend, you ugly skank.'"

"Oh. How strange."

"You going out with any teenage girls, Danny?"

"Certainly not. She must have got you confused with somebody else. Or else she was referring to your previous boyfriend, the one with the cat-hating dogs."

"That I doubt. I haven't seen him in months."

"Good. Are you coming over to my place tonight, darling?"

"I don't know, Danny. Do you want me to?"

"More than anything else in the world."

"I may show up. And I may not. My knees are stiffening up."

Not a condition that's conducive to vigorous intercourse. I expressed my sympathies again and got her to cough up Floyd's phone number.

I waited to call him, but he still answered sounding groggy. I told him I knew a girl who was interested in meeting him.

"I don't know, Danny. I still haven't finished my van."

"I think she would be open to a partially finished van."

"What does she look like?"

"She's cute. Her name is Vera. She's 33."

"Is she fat?"

"No, she's quite slim and attractive."

"Would you go out with her if you weren't shackled to my sister?"

"In a New York minute."

"OK. I guess I could call her."

I gave him the number.

"Why don't you call her right now, Floyd?"

"I don't know. I haven't had my coffee yet."

"After you have your coffee, do yourself a favor and give her a call."

"I'll think about it."

"Don't think about it. Do it. You'll like her. She's nice."

"Does she know I have a limp?"

"She does. She has no problem with that."

"I wish my van was done."

"Not a problem, Floyd. I'm sure it's very impressive the way it is now."

"OK, Danny. I gotta run."

"Do it, Floyd! Call her!"

Jesus, what does it take to get two lonely people together? And here's another question: Why the fuck do I care?

This poem came to me anonymously via aerial drone:

I'd Like You To Meet . . .

Matchmaking: what's the appeal?
Bringing strangers together:
We do it with such zeal.
Then wait and watch whether

Any sparks ignite.
Is voyeurism the payoff?
Earning some frisson slight
As their coupling takes off.

Or are we there for reasons darker?
Could it be just an intrigue
Intended to mark her
Or him as not in a league

Where love succeeds?
Do we watch with secret pride
As their amity recedes
And happiness is denied?

Fourteen/FEELIN' GREEN

Olivia hasn't been answering my calls. That's not entirely a surprise. And Wenda never showed up here last night on a mercy mission to relieve my ever-gnawing sexual frustration. I can't believe I had her stripped naked in my bed that time and couldn't get it up. Even ancient Mrs. Goodsolm is starting to look good to me these days.

Sunday afternoon I went to the mall to see if Olivia would show for our scheduled movie date. There she was looking alluringly unrepentant. Skipping the film, I bought her some nachos at the food court.

"I hope you're ashamed of yourself," I said, sipping my beer.

"Not very," she replied. "In the words of Hunter S. Thompson: 'I hate to advocate drugs, alcohol, violence, or insanity to anyone, but they've always worked for me.'"

"You only know about him because I recommended him to you."

"So actually it's all your fault."

"You hurt her, you know. She banged up her knees pretty bad."

"Good. I'm only sorry she didn't break her neck."

"You could get arrested for assault."

"Hwan's not going spill. He likes me too much."

"There's a video camera trained on the front of the store. Wenda could take the tape to your high school and have you identified."

"I'm too smart for that, Danny. I kept my back to the camera. And I was wearing an old coat of my mother's that no one's going to recognize. I pulled off the perfect crime."

"I'm amazed you got up that early."

"I'm amazed you're engaged to that slag. I'm sure it's only for sex. Did you get that wig for her or me?"

"For you, of course," I lied. "It's so I can take you to the Christmas dance without raising suspicion."

"Dream on, dude. You look like you're on your way to a meeting of Perverts Anonymous."

"This is a very expensive hairpiece, darling. I've been assured it's virtually undetectable. How's it going with you and your dick pic fellow?"

"His name is Kyle. I had lunch in the cafeteria with him this week. He has the I.Q. of a cactus, but I may let him do me."

"Why would you do that?"

"Somebody's got to. And you're not stepping up to the plate."

"I'll report him to the cops. I'll have him arrested!"

"In that case, you're not going to know anything about it."

"The guy is a bastard, Olivia. You deserve better."

"We could go back to your place right now."

"Don't tempt me, darling."

"Anyway I expect you're too exhausted from screwing that skank of yours."

"For your information, we haven't done anything yet. She's a devout Catholic."

"Glad to hear it, Danny. I only hope she doesn't call the cops when you rape her."

"You have an overly vivid imagination, dear one."

"I don't see you marrying first and banging later, Danny. Your honeymoon could be a disaster."

"Let's change the subject, shall we? Is Hwan keeping his hands off you?"

"His hands no, other parts yes. That's the best you can hope for, Danny."

"Yes, I suppose it is," I sighed.

I drank two more beers, some of which Olivia guzzled. She managed to worm it out of me that I had once struck a woman.

"What did she do to provoke you?" asked Olivia.

"She threw a glass of beer in my face."

"Just the beer or the glass too?"

"Just the beer thankfully."

"What had you done to her? Probably something diabolically outrageous."

"Not at all. I was trying in my polite way to drop her. Some chicks don't take well to being dumped."

"I'm sure I'd be horrible at it. You'd probably get way more than a glass of beer in your face, Danny. I know where my dad keeps his gun."

"That's it, girl. No more Hunter S. Thompson for you!"

Later, snoozing at home prior to reporting for work, I got a call from Owen.

"We're inviting you to Thanksgiving," he said.

"Good. I'll be there. I hope you don't expect me to bring anything."

"Just your charming self. According to Maeve, there are reports you've been seen bringing girls to Tim's condo."

"I've started a little business coaching people on quitting smoking. I'm using the condo since it's empty."

"How can you do that, Danny? You smoke like a chimney."

"It helps to be an expert on addiction. I cured one gal in a single session."

"That's amazing. How do you do it?"

"Pony up $500 for a consultation and I'll be happy to show you."

"See you on Thursday, Danny. Try not to be late."

Naturally, I couldn't blab my real use for the condo since I'm not licensed to shrink heads. I would have confided everything back in the old days, but I'm not sure I trust Owen any more. The guy is too upright for his own good.

When I got to work, Mr. Park said the cops wanted to talk to me about the mugging.

"Why?" I asked. "I don't know anything about it. I was home in bed at the time."

"You the only guy she engaged to, Danny. They think maybe you know who did it."

"That is a vicious lie. Anyway, Wenda may have misheard

what the assailant said. She might have been pissed about a bad donut experience."

"I hope you not mixed up in this. If so, you fired! I like your new fake hair, Danny. Maybe you sell more lottery tickets now."

"I'm only wearing it to keep my head warm in your unheated store."

"This store plenty warm from lights and refrigeration units. Also plenty heat from coffee pots and hotdog roller. You should see my electric bill. How many days you wear that shirt?"

"It's fresh out of the laundry today," I lied.

When Wenda arrived with the donuts in the morning, she asked me to stand guard with Mr. Park's baseball bat while she unloaded.

"How are your knees, darling?" I asked, knocking imaginary dirt off my cleats like Barry Bonds at the plate.

"Not too bad today. No thanks to you. You're getting a second chance, Danny."

"Hey, I don't know anything about that girl who attacked you."

"I was referring to darling Trevor. He came back."

"Really? How come?"

"They claimed he was attacking their furniture."

"Cats do that, Wenda dear. The little vandals are single-handedly keeping all those furniture stores in business."

"You don't have to worry about that, Danny. I've been in your apartment. Some cat scratches could only improve your furniture."

"I wouldn't mind some love scratches on my back, sweetheart. Are you free this evening?"

"I've been to confession again. That new priest is expressing some reservations about you."

Damn. I swear it's like dating the sister of the Pope.

* * *

A few hours later a cop roused me out of bed to inquire about the donut assault. I claimed complete ignorance of the entire affair.

"Are you acquainted with the victim?" he asked.

"Of course. We've gone out a few times."

"Have you been dating any teenage girls?"

"Certainly not. What do you take me for?"

"I see there's a restraining order filed against you."

"That was from an unfortunate prior misunderstanding. It's not relevant to this incident."

"It's relevant if your love life continues to involve the police. It seems kind of, uh, tumultuous. Why do you suppose that is?"

"I couldn't tell you, officer. I'm the dullest and most boring guy I know. Tumultuous is one of the few words in which the letter U appears three times. Muumuu, of course, has four."

"It's true," said the cop. "You are kind of boring. Here's my number in case you think of anyone who might have it in for your girlfriend."

"Thanks. I'll be sure to call you if any insights occur to me."

Since it took three days for the cops to get around to talking to me, this case must not be at the top of their priority list. I can take comfort in that.

Yet again, I had to explain to my landlady why the police were visiting her tenant. "There was a mugging in the parking lot of the mini mart," I said. "I wasn't working that day, but the victim's a friend of mine."

"That place attracts the criminal classes, Danny. It's like a magnet to the unwashed. You really should carry a gun. And wear a bulletproof vest."

"I don't know, Mrs. Goodsolm. I feel fairly safe."

"Don't say I didn't warn you!"

The good news is I have two more appointments with possible therapines. I may be able to pay my rent this month.

Clerking was boring that night until Abby breezed in.

"Hello, Danny," she said. "I see you're putting Mrs. Bizal's gift to good use."

"That I am, dear one. How do I look?"

"Fine. I think it works quite well as long as you don't conceive of it as hair."

"A very artistic approach, Abby darling. Oddly enough, I've noticed I don't drink as much when I wear my rug. And I sometimes go three or four hours between smokes."

"That's remarkable, Danny. Perhaps you're channeling the late Mr. Bizal via your scalp."

"I wonder if that's possible? Do you know anything about him?"

"All I know is he owned a couple of pawnshops in L.A."

"The lender of last resort to the financially desperate. Always an enviable position. I should be so lucky. So what are you doing for Thanksgiving, Abby dear?"

"I haven't decided yet."

"Want to come with me? I'm having turkey and all the trimmings at some friends' house."

"They wouldn't mind my tagging along?"

"Of course not, dear. They suggested I bring a guest."

"OK. Sure. Why not?"

"Good. How's Mrs. Bizal?"

"Still breathing, alas."

"We must have faith that all will turn out for the best. What can I get you, darling?"

"I feel like something sparkling tonight."

"Too bad. I don't get off until eight."

She settled for a bottle of sparkling wine. I couldn't help but wonder with whom she'd be sharing it.

I had to guard Wenda again with my baseball bat during her delivery. She said Floyd was baking a turkey on Thursday and did I want to come over. He bakes his buried up to the neck in rock salt. I assumed she was referring to the bird and not the cook.

"Sorry, darling. I already accepted an invitation from Owen."

"I thought you said he was a mental case bugging you for money."

"Well, he is, but we all have to do what we can to help the mentally challenged. Did your brother call that girl I told him about?"

"I haven't heard about him calling any girls. Was it the one who attacked me? Are you trying to sic her on my brother?"

"Not at all, dear. It's this very nice girl I know who's having trouble getting a date."

"If she's so nice, why aren't you dating her?"

"Because I thought we were engaged to be married."

"That new priest wants to check you out. We have an appointment with him on Saturday."

"What!"

"It's at two at the church. Don't be late. Wear your suit and your wig. And try not to show up drunk."

"But I'm not a Catholic!"

"But you want to marry one. So you have to pass muster with our priest. No big deal if you love me."

"Oh, all right."

That evening I called Floyd to inquire if he'd phoned Vera.

"Not yet, Danny. I installed the flat-screen TV in my van, but I'm still working on the blu-ray player. I had trouble finding one that runs on 12 volts."

"Forgive me for saying this, Floyd, but never quite finishing your van is a way of putting your life on hold."

"I intend to finish it soon."

I could see it was time for an ultimatum. "If you don't call her, Floyd, I won't be able to take over any of your donut-frying shifts. Not ever."

An idle threat since I had no intention of doing so.

"OK, Danny, I'll call her."

"Now's a good time."

"After I have my coffee."

"You promise?"

"Yeah, sure."

Medical question of the day: does having a limp interfere with a guy's desire to get laid?

Floyd had something on his mind too.

"I hear you're facing the Inquisition on Saturday, Danny."

"Yeah, a tête-à-tête with a busybody priest. Got any advice?"

"Just tell him what he wants to hear, guy. Lie through your teeth if you have to. Don't give up an inch to the bastard. Remember: he's the guy wearing the skirt not you."

"Thanks, Floyd. I'll keep that in mind."

I had two therapy sessions on Wednesday: with Gene, my car-towing klepto, and a new guy named Luke. He's a wannabe actor around 30 who works as a meter reader for the utility company and claims his life feels unreal, like he's living "inside a movie." Of course, I asked him if he'd seen the film "The Truman Show," but he said he hadn't. He's in love with his roommate (a chick), who has guys over and treats him to the sounds of their lovemaking through the wall. If Luke smoked, drank, and was underemployed, I'd think he was almost as messed up as me. As it is, he's losing his hair big time.

I got both Luke and Gene talking about their parents, since as Philip Larkin reminds us: "They fuck you up, your mum and dad." Opening up about that dreaded pair is a good way for therapines to feel like they're getting their money's worth. Personally, I could grouse about my crummy parents all day, every day.

I learned today that ol' Gene has been a thief pretty much since day one. As a mere tot he used to filch candy bars while riding in a cart as his mother shopped for groceries. In high school he kept all his football teammates supplied with purloined condoms. He shoplifts from stores all the time and has never been caught. The guy is every mini-mart owner's worst nightmare.

I asked him his annual income.

"I'd rather not say, Doc, since you charge on a sliding scale."

"Am I right in thinking you make a comfortable living?"

"Probably not comfortable for you, but OK for me."

"So you don't steal through economic necessity."

"It's a hobby, Doc. At least I'm not out in the woods with binoculars spying on birds. I'm not getting little kids at the playground to pull down their pants."

"Do you fantasize about doing that?"

"Not at all. I'm happy pocketing the occasional salt shaker. Yesterday I bagged a frozen turkey for the wife."

"You walked out with a turkey? How did you get away with that?"

"I went in the back and asked if they had any cardboard boxes to spare. On my way out I dumped a turkey in the box."

Pretty smart. I'll have to remember that technique if I wind up penniless and starving on skid row.

* * *

Thanksgiving dinner started off pleasant enough. Maeve and Owen were most welcoming to Abby. Maeve's brother and his wife brought their two kids, who weren't that obnoxious considering they were in the problematic eight-to-ten age bracket. I immediately forgot the parents' names, but the kids were James and Jamie. Come to think of it, their dad might have been named Jim.

So Owen was giving me the eye as if to say, "Damn, I appreciate your taste in women even if you are wearing a second-hand toupee," when the first sour note was sounded. Nobody had brought any booze–not even wine. The beverage d'jour was chilled sparkling cider–sparkling with bubbles not alcohol. I dumped in some gin from my flask, but the taste was more medicinal than festive.

The food was all you could want in a Thanksgiving feast except Maeve had decided to go full gourmet on the stuffing. It had been thoroughly adulterated with oysters.

I am willing to eat oysters if a gun is pointed at my head or someone is paying me $1,000 per bivalve. Otherwise, forget it. The kids at the table felt the same way. We skipped the stuffing, while the rest of the party shoveled it in. All went well until the meal nearly was finished. Faint rumblings could be heard, like distant thunder across the Serengeti plain. Then the sounds grew louder like a herd of elephants stampeding beyond the water hole.

The cook was the first to excuse herself. Maeve dashed to

the bathroom, followed by her sister-in-law. Owen looked at me in a blind panic.

"Danny," he gasped. "Did you bring the key to Tim's condo? I need a toilet fast!"

"Sorry, it didn't occur to me," I lied.

I had the key, but I didn't want Owen inspecting my fake diplomas and licenses framed on Tim's wall.

Desperate, Owen and Jim had to resort to using the exterior landscaping. After they left, I unlocked Tim's condo for Abby, then returned to the table.

"What's happening?" asked Jamie. "Mom's making gross noises in the bathroom."

"Sounds like a rapid evacuation from both ends at once," I replied, refilling my glass.

"Are they going to be all right?" asked James. "Should you call 9-1-1?"

"I expect they'll be fine," I said. "Your aunt must have procured some suspect oysters. The purge will be wonderfully purifying to the digestive system. When they're done, they'll be starting afresh like Adam and Eve on Day One. Now, who wants pumpkin pie?"

"I do!" shouted the kids in unison.

They both said "thank you" when I dished up generous servings from Maeve's fresh-baked pie. Just in time, Jamie remembered the bowl of whipped cream in the fridge. We scooped on big dollops and dug in. The pie was excellent.

"Who wants seconds of pie?" I asked.

"Mom doesn't let us have seconds of dessert," confessed James.

"Fortunately, your mother is indisposed. And likely will be for some time."

Everyone had seconds of the wonderful pie, then I sat back and lit a Chesterfield. A cappuccino or a glass of port would have been welcome, but I made do with my smoke.

"Aunt Maeve doesn't permit smoking in her house," said Jamie, already a junior smoke Nazi.

"Except on Thanksgiving," I said. "That's a long-standing tradition."

I offered my companions a cigarette from my pack, but they both declined.

"Do you kids like Thanksgiving?" I asked.

"It's OK," said James. "It means Christmas isn't too far off."

"I prefer Halloween," said Jamie. "Thanksgiving is kind of boring."

"Not this year!" pointed out her brother.

"Yeah," she admitted. "This year was kind of interesting."

James got up from the table and looked out the window.

"Dad's mooning us from the bushes," he said. "And so's Uncle Owen."

"Come away from the window," I said. "Let them preserve a shred of their dignity."

Eventually Abby returned from across the hall.

"You're the first one back," I reported. "Want some pie?"

"Let's blow this joint," she said weakly.

"Tell your aunt we had a good time except for the food poisoning," I said to Jamie and James. "Feel free to finish the pie and blame it on me."

"I think I'm too full," said Jamie.

"Me too," said James. "See you at Christmas."

"Not if we can help it," I replied.

We drove back in Abby's Prius. (She continues to refuse to ride in my Cordoba.) Naturally, I had to 'fess up about my new career as a bogus psychotherapist.

"Sounds semi-lucrative, Danny. Just make sure you don't take on anyone suicidal or homicidal. If they act up, you can really land in the soup."

"Not to worry, darling. I'm weeding out the serious nut cases. Would you like to stop at my place for a drink?"

"Only if you're serving Pepto-Bismol."

I wasn't, so she dropped me off at the curb and went on her way.

If I never see her again, I'm going to be so pissed at Owen.

This poem was deciphered recently from ancient Sumerian clay tablets:

Holiday Voodoo

Holidays once were holy days,
When everyone got a dose of God.
Now we eat and drift in a malaise
Of TV sports and talks that plod

Along until everyone has jawed
Themselves into a stupor.
Or, fed up, you punch that clod
Who's ever the party pooper.

The jerk your sister let swoop her
Up in disastrous wedlock:
Liquored up he's a whooper
You just want to cold cock.

But it's better not to squawk
'Cause relatives stick like glue.
So have a beer and sleepwalk
Through all that holiday voodoo.

Fifteen/GROOVY SCENE

Maeve called me the next morning to apologize. I let her grovel for a bit and then said I'd had a thoroughly good time. I said the eats were excellent, especially the pie, but I resented the paucity of beverage choices.

"I've made that recipe several times, Danny. It turned out fine before. The oysters came from a reputable fish market."

"If God had intended us to eat oysters, he wouldn't have made them so slimy and revolting."

"I want to apologize personally to your friend. Can you give me Abby's number?"

"I only have the number of her answering service."

"That will do. Are you two an item? She seems very nice."

"I'm not sure I'll ever see her again after your attempt to poison her. She did say it was the fastest she'd ever lost eight pounds."

"Oh dear, I'll call her right away and try to put it right."

"I hope so, Maeve dear. The existence of my future children may depend on it."

Always a pleasure to start one's day with a bruising guilt trip.

Today's recliner whiner was another neurotic in her late twenties. This must be the age when people realize they've fucked up their lives. First gal I ever met with the given name Culver. I remember reading somewhere that people with common, ordinary names (Michael, Jennifer, etc.) wind up better adjusted and more successful than folks with esoteric, oddball names. Culver could be an example of that. She said she needed help with her constant worrying.

"What do you worry about?" I asked.

"My biggest worry is that my husband might leave me."

"Does he show signs of being so inclined?"

"Sometimes he stays away for days at a time!"

"That doesn't sound good. Does he say where he's been?"

"He's a firefighter. He claims he was at the firehouse. They have to sleep there on their overnight shifts."

"Do you have reason to doubt his explanation?"

"I do worry about it. I call there frequently to check up on him, but he doesn't like that. He says the other guys in his crew rib him about me."

"How long have you been married?"

"Six years. I'm worried Bryce, that's my husband, is due for the seven-year itch next year."

"Do you have kids?"

"I wouldn't dare. I'd worry about them too much."

"How does Bryce feel about that?"

"He wants to have kids. But he's not the one getting his insides torn out giving birth to them. It's like having a giant parasite in your body for nine months."

"Women do give birth by the millions every year. Many are happy to repeat the experience."

"I couldn't cope, Dr. Nixon. I'd worry non-stop that the baby would stop breathing or strangle on his diaper or catch a horrible disease or stick a bobby pin in a wall socket. Bryce says we should take a first baby step like adopting a cat. But I worry I wouldn't be able to cope."

"I know a cute cat that's available for adoption. His name is Trevor."

"I might consider that if my therapy works out."

"What else do you worry about?"

"Lately I've been worrying about Bryce at his fitness gym. I followed him there and peeked in through the windows. There are attractive girls working out on those machines in practically nothing. Don't tell me those jogging bras stop the bouncing. And those yoga pants leave nothing to the imagination. Plus, the gym fee is $83.49 a month. I tell Bryce we could save the money and he could get fit by digging a bomb shelter in the back yard."

"You're worried about nuclear war?"

"All the time. Plus tornadoes, hurricanes, typhoons, earthquakes, tsunamis, mud slides, exploding gas mains, and urban conflagrations. Over 20 people died in the Oakland hills fire. It was horrible. We could be next!"

"Does your husband know you're seeing a therapist?"

"Lord no. I'd worry about what he thought of me if he knew."

"How do you intend to pay?"

"I got a small inheritance from my late aunt. I intend to use that."

In that case I quoted her a figure of $150 per session. She said she'd worry about my competence if I charged her any less. I asked her how she came to be called Culver.

"My mother got pulled over for running a stop sign in Culver City. She subsequently was charged with driving on a suspended license and DUI. My dad was the cop who nailed her."

"Was your mother a worrier?"

"Heavens, no. She's floating through life free as a bird. Not a care in her head. It was everyone else who had to worry about *her*."

"Starting with you?"

"Why yes, I suppose so."

Not a surprise. It's always the parents who mess you up.

I had another question for her. "Did your mother drink?"

"Oh, yes. Like a fish. She still does."

I thought so. I can't believe people think you have to go to school to do this job.

* * *

Bad news this morning from Vera (formerly Veronica). She has received zero phone calls from Floyd.

"That's the story of my life, Dr. Nixon," she said, settling back in Tim's recliner. "Guys just don't want to date me. Not even guys who've only heard about me secondhand. It's my aura: it casts a pall that repels men. I'm thinking maybe I was an ax murderer in a previous life."

"My heartfelt apologies, Vera. The fault does not lie with

you. I discussed you with Floyd in the most glowing terms. He's just, uh, somewhat more shy than I expected. My mistake was in taking him at his word that he wished to meet someone."

"I don't mind shy guys. I expect they'd be an improvement over the creeps I've gone out with in the past."

We spent the hour discussing her previous boyfriends. What a motley crew of cheating lowlifes. And I thought I was bad news for chicks. At least I never pilfered cash from a girlfriend's purse. Or borrowed her car and misplaced it because I was too drunk to remember where I parked it. Or took her mom out for Mother's Day and tried to hit on her when my girlfriend went to the restroom. I asked Vera why she was attracted to men of this type.

"All three were very charming starting out. All had this boyish, crooked grin. I must have a weakness for that. The ugliness creeps in slowly so you sort of don't notice it at first. Or you try to dismiss it. And then before you know it you're buried up to your neck in the kudzu. I never did give up. It was always them who dropped me. Or just disappeared one day with my credit cards."

"No offense, Vera, but these men all sound like sociopaths."

"Yeah, I guess that's my type. I think there must be a club somewhere for sociopaths with my phone number scratched on the wall."

I said we'd work on changing that aspect of her love life.

"What love life?" she replied.

That afternoon was my date with Wenda's nosy priest. Driving to her church, I was in a foul mood. No one should have to consult a priest in order to get laid. I'd rather walk over hot coals. I was only ten minutes late and virtually sober, but Wenda greeted me coldly. She led me down a hallway, which smelled of incense and unwashed altar boys, to a cramped office where the priest was waiting behind a cluttered desk. His portrait of Jesus on the wall was one of those spooky paintings where the eyes follow you about.

"Father Thomas," she said, "this is my boyfriend Danny Nix-on."

Both guys gave a start. I'd seen that priest before.

"Jesus, is that you, Matt?" I said.

"Danny Nixon, as I live and breathe," he said. "The last time I saw you, you were peddling fake I.D.s in Modesto."

"Didn't I sell one to you?"

"I really don't recall," he lied.

"You know each other?" asked Wenda.

"I went to a public high school in Modesto," I replied. "Matthew here went to the Catholic high school. He had some business dealings with my friend Owen. Also some personal dealings."

"That's all in the past," he replied, blushing. "Did you ever marry that girlfriend of yours? What was her name?"

"Monica. No, I never got anywhere in particular with her, although Owen did later. I'm surprised to see you here, Matt. I never pegged you as someone to go in for full-time Bible banging."

"I have two uncles who are priests. It's kind of a family profession. How about you, Danny? Have you had any spiritual awakenings?"

"Not so far, Matt. I'm a secular humanist of the worst sort."

He had us take a seat and tried to regain his priestly demeanor.

"Danny, I must ask you: Do you have a sincere affection for this woman? Do you wish to marry and make a home with her? To give her children and raise them according to the law of Christ and his holy church?"

"Sure, why not?" I replied.

"Do you have a means of supporting her?"

"Yeah, I got a job. And I started a business recently that's doing well."

"And are you drinking to excess, Danny?"

"Not to excess, no. Certainly not like you on Saturday nights back in Modesto."

"We were both young back then, Danny. I trust we've both matured."

"I hope so, father. I'm sure your parishioners hold you to a high standard."

"I have to ask, Danny. Is that your real hair?"

"It's mine in that I own it. I hold legal title to it."

"It looks good," he said. "Wenda, do you have any questions for Danny?"

"When do you want to get married, honey? It will have to be when Father Thomas has an opening in his schedule."

"We can talk about that later, dear," I replied. "We don't want to take up the good padre's time."

"How's Owen?" he asked, as we were leaving. "I was sorry to hear about his accident."

"He's doing well," I said. "He met a girl here and they're talking about getting married."

"Good for him," he said. "Tell him to drop by sometime. I'd like to see him."

"Will do. And thanks."

"I'm amazed that you knew Father Thomas back in high school," said Wenda as we walked toward the parking lot.

"Yeah, he was a pretty wild kid."

"Wild in what way?"

"You should ask him. I don't want to tell tales out of school."

During our senior year Owen scaled up production and did a bit of wholesaling. He used the profits to drop a big-block 396 into his dad's old Chevelle. A fast car with virtually no brakes. Kind of like us. Matt was his distributor to the Catholic kids. They spent some time together, and Matt's interest got to be more than purely business. But Owen was strictly into girls, so nothing happened. All of which I kept to myself. It wouldn't help my cause to antagonize Wenda's priest.

"Who's this Monica person?" asked Wenda.

"My girlfriend in high school. She was vice president in charge of keeping me celibate. Kind of like you are now."

"It's not my fault you couldn't perform. Father Thomas says that was God's will."

More good news: her priest thinks I have impotence issues.

"Want to go to my place and try again?" I asked, flashing my version of a boyish, crooked grin.

"Not likely, Danny. I'm due at the cat store in ten minutes. We're having a 20 percent off sale today. I'm sure it will be a madhouse."

"Any chance I could drop by later and remove 80 percent of your clothes?"

"Sorry, I promised Floyd I'd help him test his blu-ray player in his van."

"Fine. Have a good time–on Saturday night–*with your brother!*"

I ask you, Jesus, is it any wonder I drink?

"And tell Floyd I think he's a stinking coward for not calling Vera."

"Floyd was never much of a ladies man, Danny. He talks about getting laid, but only theoretically."

"Has he ever had a girlfriend?"

"Not that I'm aware of."

"Is he gay?"

"Certainly not. He was born in Oklahoma, just like me."

* * *

Owen called me as I was mixing a highball for dinner.

"I'm pissed at you, Danny."

"What for, pray tell?"

"Lying about not having a key to Tim's condo."

"That wasn't a lie," I lied. "It occurred to me after you left that I had a spare key on my key ring. How was it out there in the bushes?"

"Only slightly less horrible than setting my face on fire. It's a wonder the neighbors didn't call the cops."

"That will teach you for grubbing for calories off the bottom of the sea floor. Anyway, I should be pissed at you guys for trying to poison my girlfriend."

"Is she really your girlfriend? She's quite a looker."

"I'm working on her. Did you find a job?"

"Yeah. Driving a truck. I deliver produce to restaurants and neighborhood markets."

"How's the pay?"

"It's decent. I just hope my back holds up. You'd be amazed what a box of cabbages weighs."

I told him about running into our old pal Matt.

"Wow, Matt's a priest. That's kind of mind boggling."

"He wants you to drop by and say hi."

"I could do that I guess. I have a route in that neighborhood."

"Did anything ever happen with you two? You could fry an egg on the love vibe that used to emanate from that dude."

"I might have kissed him once. As an experiment."

"I admire your versatility. How was he?"

"We were both high at the time. As I recall it was pretty intense."

"Damn, Owen. You've made out with a future priest, banged my first girlfriend, and are now living with a chick I wanted to date."

"Yeah, I'm a regular Don Swan."

"That's from 'Bringing Up Baby,' 1938, spoken by Katherine Hepburn while swinging on a jailhouse cell door."

"You were always the movie expert, Danny. Why not ask Abby if she wants to double date sometime?"

"OK. That might be fun. We could all go out for oysters."

Loud banging on my door sometime after midnight. I put the DVD player on pause, took another swig from my highball, and stumbled over to the door. It was Olivia and another girl. They waltzed in uninvited and looked around.

"Just as I suspected," said Olivia. "This place is a dump."

"More like a pig sty," said her mystery friend.

"I have big plans for its renovation," I said.

"I'd start with a can of gas and a match," said Olivia. "Danny, this is Clare."

"Nice to meet you," I said.

"My pleasure, I'm sure," she replied.

Clare was a big-boned girl with a square jaw and pretty dark eyes.

"How did you girls find me?"

"It wasn't hard, Danny," said Olivia, slumping on my sofa. "We walk by this place every day. Anyone can see your aging pimpmobile parked out back. Have a seat, Clare. Take a load off. Danny, we'll both have what you're drinking."

"Not likely, dear one. Isn't there a curfew for teenagers in this town?"

"We're not out on the streets, Danny. We're safely inside with you. I'll take a wine cooler and so will Clare."

"Fresh out, darling. I could offer you ginger ale with a modest splash of bourbon."

"Go for it, Danny. And why not phone out for a pizza while you're at it?"

I let Olivia do that while I mixed the cocktails. She had her favorite pizza joint on speed dial. She knew the delivery boy by name and insisted I hand him a $5 tip. She also insisted I retire to the bedroom to don my toupee.

"What do you think, Clare?" she asked, when I returned.

"Well, I guess it's an improvement."

Not generous with the compliments was Clare.

"I think it's a blast," Olivia replied. "I think all guys should shave their heads and wear fake hair. It could be a status thing like bling jewelry, tattoos, and pricey shoes. You know: guys competing to flash the latest styles and colors in wigs. How about it, Danny?"

"Another brilliant idea, dear one. I expect you'll be a billionaire before you're out of your teens."

"You'll be my first hire, Danny. You'll be Head of Design, my chief fashion maven."

"I can't wait," I said. "Do you mind if I smoke?"

"We'd be disappointed if you don't," said Olivia. "I'm getting a nicotine rush just breathing the air in this joint." She held out her glass. "I'll take a refill. And don't be so chintzy with the booze."

I freshened both of their drinks, this time splashing in even less from the bourbon bottle.

"Any news of that exhibitionist Kyle?" I asked.

Clare directed a warning glance at Olivia. "Don't say a word about it," she hissed.

"Danny, I'm not supposed to tell you that Clare did the big nasty with Kyle."

"You promised you wouldn't say anything!" wailed her friend.

"I promised I wouldn't tell anyone at school, Clare. And I'm not. Danny doesn't know anyone except us, and his lips are sealed. Too bad for you that Kyle's probably aren't."

"Guys do have an unfortunate inclination to blab about such things," I admitted.

"Clare says it was not at all fun and more than a little creepy," reported Olivia.

"We shouldn't talk about this if Clare doesn't want to," I said. "We should respect her privacy."

"It's OK," Clare said. "I don't see what the big deal is. About sex I mean."

"I know it's a cliché, Clare," I said, "But it does get better with time. People generally don't have much fun their first time, especially girls."

"Especially if they're doing it with a lump like Kyle," added Olivia, flashing me a lascivious wink.

"At least it was over quick," added her friend.

"It lasted eight seconds!" exclaimed Olivia. "I timed it with my phone."

"How on earth did you do that?" I asked. "Were you there?"

"I was listening outside in the hall. I could hear the springs creak."

"That was the creepy part," said Clare.

"I'm planning on doing it with an experienced guy," said Olivia, helping herself to the last slice of pizza. "None of those novices for this girl. Either with Danny or Hwan. Whichever mans up first."

"Good luck with that," said Clare. "I could leave if you guys want to be alone."

"Danny's had too much to drink," said Olivia. "Guys his age are useless past a certain blood-alcohol level."

"I'm not rising to the bait, dear one. Your strategy is blatantly obvious."

"We'll never be more alluring than we are right now, Clare. And I can't even get a nibble out of him. What's wrong with men these days?"

"I expect they've all been emasculated by the pressures of modern life," said Clare with a yawn. "Are we sleeping here or what?"

"We have to," said Olivia. "We both told our parents we were staying at the other's house, so neither of us can go home. You can crash on the sofa and I'll sleep with Danny."

"In your dreams, darling," I said. "Not happening until you're safely 18, if then."

"We won't do anything, Danny. We'll just sleep. I hope you changed your sheets since the last time you had that skank over."

I suppose it was too late to argue that point. We retired as Olivia proposed. I made her wear a nightgown left behind by Kimberly. She attempted some snuggling, but I removed her hand and pushed her over to her side of the bed.

Had I been sober, I doubt very much I would have passed the night in bed with a horny 16-year-old virgin. I can only hope this is not the camel nose under the tent flap.

This poem I once found scrawled in lipstick on a badly cracked motel bathroom mirror.

Sleeping with Strangers.

I'll no longer sleep with strangers
Announced Frank O'Hara in 1959.
That's the poet, art critic, and libertine,
Not the dentist, undertaker, or
Other Frank O'Haras of local repute.

No more BJs for colored attendants
In parking lot shacks or lonely
Toll-takers fighting sleep on foggy nights.
No more sliding low in the seats of high
Balconies while guns blazed on the silver screen.

But who hasn't slept with a stranger?
That warm body on the other side of your lips.
And hips. The one with the alien smell
Who groaned as you came in their
. . . What? Take your pick. It's all the same.

It's all the same awkwardness the first time,
Wondering how you scored on their
Checklist. Whether you'll be granted
Another intimacy. Or be banished:
Your face and touch soon forgotten.

Sixteen/MEET THE QUEEN

Loud shrieking woke us the next morning. It was Clare not getting the hang of my shower faucet. A safecracker's touch was required on the lever, lest the hot water shut off entirely.

"She'll be all right," I said to Olivia, removing her hand from my pajama bottom. "In Europe people love taking cold showers."

"I thought guys always woke up with erections."

"You can check that out with your future husband. Here's the thing, sweetheart. You can't mention to Hwan that you spent the night here. He'll call the cops for sure. I'll be sent to the slammer. And you girls will be headed toward careers in outcall massage. Believe me, you don't need the disgrace. Or the hassle."

"I'm not telling anyone, Danny. Besides, you might be my future husband."

"God knows, Olivia dear, stranger things have happened. More likely you'll look back on the time you spent with me and shake your head in disbelief."

"Never going to happen, Danny. I like you too much."

"Says the voice of an immature girl."

She climbed out of bed and slipped off her nightgown, making no effort to conceal her nakedness. Not voluptuous, but well past the coltish stage. I made an elaborate show of ducking under a pillow.

"Can't take the pressure, huh, Danny?"

"Put your clothes on, dear. I'll take you both out to breakfast."

Taking no chances, I drove us to a café two towns over. Fortunately for my wallet, neither of my guests was a big-time breakfast eater. They munched their bagels and watched me eat my eggs and bacon. I was finishing a second cup of coffee when Deputy Grizzoffski walked in. I tried to make myself inconspicuous, but he spotted me.

"Danny Nixon," he said, strolling over. "I thought that was your car in the lot. You're up early. And with your Girl Scout troop. Care to explain?"

"These are some underprivileged girls from my Bible study group. I treat them to breakfast before we go to church."

"We always say prayers for you policemen," said Olivia, feigning piety.

"Uh, right," said the deputy. "I found out your pal Tim hightailed it to Mexico. I have contacts in the Federales looking for him. When they nab him, they're going to hold him until I get there. It's even easier to dispose of a body down there. The head I'll bury separately or keep as a souvenir. I watched a video on YouTube of how to shrink a head. It looks like fun."

"Girls, he's only teasing," I said, "although that's hardly appropriate talk for the Sabbath."

"I'm still keeping my eye on you, Nixon. One slip up, and you're going down."

"Who was that scary dude?" asked Olivia after he departed.

"His name's Fred Grizzoffski. A former coworker had the poor sense to sleep with his underage daughter. He's vowed to track him down and kill him. Now do you understand why I'm so jumpy around you girls?"

"But he's a cop," she replied. "He can't go around snuffing people."

"He can if this guy Tim is black," said Clare. "Cops always get away with that."

"Tim's white. But Grizzoffski still intends to waste him if he gets his hands on him."

"Can't you snitch on him to his bosses?" asked Olivia.

"I could if I was feeling especially suicidal."

"This is just like in a movie," said Clare. "Did your friend rape his daughter?"

"Hardly. She seduced him. And he wasn't her first."

"See, Clare," said Olivia. "I told you it gets better with practice."

"Yeah," said Clare. "Too bad Tim isn't around. I could practice on him."

I got my ass chewed by Mrs. Park when I showed up for work. She'd been reviewing the surveillance tapes. Allegedly someone last week walked right past me and out the door with a big box of Pampers. I sure didn't see that. Anyway, if someone is desperate for diapers at two in the morning, does she really expect me to run after them and tackle them in the parking lot? Hell, they might have been trying to patch up a hemorrhaging gunshot wound. She said she was deducting the price from my next paycheck.

"The retail price or the wholesale price that is your actual cost?" I asked.

"We deduct the full price that the customer didn't pay! You want to argue about that?"

"Not at all, Mrs. Park. I merely was seeking clarification on that point."

That woman is more than a bit scary. If I can round up a couple more therapines, I'm going to ditch this lousy job. At least it's a way to see Abby. She pulled in at her usual late hour.

"Hello, Abby dear," I said. "How's your digestive tract?"

"Oh? Have we arrived at that level of intimacy?"

"I consider you to be one of my closest friends. What's up?"

"I'm going to a funeral on Tuesday."

"I see. Good news for the orphans?"

"The best."

"Please offer my condolences to the Bizal family, darling."

"I'll be sure to do that."

"Owen and Maeve are proposing a festive double date. Any interest in that?"

"Are you paying?"

"Certainly, sweetheart."

"OK, I'll consider it."

This time she bought a pint of Southern Comfort, a tin of mints, and a box of tampons. I put it all in a bag with my usual non-judgmental dispatch.

"It's lovely to see you looking so well, Abby dear."

"You too, Danny. Although that rug of yours could do with a shampoo."

"It's on my agenda for tomorrow, dear one."

Later in my shift I got some bad news while guarding Wenda with the baseball bat.

"I went to confession yesterday, Danny," she said.

"Again! What could you possibly have to confess? That you watched a DVD with your brother in his van? That you gave someone the wrong change at the thrift store? That you underfilled a jelly donut?"

"Confession is a private matter, Danny. Father Thomas said we shouldn't be in a rush to get married. He said we should take it slow and get to know each other better."

"Meaning what? No sex?"

"He said we should take that slow too."

Great. My sex life is now being run by a former teen dopedealer who once had the hots for my best friend.

She had more news.

"I talked to Floyd about that girl you want him to meet. He said he was going to call her, but lost her phone number."

"A likely story. I gave it to him twice."

"Well, give it to me, and I'll make sure he calls her. I do worry about him never having any dates."

"You should try worrying about me, darling. I don't have any either."

"We need another volunteer at the store, Danny. That would be a good way for us to spend some time together."

"We could spoon in between customers."

"Think about it, Danny. It could be fun. And Trevor would love to see you."

* * *

I shampooed my toupee. I taped it to my skull and washed it in the shower along with the rest of me. Then set it out to dry on a foam head donated by Mrs. Goodsolm (a big-time wig wearer). She favors old-lady styles in easy-care polyester.

I was settling in for some late-afternoon TV-watching when

my phone rang. It was Lizzie Harger, that cute brainiac from my high-school class who instructs future Steve Jobs-types about international relations at Reed College. I asked how things were up in Portland.

"I'm down here in Walnut Creek, Danny. You remember my sister Delia?"

"I remember she was pretty and popular. I remember she was a cheerleader and president of the student council. Also homecoming queen. She had an extensive wardrobe of sweaters that showed off her perfect silhouette. She drove a vintage MG sports car and only dated handsome college guys. Her golden aura parted the crowds as she walked down the halls. Not at all stuck up though. As a senior she was even nice to us lowly sophomores."

"Sounds like she made quite an impression on you."

"Yeah, she's lodged in my mind on the same synapse as Jackie Kennedy, Lana Turner, and Reese Witherspoon. What about her?"

"She's having a spot of trouble. She has a new baby—her first—and her rat of a husband walked out on her. I'm down here trying to help out. But I'm going nuts. I need a break. You want to go out for coffee or something?"

"I could be there in under an hour. What's the address?"

I picked her up and drove to a nearby bar where I was once summarily ejected. Same bartender, but this time I was wearing my topper, so we were served without incident. Lizzie had coffee; I had an Irish coffee.

"Do people comment on your toupee or pretend they don't notice it?" she inquired, studying my hairline.

"What toupee?" I asked icily.

"Oh. My mistake."

"Just kidding, Lizzie. It's a fashion accessory. Please don't think of it as hair, I don't."

"Right."

"It's like that trend of women letting their bra straps show."

"Exactly, Danny. Or men who aren't Swiss showing up in lederhosen."

"Or folks wearing tie-dyed tunics when they're not long-haired hippies strung out on acid."

"I'm glad we got that straightened out, Danny. How are you these days?"

"Great. I quit my county job and am now doing psychotherapy."

"Really? I didn't know you'd been trained in that."

"Oh, yes. Studied it in college. Got my license, then let it drop for a few years. Back into it now."

"I thought you majored in English."

"Nothing so grim and useless as that."

"That's interesting. Delia's been talking about seeing a therapist. She's very stressed out."

"She should give me a call. I have one opening in my busy schedule. Why did her husband split?"

"Wasn't ready for fatherhood, I guess. I never much liked the guy. Dennis claims their baby looks Chinese."

"Newborns usually look like something dredged out of a swamp. Doesn't he know they look less repulsive with time?"

"Delia's baby happens to be very cute. Remarkably healthy lungs too. He has a scream like an air raid siren. The thing is, Delia's best friend is Lee Chu, the Chinese painter."

"Never heard of him."

"He's quite big in the art world. Delia's an art consultant you know. She advises corporations and rich people on what art to buy."

"Does her baby look Chinese?"

"Well, half-Chinese maybe. But Delia's claiming it's her husband's. Lee Chu is married, and now he's not returning her phone calls. It's a big mess."

"Have they done a DNA test?"

"No, and she doesn't want to either. She says her baby's in distress because he can sense that he's not wanted."

"I doubt that. So how long are you going to be down here?"

"It's open-ended. I'm on sabbatical this semester."

"Good, Lizzie. We should go out and pick up where we left off."

"Left off from what? We never did anything except see each other in class. Monica barely let you talk to me."

"That's no excuse for running off and getting married. And disappearing for 20 years. I suppose you're stuck on your husband."

"I'm not sure I like him as much as some of the gals he's cheated on me with."

"What's the name of this turkey?"

"Dennis."

"You and your sister married the same guy? Is that legal?"

"No, we both married men named Dennis. Anyway, she copied me. I married my Dennis first."

"Any kids?"

"Not so far. I'm not sure my husband is father material."

"Your clock is ticking. Does that concern you?"

"It's caused me some sleepless nights. On the other hand we have Delia's screeching infant. He's a real deterrent to reproduction. Now I see why people get this baby business over in their twenties."

"I know. Back then I slept like the proverbial log. Once when I was 26 I left a candle burning and slept through the smoke alarm and the sirens. It was the fireman dragging me down the stairs by my ankles that woke me up."

"Damn, Danny! You could have been killed."

"Not likely. You can't kill a smoker with a bit of smoke inhalation. We've built up a tolerance. So what's Delia's baby's name?"

"I'll give you three guesses."

"Not Dennis Junior I hope."

"You guessed it."

"I suppose your sister married some hotshot executive or doctor," I said.

"No, her Dennis is a plumber."

"Delia Harger married a plumber! I can hardly believe it. I expected her to wind up First Lady and living in the White House."

"That's rather sexist, Danny. Why not imagine her becoming President in her own right?"

"Yeah, I see what you mean. She's President with a half-Chinese baby and First Husband Dennis is in charge of emergency White House toilet repairs."

"That works for me. How come you're not married?"

"Just lucky, I guess. Either that or I was waiting for you to reappear."

"I don't recall you being this charming in high school."

"I had to suppress it. Being charming in Modesto could get you beat up."

"How did we ever live there all those years?"

"Some of us smoked dope."

"Yeah, you and Owen. What a pair. I always thought of him as the Bebe Rebozo to your Dick Nixon."

"Thanks. I think."

I filled her in on Owen and Maeve.

"That sounds promising, Danny. I always liked Owen."

"He nailed Monica. Something I never accomplished."

"I think I heard about that. Don't ask me how."

"Chicks always know about stuff like that. Guys are usually clueless."

"Monica never came across, huh? That doesn't surprise me, Danny."

"Why not? Do you doubt my powers of seduction?"

"You never seemed that enthusiastic about her. And I showered with Monica in gym class. She didn't seem all that steeped in eros."

"So you got to see Monica naked and I never did."

"It's a cruel world, Danny. And then you die."

I invited her out to dinner, but she said she had to get back lest Delia go off the deep end.

"So whom did you date in high school?" I asked, driving her back.

"Mostly I didn't. Jeff Tobeck took me to the prom."

"I remember that dork. He made all-state in wrestling."

"He certainly demonstrated some adroit moves on me."

"You got nailed by Jeff Tobeck?"

"No comment."

"Here's another question, Lizzie. How come your sister was driving that classic M.G.?"

"It was my dad's baby. He loved it only slightly less than my sister. So she got to drive it. When she went off to college, I assumed I would inherit the keys. I was counting on it to be a powerful boy magnet. No such luck."

"Your father wouldn't let you drive it? Why the hell not?"

"I guess he loved me slightly less than his car. He claimed he wasn't impressed with my driving skills. I drove my mother's Ford Escort instead, attracting admiring glances from no one."

"I wonder where that car is now?"

"The M.G.? Gone down the highway. My mother sold it when my father died."

"I forget. Was it green?"

"Blue, Danny. It nicely complemented my gorgeous sister's eyes. The Escort was brown like my eyes."

"I like your eyes."

"Thanks. They kind of match your hairpiece."

"What hairpiece?"

"Uh-oh. I stepped in it again."

I pulled to a stop in front of Delia's modest ranch house.

"Want to come in and say hi to my sister?" she asked.

"Nah, I prefer to remember her as the blissfully regal homecoming queen. When can I see you again?"

"I'll call you when I get a free minute. It was nice to see you, Danny."

"Yeah. Same here."

I almost leaned over and kissed her, but couldn't quite work up the nerve.

* * *

That night at work in the mini mart I was thinking it over. I could ditch Wenda as a lost cause and take up with Lizzie. I have history with that gal. I've known her for 27 years–since junior high school. Wenda I've only known a couple of months. Here's the problem: sooner or later Lizzie is going back to Portland. Sure, that's a groovy and happening burg, but it snows up there. They have real winters. I wasn't born in sunny California only to move north and freeze my ass off. I have zero interest in shoveling snow, chipping ice off my windshield, being impaled by falling icicles, or skidding around on icy roads while playing bumper cars with my Cordoba. Plus, all that salt on the roads will corrode its vintage fenders.

The only direction I'd consider moving is south. If Lizzie dumped her husband and got a job at San Diego State, I'd think seriously about joining her there.

Olivia showed up at 1:47 a.m. I asked her if she ever slept.

"I can't turn my mind off, Danny. It just buzzes along for hours."

"Thinking about what, dear one?"

"About you, for example. I think it would really calm me down if we had sex."

"It might," I admitted. "Except it would make me very, very anxious. Like Burt Lancaster in the movie 'The Killers.' He was waiting for a couple of hit men named Max and Al to show up and pump him full of lead."

"Do they kill him?"

"Yes, they do, hence the title of the film. You're lucky you're not growing up in the 1940s. Back then your parents would be signing you up for a therapeutic lobotomy. They'd stick an ice pick up your eye socket and poke around in your brain. They took a very dim view of budding adolescent sexuality back then."

"If you sell me a wine cooler, Danny, I'll let you feel me up in the dead zone."

"Oh, all right. If you insist."

It was a school night, but we went at it anyway. Very steamy as usual. Call me a degenerate, but I do like kissing that girl. She did most of the groping. I had to tug her busy hand out of my pants.

Later, Wenda had some news as I was guarding her with the baseball bat.

"Floyd called that girl Vera," she said, unloading her pink boxes. "They have a date for tonight."

"Good. I never thought he'd call her."

"He was kind of resistant. You have to be firm with Floyd. I said I wasn't filling, dipping, or sorting any donuts until he made the call."

"Blackmail. I'm glad that worked."

"I also heard from the cops. They looked at the surveillance tapes. They couldn't make out the mugger's face, but they said her coat didn't look like anything a teenager would wear. What other violent females are you going out with?"

"Only you, darling," I lied. "Are you coming over tonight?"

"Sorry. But I will let you take me out to dinner."

"Uh, some other time, dear."

I'm done forking out the dollars to watch her eat brains.

Later that morning Lizzie phoned while I was in deepest dreamland to invite me to lunch.

"I had a very late night last night," I yawned. "How about dinner instead?"

"I can't tonight, Danny. Delia's husband is coming over, and we're going to hash things out."

"How about dinner tomorrow? I'll pick you up at seven."

"Sounds good. How come you had such a late night? Entertaining some slinky blonde?"

"Hardly, Lizzie dear. I got absorbed in reading Wilhelm Reich, and the hours just flew by."

"I hear he has that effect on people. See you tomorrow, Danny."

"I'm looking forward to it, darling."

Could it be that winters in Portland aren't really that bad? Good thing it's the Portland in Oregon and not the one in Maine. No way I'd ever move to that blizzard-prone state.

Owen called me that evening. We're on for a double date Friday night, assuming I can rope in Abby. I left a message with her phone service with the details. I never know where she is or what she's doing, except I recall that today was Mrs. Bizal's funeral. Sorry I missed it.

Saw my two therapines Gene and Luke on Wednesday. I did some role-playing with Gene where I was a restaurant manager catching him in the act of pocketing some shakers. I thought this might impress on him the seriousness of getting caught, but he found it all great fun. Oh well, I'm not looking for a fast cure. I need his weekly check more than the world needs one fewer kleptomaniacs.

Doleful Luke said he'd watched the movie "The Truman Show" and was now looking for hidden cameras filming his every move. I think mentioning that film might have been a mistake. I've decided he's a masochist with an overactive ego. We're just slogging through his past (kind of boring so far) and hoping to dig up some nuggets of buried trauma. So far his parents seem fairly normal. Clearly, the guy needs to get laid even more than me, if that's possible.

Since it was the last day of November, I knocked on Mrs. Goodsolm's door to give her my rent check. As is her custom she invited me in for a glass of sherry. She was wearing her brown pixie-cut wig with the frosted highlights. Probably not as fetching on her as it looked on the model in the catalogue. We discussed our mutual interest in fake hair for a time, then she said it was too bad about that awful news.

"What news was that, Mrs. G?" I asked.

"Oh, that nut case who shot those two girls and then turned the gun on himself. At least he spared the baby."

A cold chill ran down my back.

"Uh, where was this?" I asked.

"Somewhere in Contra Costa, Danny. Walnut Creek I think. It's all over the news."

"Oh, my God. Is everyone dead?"

"Just the shooter and his sister-in-law. The wife's in intensive care. Shot four times, but nothing vital got hit. They're calling it a miracle. And the baby's OK, of course."

"Fuck! The sister-in-law is dead?"

"That's right, Danny. Why? Do you know them?"

She had saved the newspaper. It was Lizzie all right. Gunned down last night by that lunatic plumber.

If only I had taken up her invitation for lunch. We might have wound up back at my place. Who knows? We might have been having such a good time, she might have decided to blow off that meeting. Not likely though. I expect she would have wanted to be there to support her sister.

Why are these bastards always reaching for their guns?

This poem I found under a rock in Mrs. Goodsolm's back yard:

Happenstance

Yielding to the enchantment:
Blame it on the dim hope that
Existence is more than daily toil
Ending in a cold final nowhere.

A long life: your reward for years
Well spent? Or just a further lap in the
Long dodge past disease, turmoil, war,
Happenstance, and homicidal rage?

Said the old survivor in his cups:
Staying in the fight is an exercise in
Masochism, hypocrisy, and futility
I would not care to repeat.

Then enchantment be damned.
Re-entrenchment it must be.
Let us withdraw to the bunkers.
Let us get on with the dreary slog of life.

Seventeen/UNSERENE

I made a trip to Bottle Chalet for reinforcements; after that the details get blurry. Owen called at some point to ask if I'd heard the news. I said I had and cancelled our date for Friday. Which is just as well because I never heard back from Abby. Monica and my mother also phoned to chew over the incident. People seem to come out of the woodwork when someone they know gets murdered. I also got calls from several potential therapines, who–not impressed by my coherence–quickly rang off. In one of my more sober moments I cancelled my sessions this week with Culver and Vera.

Late Friday night Olivia showed up alone and spent the night again, this time foregoing the nightgown. I gave her an orgasm with my hand–for which good-deed molestation I'll probably rot in prison. I made her promise not to tell Hwan, but who can trust the word of a 16-year-old? She slept long and hard, and kissed me upon awakening. She made her own breakfast and departed a well-rested virgin, though with her innocence now besmirched. Perhaps Kyle should rise to the challenge and take that burden off my radar.

An hour later Wenda phoned and said I was due at the thrift store at noon for my shift as a volunteer. I told her I had a bad cold and was staying home in bed.

"You can't be drinking this early in the morning," she said.

"Just a bit of a gargle with hot whiskey and lemon," I lied.

"I was counting on your taking me out to dinner after our shift today."

"You must have me confused with some billionaire playboy, darling."

"I thought you said you started a successful new business."

"It's going great guns, but not yet showing much of a profit.

We have entered an Age of Equality, dear one. Women now pay their own way."

"Not gals from Oklahoma, Danny. We cherish our traditional way of life."

"You're in California now, sweetheart. This is a progressive state. You must change with the times."

"It's a moot point anyway, Danny, since you're currently diseased. Call me after you lick that virus."

"Will do, darling. Any report on Floyd's date with Vera?"

"He made Spanish braised chicken with sherry and saffron. Apparently, she liked it."

Perhaps I should drop the sister and start dating the brother. At least I would eat better.

Restless, I switched on the radio. Christmas music already. I switched it off. I phoned my landlady.

"Mrs. Goodsolm, do you know the hospital where they took that shooting victim?"

"Sure, Danny. It's the big Kaiser in Concord."

So I drove to Concord, stopping at Safeway on the way for their budget bouquet. Delia was out of intensive care and receiving visitors. I almost turned around in the corridor, but I had invested $8.99 in wilting carnations, so I knocked on her door and entered.

Still pretty at 40, though showing the strains of her ordeal. The dark circles under her eyes were the biggest change from how I remembered her. I introduced myself and added my meager bouquet to one of the numerous floral piles crowding the room.

"Thank you for the flowers," she said. "The nurses have run out of vases."

"You must have lots of friends."

"A few are from friends and clients. Most of them are from people I don't even know. I'm sorry I don't remember you, Danny, but Lizzie seemed excited to reconnect with you."

"Yeah, I kind of had a thing for her back in high school."

"Her husband was here. He left yesterday. She's being buried up in Portland. The funeral's up there on Tuesday."

"That's OK. I don't really do funerals."

"I don't like them either, but they're a necessity I suppose."

I didn't inquire about funeral arrangements for her late husband.

"Are you in pain?" I asked.

"Doped up to the gills. The doctors aren't telling me yet when I can leave. Lizzie said you're a psychotherapist."

"Yeah, something like that."

"Are you taking on any new patients? It might be nice to talk to someone who's not a complete stranger."

"I don't know, Delia. You've been through a lot. You might be better off with someone who's had more experience."

"I'd like you to consider me, Danny. Lizzie said you have a good heart."

"She may have been overestimating me."

"We should figure out who we know in common."

We went through our Modesto connections. Not much overlap, except she had once dated Matt the priest's older brother.

"My parents weren't thrilled that he was a Catholic. Fortunately for them, they had passed on before I fell in love with a married Chinese Buddhist."

"Lizzie told me about your artist friend. Has he visited you?"

"Not a word from that camp, Danny. Nor do I expect there to be."

"Sorry to hear that. Who's taking care of your baby?"

"Dennis's mother. I'm not too happy about that, but there's no alternative right now. I think my baby was trying to warn me. I think that's why he was in such distress."

I agreed that babies might be more intuitive that we realize. I gave her my number and told her to call me if she needed anything. She said she "very much" hoped I'd visit her again.

I don't expect I'll see her again, but I wish her the best.

* * *

On Sunday I ran out of booze and cigarettes. So I switched to beer and nicotine gum.

Wenda showed up unexpectedly bearing a container of chicken soup.

"Gee, Wenda, you shouldn't have."

"I didn't. Floyd made the soup. You look like death warmed over. I can tell you've been drinking too."

"Only therapeutic gargles."

"I just came from confession."

"Again? If Father Thomas gets paid by the absolved sin, he's due for a bonus this month."

"He said I shouldn't expect the man to pay for everything. He said times have changed."

"How enlightened."

"I guess you can't have much money if you're working nights at a mini mart."

"I don't expect to be doing that much longer."

"So when you take me out to dinner, we can, uh, split the check if you want."

"OK, we'll see. Care to have a seat? Or take your clothes off? I could hop in the shower and be daisy fresh in a jiffy."

"I thought you had a cold."

"All gone. Those gargles worked wonders. How about a kiss?"

"I don't know, Danny. It's Sunday and I've just been to confession."

"In that case you have a clean slate for racking up some sins."

Someone knocked on my door. I walked over and opened it. Olivia smiled and said, "Hi, Danny baby." She looked in and spotted my guest.

"The skank!" yelled Olivia, pointing.

"The mugger!" screamed Wenda, pointing back at her.

Olivia socked me hard in the stomach, turned, and ran down the stairs.

Wenda grabbed her purse and rummaged for her phone.

"What are you doing?" I gasped, bent over from the punch.

"Calling 9-1-1."

"Please don't," I said, wrestling her for the phone.

"You know that girl!" shouted Wenda. "You want her to get away! Give me back my phone!"

"Relax, darling. Let's discuss this like adults."

Wenda reared back and clipped me on the jaw with a right hook. My glasses went flying and I dropped her phone. The back flew off and the battery rocketed under the sofa. Wenda groped about in the murk for it, but came up only with dust bunnies, empty booze bottles, and a pair of Kimberly-era panties.

"Where's your damn phone?" she demanded.

"It's no use, darling. She's far away by now. The cops won't find her."

"Who the hell is she? What's her name?"

"I swear I don't know. She's some nut case. Obviously, she followed you here."

"She addressed you as Danny baby!"

"My name is right on the door: R. Daniel Nixon. Plain as day. Besides, didn't she assault me? You saw her punch me. I got mugged just like you."

"Yeah, I guess so. That's true."

"Jesus, Wenda," I said, rubbing my chin, "you could have dislocated my jaw."

"Sorry, Danny. You shouldn't have grabbed my phone."

"No harm done. Want to retire to the bedroom?"

"I can't. I'm due at the thrift store in ten minutes. Help me find that damn battery. Why is it so disgusting under your couch? Whose panties are these?"

"Don't ask me, dear one. It's not my doing. It's all from the previous tenant. And while you're at it, help me find my glasses. I can't see a thing without them."

After she left and I calmed down, I heated up the soup. Delicious, with a hint of saffron in the broth. Made with leftovers from his get-acquainted dinner with Vera?

Olivia phoned later as I was smoking a cigar excavated from under the sofa.

"What was that slag doing in your apartment?" she asked, sounding hostile.

"She was bringing me some comforting soup. You know

how upset I've been about my friend being murdered. And why the hell did you punch me?"

"Why do you think?"

"I'm not getting into guessing games with some kid."

"I'm hardly that. I punched you for your treachery."

"If you're going to resort to violence all the time, I don't intend to have anything to do with you."

"You told me you weren't screwing that slag."

"I'm not. I'm not screwing anyone, if you must know—including you, because you're just a kid."

"I love you, Danny."

"No, you don't. I am not at all a lovable person. I'm a drunk with no scruples. You should stay far away from me."

"I'll see you at the store tonight, Danny. You can feel me up."

"You should stay home and sleep in your bed like a normal high-school kid. Hanging around me is a very bad idea. I'm corrupting a minor."

"No, you're not, Danny. I am not a child any more. I buried my Barbie doll in my back yard a long time ago."

"Well, you should dig it up and play with Barbie, not me."

"I prefer you, Danny. You're anatomically correct."

"As is your pal Kyle. I suggest you give him a call."

"I may just do that."

"Great. That suits me fine!"

I hung up. Damn, that girl sends my blood pressure into the red zone. The scary thing is I'm more than a bit fond of her too.

That night at the store I wasn't feeling very alert until Abby breezed in for a pint of Old Forester. I continue to be impressed by the diversity of her refreshment choices.

"I got your message about your invitation, Danny. I was away in Nevada."

"Las Vegas?"

"Mostly."

"Business or pleasure?"

"If you enjoy your work, that distinction doesn't apply."

"Do you go there to gamble, see shows, or what?"

"Or what mostly."

"Sounds like fun. I've been wondering why you buy your party supplies here. You could save a lot by stocking up at Bottle Chalet."

"Same reason I don't buy my underwear at K-Mart. Besides, I sort of like the help here."

"Are we going out on Friday with Owen and Maeve?"

"I need to check my calendar. I'll get back to you on that."

Olivia arrived as Abby was leaving.

"I saw you talking to that girl, Danny. I watched you through the window."

"This is a store, darling. I'm expected to talk to the customers."

"You were more than talking. You were flirting!"

"Guilty as charged. Guys generally flirt with attractive women. It helps us feel like we're not yet moldering in our graves."

"How come you flirt with girls that are totally out of your league?"

"To a well-functioning male ego no woman on the planet is outside his realm–minors excepted, of course."

"I bet you'd be all over me if it wasn't against the law."

"In a minute, dear one. You'd experience several lifetimes of intercourse in just a few weeks."

"Hah. I doubt that. Are we retiring to the dead zone?"

"OK, sweetheart. But please keep your hand out of my pants."

* * *

The curse of the day sleeper: my phone jolted me away Monday morning. It was Delia calling from the hospital.

"I feel bad, Danny, that I didn't apologize to you for what happened. After all, it was your friend who got murdered."

"No apology needed, dear. It wasn't at all your fault."

"I married the man, Danny. I cheated on him."

"Happens millions of times a day, Delia. He's the one who crossed the line. He's the one who resorted to violence. It was terrible what happened to you. And it's not your fault."

"Are you coming to visit me today, Danny?"

"I could I suppose. If you want me to."

"Please do."

"OK. It will be later. I have a full slate of appointments to-day."

"Any time you can make it would be great, Danny. I'm not going anywhere."

Wenda phoned that afternoon as I was grinding through a bowl of cornflakes. I was out of milk, so I had splashed on some tequila and a squeeze of lime.

"I went to confession today, Danny."

"Wow, you must be a shoe-in for Parishioner of the Month."

"We discussed that incident in your apartment with the mugger. Father Thomas thinks I should go out with a good Catholic man who doesn't drink and run around with teenagers."

"So this is the big brush-off, huh?"

"I'm afraid so, Danny. I hope we can continue to be cordial when I'm delivering my pastries."

"Not a problem, darling. I'm not the type to hold a grudge."

Dumped by Wenda. There goes my most promising prospect for a legal lay. She had a nice body too, although her little-girl voice and religiosity were grating seriously on my nerves. At least I got out of the deal without adopting a cat. And I'll never again have to watch her fork in a plate of fried brains. So I'm rating this breakup only a two on the R. Daniel Nixon emotional heartbreak scale. (Zero being serenely blasé and ten being actively suicidal.)

For some reason I find it difficult to walk into a hospital room empty-handed. This time I brought some budget chocolates. "Rum-filled" alleged the label on the box. Delia said she would try one when her doctor said it was OK for her to have alcohol. I ate six and received no buzz at all.

She was looking better. Her hair had been washed and styled. A bit of make-up daubed on. But no one looks their best under the harsh lights in a hospital room. I'm sure I looked even more repellent than usual.

We chatted for a bit. She said she was remembering more about what happened that night. It had all been a blank before.

"I'm feeling very bad about it, Danny," she said, taking my hand.

"I'm sure you are, Delia. It was a terrible trauma."

"I'm wishing Lizzie had lived and I was the one who got killed. She could have taken my baby and raised him as her own."

"That wasn't fated to be, dear. It's fortunate that both of you weren't killed."

"I feel like 40 years of my life have been negated. Like it's all a big zero now."

"You have a lot to live for, Delia. There's your son, your family, your work, your friends."

"Lizzie was my only real family. I have some cousins I never see. We weren't that close growing up. I was my dad's favorite and Lizzie resented that. She had a right to. We were very different too. Dennis never liked her. He shot her first, you know. He shot her in the face."

That was something I could have done without knowing. I told her again I was sorry for her pain, and to tell me about it if she wished. So she talked some more about that evening and her troubled life with Dennis until a nurse came in and said it was time for her to do some walking. I helped her amble up and down the corridor a few times. Then her mother-in-law showed up with Dennis Junior, I got introduced, and left as soon as I could.

Did Delia's baby look half-Chinese? I'm no expert, but I wouldn't be surprised if he masters chopsticks by age two.

This whole business of letting Lizzie and her sister think I'm a mental-health professional was a serious mistake. I've never been a helping person, and I'm useless around someone in need. I'd tell Delia I'm a total fraud, but that's one more blow she doesn't need.

I stopped at my local dive bar on the way back and let Sam the bartender pour me a double tequila.

"I like the rug, Danny," he said, inspecting my faux hair. "Looks like you're moving up in the world."

"I'm trying to. Do you get a lot of depressed people in here, Sam?"

"It's my stock in trade. Why?"

"What do you do to cheer them up?"

"That's not my job, Danny. I fill their drink orders and I listen to their stories. If that makes 'em feel better, I'm fine with that. But I don't have any skin in the game."

"I admire your detachment. I need to be at work at midnight. Don't serve me more than one more drink and make sure I leave here in time."

"Even if you beg and plead, Danny?"

"Even if I beg and plead."

More proof that my anonymous pal is not a poet:

Destinations

Recovery Room, Alibi Club, Drift On Inn,
The Oasis, Safety Valve, Ease On Inn,
Safe Haven, The Pour House, Wander Inn,
The Bent Elbow, Storm's Port, Half Way Inn.

The Antidote, A Swill Place, Way Out Inn,
Strange Brew, The Golden Stool, Step Right Inn,
Relief Station, What Ales You, Stagger Inn,
We're Not Hostel, Last Chance, Dew Drop Inn.

Eighteen/VENTIN' SPLEEN

I made it to work on time, appeared to be sober enough to operate the cash register, and my presence with the baseball bat was no longer requested by Wenda. Naturally, now that she's off-limits, she was looking quite sexy. But not jonesing for another restraining order, I kept my distance.

Just after midnight Hwan came in to buy a tin of mints and a three-pack of Trojans.

"Looks like you've got a date," I said. "It better not be with Olivia."

"It's not. That wig of yours looks really, really cheesy."

"Do you want your change in lottery tickets?"

"Stuff that one, Danny. Are you taking Olive to the Christmas dance? It's this Saturday you know."

"Not me. Are you?"

"I'm volunteering my brother Jin."

"What's his middle name, Tonic? Or Fizz?"

"His name is Jin, J-I-N. He's 17. He's kind of shy around girls and doesn't dance."

"He sounds absolutely perfect. What are his other qualifications?"

"He's a nice kid. He's tops in his class and hopes to get into Stanford."

"He sounds OK–as long as he doesn't hope to get into Olivia."

"I told you. He's shy around girls."

"Good. Let's hope he stays that way. How does your mother feel about this blind date?"

"She's not going to know anything about it."

"And this rendezvous of yours, Hwan, is it with a Korean girl?"

"Butt out, Danny. And drop dead."

"No, please, you first."

Later that morning Delia woke me again to inquire what time I would be visiting.

"Uh, late again, dear. I'm busy all day. Do you need anything?"

"Just a visit from my favorite therapist."

What happened to me? I used to run from troubled chicks like a scalded cat.

Olivia showed up after school as I was getting out of the shower. I made her wait in the living room as I dressed.

"I thought you were going to call before you came over," I called.

"I tried, Danny. Some idiot had his phone switched off."

"It was so I could sleep in peace. What's up, darling?"

"It's the Christmas dance. Do you think I should go with Hwan's baby brother?"

"He's older than you are," I said, emerging from the bedroom in all my owlish glory. "What do you know about him?"

"Nothing. I never met the dude. He doesn't go to my high school. Hwan says he's cute."

"Go with him, dear one. What have you got to lose?"

"Only my time and possibly my virginity. Also the respect of my peers if he turns out to be an embarrassment."

"Nothing ventured, nothing gained, dearest. I've got to go. Shall I drop you somewhere?"

"Where are you going all dolled up? To meet that girl you were flirting with?"

"I wish. I'm going to see a friend in the hospital."

"Is she knocked up with your kid?"

"No, dear. These days I'm getting even less sex than you are."

"Then you are in very dire straits."

"I am. And you'll be happy to know I broke things off with the donut queen. You don't have to terrorize her anymore."

"Hooray, Danny! Way to go, dude!"

"Yes, I thought that might make your day."

Delia had some news. Her doctors are saying she may be able to go home on Friday.

"Kind of amazing, huh, Danny?" she said. "Surgeons dig four bullet out of you, pump in eight units of blood, and a week later you're waltzing out of the joint."

"I'm glad you're a fast healer."

"My body is. I'm not so sure about the rest of me. I need your opinion on something. Do you think I should change my son's name?"

I gave it some thought.

"Sounds like a good idea to me, Delia. It could be part of a fresh start for you both."

"You don't think it would be confusing to him?"

"Not at his young age. Do you have any new names in mind?"

"I'd like to name him after my dad, except his name was Howard."

"Right. That name has pretty much had its day. Killed off by the antics of Howard Hughes, Howard Stern, and the rest of those flaky Howards. Did your father have a middle name?"

"Lewis."

"That's not bad."

"I'm thinking it might work as a middle name."

"I always thought if I had a kid, I'd name him Smokey Joe."

"Smokey Joe Nixon. I like that. I see him growing up to become a forest ranger. Or a fireman."

"Jesus H. Nixon also has a certain appeal."

I got a rare laugh out of her for that one. We trotted out dozens of names to try them on for size and came up with a few possibilities.

"What I need to do is get married fast," said Delia. "That way I can change his last name too."

"Uh, right."

The look in her lovely blue eyes could be characterized as warm, but I felt fairly secure. Very few wannabe brides wish to marry into the name Nixon. Nor are tall bald alcoholics with bad eyes at the top of their list.

Owen called me later as I was easing into a bottle of Walgreen's tasty scotch.

"Are the four of us going out on Friday?" he asked.

"I put it to Abby. I'm still waiting to hear back from her."

"I'm not interested in your sex life. What did she say about going out?"

"Ha-ha-ha."

"I stopped in and saw Matt the priest yesterday."

"Was it a poignant reunion?"

"It was kind of embarrassing. He started crying. I think my crispy face rattled him."

"It's obvious, Owen. The guy still loves you."

"Don't say that, Danny. He's a priest."

"As if that changes anything. What did he say?"

"Not much. We were both sort of tongue-tied. I didn't stay long."

"Did you at least offer him a joint for old time's sake?"

"I did. He took it too."

"Any farewell kisses?"

"Just a hug. I couldn't be a priest, Danny. Too lonely a life."

I agreed that celibacy sucks. On that subject I'm an expert.

* * *

When I got to Tim's condo on Wednesday for my appointment with Gene, the tow-happy klepto, I found an official-looking envelope taped to the door. It was a demand from the bank holding the mortgage for immediate payment of all funds in arrears. Dream on, you foolish usurers. Kind of troubling though. They could seize the condo and I'd be out on my ear. I'm not making enough money yet to live, let alone rent an office. I wonder if Freud had this trouble when he was starting out?

Gene continues to amaze me with his sordid life. Not only is he an incorrigible thief, but he also appears to be something of a sex addict. Any chicks who can't afford to ransom their cars are invited into his office to pay "in kind" on his seven-foot sofa. The back cushions lift off so it's nearly as wide as a double bed. He takes on all races, ages, and body types, though he once refused a 300-pound woman with bad eczema.

"Any guys?" I had to ask.

"Only if they're cute, clean-looking, and under 25. Don't tell anyone I said that."

"Of course, Gene. Anything you tell me is held in the strictest confidence. So you're bi-sexual?"

"Certainly not. I just need to get my rocks off as much as possible. And I fuck them. Nobody fucks me."

He said he successfully seduced the babysitter at age nine. He got it into her and came, but was not yet ejaculating any liquids. He loved it because the only birth control required was his extreme youth. He claimed the act was consensual, but it sounded like rape to me.

Then I met with Luke, whose life continues to unwind like a bad movie on a loop tape. His roommate (and love object) has a new boyfriend, who's even more of a creepy lowlife than her usual picks.

"All they do is screw day and night," he sighed. "I don't understand what she sees in him."

"Have you considered moving?" I asked.

"How could I do that? I love her. Besides, you really do need a roommate with rents so high in the Bay Area."

"Agreed, but listening to her make love with another man is not conducive to positive mental health."

"You're the expert, Dr. Nixon. I suppose you're right. But I don't want to move. I want Tina to fall in love with me."

"Don't you see the pattern here, Luke? Remember how you tried out for all those sports teams in high school because your mother wanted you to be athletic?"

"I did make the bowling team. But she never came to any of our matches. She said bowling alleys gave her headaches."

"What do you do to impress Tina?"

"I pay most of the bills. I shop for groceries and make most of the meals. I buy the beer that her boyfriends suck down. I even washed her cruddy sheets last week. Oh, and I leave cute little notes around for her."

"And what does she say about that?"

"She said if I got in her panties drawer again she'd break my face. I love it when she gets mad. She's even more beautiful with her nostrils flaring. She has the most amazing nose. And mouth too. To see it is to want to kiss it. Tina's about the only thing in my life now that seems real."

If I weren't posing as a professional, I'd be tempted to slap that guy silly.

A nurse at the hospital this afternoon thanked me for visiting Delia. Apparently, she's not getting many visitors. I asked Delia about that.

"Dennis wasn't big on doing things with my friends. Over the years he alienated most of them. He was quite charming and gallant when I first met him."

"Yeah, they usually are."

"I had this old house in Concord with lots of plumbing issues. The water pressure was a joke. You'd turn the tap and get just a trickle. The old galvanized pipes had corroded inside. Dennis replaced them all with copper. It was a big job, and by the time he had finished we were, well . . . you know."

"Right."

I felt like asking if he'd given her any sort of discount after he'd taken her to bed. Probably not. Such are the workings of the world: if Delia had better pipes, her sister would still be alive. And I might be shoveling snow in Portland next winter.

"I admired a man with such practical skills," she continued. "Now I have his van parked in my driveway and a garage full of useless plumbing tools and supplies."

"I could look them over," I surprised myself by volunteering. "And put an ad on Craigslist for you."

"Would you, Danny? That would be great. I'll pay you 20 percent of anything you get for them."

"Oh, you don't have to do that."

"I insist, Danny. You're a busy psychoanalyst. Your time is valuable. I suppose we'd have to divulge whose gear they're buying."

"I imagine they'll know already. It's not often a plumber makes the news like that."

"And his name is painted right on the van. It will be a relief to see it go."

"I expect you could use the money, Delia, since you won't be working for a time."

"I'm better fixed than I thought, Danny. I just found out that Lizzie changed the beneficiary on her life insurance from her husband to me. She'd been thinking of leaving him you know."

"I knew they were having problems."

"It's ironic. She's murdered in my home and now I hit the jackpot."

"I'm sure she'd want you to have the money."

"I suppose, but I'd rather have my sister."

My phone buzzed; I excused myself to take the call.

"Hi, Danny," said Olivia. "I talked to Jin. He doesn't sound like a total creep. We're on for the dance on Saturday, but Jin doesn't have his license. The dweeb keeps flunking parallel parking."

"And how is this news relevant to me?" I asked.

"I'm hoping you'll drive us to the dance in your cool car."

"You want me to drive you on a date with another guy?"

"Or I could go with Jin's unknown buddies, and be gang-raped by a dozen degenerates or die in a speeding car driven by a drunken teenager."

"Your parents don't drive?"

"Being hauled by your parents is much too juvenile. I'm not 12 anymore."

"You were 12 a mere four years ago."

"That's hardly relevant either."

"OK, I'll think about it."

"Good, Danny. I knew I could count on you!"

When I returned home, I left another message with Abby's answering service inquiring about Friday night. She remains as elusive as ever. I sometimes get the feeling I'm not high on her list of priorities. But then, when you think about it, why should I be?

* * *

On Thursday I met with Vera, the gal who can't get a date. I asked her how things went with her and Floyd.

"OK, I guess. He was kind of nervous at first, but he sort of settled down. He said you're engaged to his sister."

"Not engaged, no. We were going out for a time, but not any longer. And you and Floyd?"

"Well, I don't think he's a sociopath. That's a switch for me. At least I wasn't getting that vibe, but then I never do until it's too late. Did you know he watches the Food Channel all night while making donuts?"

"No, I didn't know that."

"Yeah, he's got a big-screen TV mounted right above the deep fryer. The guy can cook anything. He really should get a job as a chef and get off that nightly donut treadmill. I can't believe he works seven nights a week."

"I know. He needs to hire people to ease up on his workload."

"He showed me his van. It's truly a work of art. Like something you'd see in a car museum."

"So you like him?"

"I don't know, Dr. Nixon. I like that he's a living, breathing guy willing to make me dinner. But I'm not sure about what's there once you get past the van, the bachelor pad, the donuts, and the expertise with a sauce pan."

"You'll just have to get to know him better."

"I'd kind of like to, but he hasn't called me since that night."

"What?"

"Not a word back from Floyd. It may have occurred to him that I'm not the sort of girl that guys date–even if they've never dated anyone else before."

"That's not true, Vera. Floyd just needs some coaxing. I'll make sure he calls you back."

"Why do guys need coaxing to phone me?"

"It's not you, Vera. It's Floyd. He has issues stemming from his motorcycle accident."

"I hope he didn't hit the handlebars at 80 miles an hour. I am hoping for a guy who's intact down there."

"I'm sure he is. He's just self-conscious about his limp."

"He's kind of cute. He reminds me of Montgomery Clift after his bad car wreck. Not put back together exactly right, but still interesting."

"Bob Dylan, Billy Idol, and Duane Allman all had motorcycle crashes," I pointed out.

"That's a point in Floyd's favor," she conceded.

"And Bob Dylan won the Nobel Prize," I added with barely a pang of envy.

After she left, I phoned Wenda.

"Why hasn't your damn brother called Vera?" I demanded.

"He told me he did. He said she declined to see him again."

"That's a flaming lie! She's wondering why he hasn't called."

"Thanks for letting me know, Danny. No jelly rolls or cream sticks will get filled until he calls her."

"Right. And make sure he asks her out too."

"OK, Danny. I'm on top of it."

"One more thing: about Floyd and his motorcycle wreck. Did he suffer any impairments? Are all of his male faculties working?"

"I never heard that they weren't. I expect they're working better than yours. Father Thomas says I did the right thing dumping you."

"Yeah, he would."

"Are you seeing other girls or just sticking with your underage mugger?"

"I'm going out with two beautiful, blue-eyed blondes–both of whom are nuts about me."

"You always were a kidder, Danny."

I'd say that boast qualifies more as an exaggeration than a flat-out lie.

I had to rearrange things for my busy day on Friday. Culver was able to come to her session an hour earlier. I asked her how the worrying was going.

"Still on full steam ahead, Dr. Nixon," she replied. "Plus, this week I was worrying your cold would get worse and you'd die of pneumonia."

"A needless anxiety," I pointed out. "I'm in perfect health."

"So it appears. I'm also worried sick my husband Bryce will hate his Christmas presents."

"What did you get him?"

"He's kind of hard to buy for. So far I got him some socks, new windshield wipers for his truck, a book on home-built bomb shelters, and a DVD titled 'The Joys of Marital Fidelity.'"

"Right. Fortunately, you still have two more shopping weeks until Christmas."

"I'm also worried I'll hate what he gets me."

"Do you generally dislike his gifts?"

"Always. He buys me clothes like you'd find in the back of his mother's closet. Horrible colors and patterns, and styles 30 years out of date. He bought me this sweater."

It was a shaggy number in muted shades of orange and green (my high school colors), knit in a pattern suggesting there had been a malfunction at the factory. Incongruously, the sleeves and neckline were trimmed in shiny orange satin. Not wishing to venture into female fashions, I decided not to pursue that line of inquiry.

"Any other worries?" I asked.

"I got some hygiene worries too. Like when I shave my legs, I'm afraid the hair is coming back thicker and blacker. And I think my deodorant is making my armpits smell like rotten eggs."

We went on like that for another 50 minutes. At the end of the session I told her the mind was like a giant jukebox–always ready to play a selection of prerecorded thoughts. And her mind loved to drop the needle on worry records.

"But why?" she asked.

"It's an obsession, Culver. It's a matter of routine: you worry because you always worry. And also it's a matter of comfort: for some reason playing these worry records is comforting to you. They've become the soundtrack to your life."

"But what do I do about it, Dr. Nixon?"

"Let's try an experiment. This week when you start worrying about something, say to yourself: 'Every day in every way, I'm getting better and better.'"

"OK. I'll try it."

The Coué method worked for some people back in the flapper era. We might as well try it out on her.

This poem hurtled out of the sky engraved on a meteorite:

Obsessions

Humans are prone to obsess
Over matters richly diverse.
Their minds love to regress
Into zones unseemly or perverse.

Some recoil from germs and dirt,
Or pluck themselves bald.
Others do obscenities blurt,
Or with thinness are enthralled.

Phantoms wrack hypochondriacs.
Shoppers strive for endless stuff.
Ceilings entrance insomniacs.
Sex nuts like it often and rough.

Gossips must ever peek and snoop.
Racists hate you for your color.
Hermits boycott every group.
Cat ladies thrive in smelly squalor.

Internet trolls must ever blacken.
Jesus fans have to spread the word.
Almost never do they slacken,
Obsessing on 'til at last interred.

Nineteen/GOIN' LEAN

Delia ate lunch in her hospital room, and then I drove her home. She was surprised by my car. Naturally, I was prepared with an explanation.

"The diesel engine in my Mercedes failed," I said. "My mechanic wanted $14,000 for a rebuild. I told Fritz to keep the car and salvage what he could get for it. A patient of mine, strapped for cash, offered me this amusing car in lieu of my fee. I decided to drive it until it dies."

"The engine sounds OK," said Delia, buckling her grungy seatbelt.

"It's the legendary Chrysler 318."

"Legendary for what, Danny?"

"Legendary for running forever."

I pressed on the gas and the engine sputtered and stalled. It took me four tries to get it restarted.

"Are we stopping to pick up your son?" I asked.

"No, my mother-in-law is bringing him by later."

"You think you'll be able to care for him by yourself?"

"I hope so. If not, I have a babysitter I can call on for help. I'm thinking of Keanu."

"Keanu Reeves? Do you know him?"

"I'm thinking of Keanu Lewis Harger as a name for my son. I'm reverting back to my maiden name."

"You like Keanu Reeves?" I asked.

"Who doesn't? Do you think that name is too closely associated with him?"

"I think people would be inclined to make the connection, him being the only Keanu around."

"I wouldn't want my son to grow up in the shadow of some movie star. OK, Keanu is out. We're back to Smokey Joe."

"Joe's not a bad name, Delia. Studies show people do better in life with less exotic names."

"He'd be Joe Lewis, Danny. Do I want to name him after a black prizefighter?"

"Why not? The Brown Bomber fought 70 pro bouts and only lost three. He spelled his name differently too."

"I'm sure the perfect name is out there, Danny. It will come to us eventually."

"Your house," I said. "Has it been, uh . . ?"

"Yes, my mother-in-law hired a professional service to deal with the disorder. Everything's been cleaned up."

I'm sure it was the least she could do for giving birth to that monster.

Delia's tastefully furnished house was crammed with bold modern art on all the walls. Her plumbing fixtures were top of the line; the water pressure could not be faulted.

"Do you want any of Dennis's clothes?" she asked, when I emerged from the guest bath. "He was about your size."

Did I want to drape myself in the cooties of a crazed murderer? I think not.

"No thanks," I said. "I'm well-fixed for clothes."

"He also has a humidor filled with cigars. He went for the expensive kind."

"Hmm, I might take those off your hands."

Cooties don't cling to fine cigars.

I wandered out to inspect the plumbing liquidation scene. The van was newer than I expected with only 37,000 miles. One bay of the two-car garage was filled with plumbing supplies, including ranks of ready-to-install toilets and water heaters. All arranged very neatly. I snapped away with my cellphone camera, then returned with a proposal for Delia.

"I can put an ad on Craigslist right now. I suggest we sell it all in one lot. We show it over the weekend, taking written bids. Then sell it Sunday night for the highest bid over $10,000."

"That sounds fine," she said, starting to weep.

"What's the matter, dear?"

"I don't know if I can live in this house any more, Danny. I keep recalling that horrible night."

"It's a process, dear," I said, putting my arm around her. "Take it one day at a time. Things will get better with time."

For not being a helping person, I was sure starting to sound like one. Could masquerading as a therapist alter a guy's personality? Or was I just in it for the fat commission on the liquidation sale?

Smokey Joe arrived and seemed happy to be returned to his mother and his familiar crib. He was a cute little bugger, if infants are your thing. Fussing and screaming appeared to be off his menu.

"He's been so calm since Dennis left us," observed Delia. "He's like a totally different baby. And see how he smiles at you, Danny."

I could see through that infantile ploy.

"Right," I said. "Like a salesman trying to sign me up for a vacation time-share."

I got take-out from Delia's favorite Indian restaurant. We were just sitting down to eat when my phone buzzed. It was Owen sounding annoyed.

"Where are you, Danny? Abby's here and we're ready to go."

"I assumed the date was off. I never heard back from her."

Owen relayed that to Abby.

"She says she left a message for you with a guy named Juan."

"I think she means Hwan," I said. "Leaving a message with him is like flushing it down a toilet. I'm tied up here. You guys go out. Have a good time."

"Really? You can't make it, Danny?"

"Nah, sorry. I'll catch the next one."

"OK, Danny. But I'm going to tell Abby about your high-school years. I have total recall of all your most embarrassing episodes."

"An idle threat, Owen, since I have just as much to spill to Maeve about you."

Delia dredged up a beer for me to drink with our chicken biryani. Dennis was dead and buried, I was drinking his last beer, eating dinner with his beautiful wife, and later I'll be smoking his prized cigars. Probably not the scenario he envisioned when he started blasting away.

* * *

I returned the next morning with a bag of donuts. Delia plopped S.J. in my lap and had me feed him a jar of strained carrots. He got bug-eyed and slurped the spoon with alacrity. Clearly carrots were high on his list. I feel the same way about a fine single-malt scotch.

Plumbers of all shapes, sizes, ages, and ethnicities arrived to inspect the goods. Some took me aside to make insulting low-ball, all-cash offers. I told them to write down their best bid over $10,000 and seal it with their business card in one of the provided envelopes. Quite a few knew Dennis personally and were curious to know who the hell I was.

"Dennis was a good guy," said a large dude sporting a modified mullet (long in back, shaved over the ears). "He must have been provoked. Are you the boyfriend?"

"I'm the psychoanalyst treating his traumatized wife. I was friends with her sister."

"Uh, right. The girl he shot."

"And killed."

"It ain't easy being a plumber," said Mr. Mullet's pal. "You want to crawl under a house on your belly through stinking puddles of backed-up shit? We do that all the time!"

"You have my sympathies," I said. "I wouldn't want your job."

"How you want to get paid?" asked another plumber. "With a bank check?"

"Cash only," I replied. "And tell your bank we'll only take the new Benjamins with the blue stripes."

"Kinda picky aren't you?" said Mr. Mullet.

"I'm just looking out for the wife's welfare."

"I hear she's a looker," said his pal. "I bet I know what you're after."

I was going to punch out his lights, but then I remembered I'm not Jason Bourne or even Matt Damon.

Delia made lunch from the groceries her mother-in-law

thoughtfully provided. She appeared to be a nice lady despite her profound failure as a parent.

"I'm thinking of Brandon," said Delia, serving me a tuna salad sandwich.

"Certainly a popular name," I conceded. "Although perhaps a source of confusion in kindergarten with three or four Brandons in his class."

"Too popular, huh?"

"You could be a little different and name him Brando."

"Or how about Brand X?" she laughed.

By the end of the day we had nine envelopes in our basket.

"It was like plumbing central out there today," I reported to Delia. "I hope we do as well tomorrow."

"I'm so grateful for your help, Danny. I don't know what I'd do without you."

Words I never expected to hear from a beautiful woman. What exactly was I after here anyway?

Delia invited me to dinner, but I had to decline due to to-night's chauffeur duties. I was nearly on time. Olivia was waiting at the curb in front of her house when I pulled up with my wheel spinners spinning.

"You're late, Danny," she said, easing into the back seat. "I really like standing around in the cold and dark in a strapless gown."

"Where's your coat, darling?"

"I'm not wearing a coat. I don't have one that goes with this dress."

"Only females are willing to die for fashion, Olivia. That's a distinctly gender-based trait."

"Guys do dumb things too, Danny. Your sex wins all the Darwin Awards."

"You mean like the fellow taking a selfie in front of an on-coming train who misjudged which track it was on? Or the guy also taking a selfie as he pulled the pin on a hand grenade which turned out to be live?"

"Exactly. So step on it. We don't want to piss off darling Jin."

Jin lived 12 miles away. Not exactly the boy next door. Despite being the younger brother, he was taller and better looking than Hwan. He reminded me of a young Korean Henry Fonda. Jin tried occupying the front seat, but I made him get in the back with his date. Being the so-called adult, I made the introductions.

"Hi," said Jin, handing Olivia a boxed corsage.

"Thanks," she said. "This dress is stuck on with double-sided tape. So I think I'll just carry the flowers."

"Tape, huh?" he said, inspecting her décolletage with interest. "If you perspire, things could get quite interesting."

"Not that interesting," she replied. "Danny here has informed me that I'm not voluptuous."

"This car is a trip," said Jin, changing the subject. "Are you the original owner?"

"No, Jin, it's a 1978 model. I wasn't buying cars as a newborn infant."

"Oh, sorry," he said.

"I like your cologne," said Olivia. "You smell better than I do."

"My brother made me put it on," said Jin. "He has some old-fashioned ideas."

"I know. Hwan is *so-o-o* old," said Olivia, doubtless intending to tweak me.

I dropped them off at the high school.

"What time do you want me back?" I asked.

"I'll call you," replied Olivia. "And try to show up sober. You've got precious cargo to haul."

"Jawohl, mein führer."

Later, I was relaxing in my attic hovel when my phone rang.

"Is the dance over already?" I said.

"What dance?" asked Abby. "Are you expecting a call from Cinderella?"

"Oh, hi, Abby dear. No, I'm just experimenting with novel ways to answer my phone. Sorry for the failure to communicate last night."

"Not a problem, Danny. The consensus was we had a better time without you."

"That's usually the case, darling. What did you do?"

"We went to a strange restaurant that Owen delivers to. They have weird dishes on the menu like fried brains."

"Ah, yes, Abby, I know it well."

"You like brains?"

"I like them in beautiful women."

"Are you smoking a joint, Danny? I can tell you're smoking something."

"It's a Cuban cigar, sweetheart."

"Too bad, Danny. I was going to invite myself over. I can't abide cigar smoke."

"Really? I could snuff it out and open all the windows."

"Too late. Maybe next time."

"Abby dearest, I notice when you call me that my phone doesn't register your number. Is that deliberate?"

"Everything I do is deliberate, Danny. Have a nice evening with your cigar."

I was just getting warmed up for our conversation, but she hung up.

Bad karma from Dennis's cigar or was that minx just messing with my head?

My phone rang again a half-hour later.

"Dance transportation central," I said.

"What?" asked Delia. "Who is this?"

"Hi, Delia," I said. "It's only me. Danny."

"Hi, Danny. I'm thinking of the name Brynn."

"How's that spelled?"

"B-R-Y-N-N."

"It would be more fun with extra Ns at the end. How about four or five of them?"

"You don't like it?"

"No, I think it's fine. Brynn is a strong masculine name."

"You don't think it's too macho?"

"It's macho but not too macho. A happy medium like Ryan Gosling. He can dance, but also can deck someone if required. I'd take him any day in a knife fight with Matt Damon."

"How about it as a name for a mixed-race child?"

"It's good. I think you should put it on your list."

"Are you smoking one of Dennis's cigars?"

"No," I lied, "I'm just breathing deeply because it's such a pleasure to hear from you."

"Lizzie said you could be charming."

"It's one of my gravest faults."

"See you tomorrow, Danny."

"I'm looking forward to it, darling."

It was after midnight when Olivia finally called.

"You don't have to drive us, Danny," she said, sounding upbeat. "We're going with Clare in Kyle's car."

"Is Kyle sober?"

"Sure, not to worry."

"How's your beau Jin?"

"Great. I can't talk now. See you tomorrow. Bye!"

Olivia's having a good time with her friends. Why does that not thrill me?

* * *

As an experiment only, we are now addressing Smokey Joe as Brynn. He was taking it in his stride as I was spooning in the strained apricots. Delia wanted to break me in on the delights of diaper changing, but I drew the line at that. The only bum I intend to wipe is my own. Or possibly hers if it comes to that. I think Wenda has the right idea. At least cats come from the factory programmed to use a litter box.

Not as many plumbers showed up today. Were they all out Christmas shopping? Were they reevaluating their careers? By the end of the day we had 13 envelopes in the basket. Delia had me do the honors. Four envelopes contained only rude notes. More proof that trolls are everywhere. The highest bid received was $16,100.

"That's kind of disappointing," sighed Delia. "Dennis spent nearly twice that just on the van."

"We could show it again next weekend if you want," I said.

"No, Danny. I want it all gone. I want Dennis out of my life A.S.A.P."

I called the winning plumber with the happy news. He said he would go to the bank first thing tomorrow morning. I reminded him we were only accepting Benjamins with the blue stripes.

"That's quite a pile of cash," he said. "You wouldn't rather have a cashier's check from my bank?"

"Cash only," I said. "We're also throwing in Dennis's entire wardrobe if you want."

"No, thanks. I don't wear dead men's clothes."

Right, except he's happy to use Dennis's pipe wrenches and drive his spiffy van.

After dinner (take-out Thai) I cleaned up the kitchen. Then things got awkward.

"I guess I'll see you tomorrow," I said.

"Right," said Delia, holding the baby.

What's the etiquette for putting the moves on an infant-clutching woman who's healing from four bullet wounds? I sure didn't know, so I left.

I did some calculations on the drive home. My share was $3,220. A nice cash windfall for Danny. Another month or two's reprieve from sleeping in my Cordoba.

I watched a video, smoked a cigar, eased into a bottle of bourbon, and was getting ready to turn in when I remembered something: I was due at work in two minutes! Oh right, I'm still a mini-mart wage slave.

"You late, Danny," said Mr. Park when I finally showed up.

"This is my last weekend," I replied. "I quit this job. You can find yourself another late-night serf."

"You been drinking, Danny. I can smell it. I happy you quit! I don't need drunks in my store!"

"I'm hardly drunk. Just a beer or two to wake me up."

"You sell lottery tickets tonight or you fired!"

"An idle threat, since I'm only working this shift and the next one."

Mr. Park stomped out looking pissed. Another guy who had gone into the wrong line of work. I see him more as a prison guard at San Quentin.

Olivia drifted in a few minutes later.

"Hello, darling." I said. "Why aren't you in strapless chiffon?"

"That's history, Danny. Get over it."

"How was your date?"

"Much better than I expected. Jin's a cool dude. He's smart, funny, and isn't nearly as inept on the dance floor as Kyle. And he's not married to his phone like Hwan."

"Damn, dear one. This sounds like love."

"It could be, Danny. I talked to him for two hours tonight. He wants to go out next weekend. His mother won't like it, but that's her problem."

"And is it my problem if I don't like it?"

"You had your chance, Danny. You took my girlish heart and punted it away."

"I did no such thing. Hell, I even spent the night with you—twice!"

"Hah! I could get more sex from a lady gym teacher. Are you selling me a wine cooler?"

"If you insist. You want to make out in the dead zone?"

"No way, Danny. I'm saving these lips for Jin. Not to mention the rest of me."

"That's extremely cruel of you, darling. Fondling you is always the high point of my work night."

"I'll meet you in the dead zone, Danny. But only to pay for my wine cooler."

"Tomorrow is my last night in this job, sweetheart. After that you'll have to use your feminine wiles on Mr. Park's wife."

"You're quitting! Why?"

"I can't take the rejection. First from the donut queen and now from you."

"I still love you, Danny. You know that. But only as a friend."

"Sorry, dear one. That's too little too late. I'm history as of tomorrow night."

"Hardly. I know where you live. I'll still show up unannounced to catch you in some gross act with an inappropriate female."

"I won't open the door, darling. I'll be in there nursing a broken heart."

"More likely nursing a bottle of gin."

"Please, Olivia, don't mention that name!"

A slow night after she left. I nodded off a few times, nearly toppling off my stool. I revived a bit when Wenda arrived with her morning delivery.

"Did your brother call Vera?" I asked.

"I made him. I told Floyd if she didn't spend the night, I'd assume he had some disability from his motorcycle wreck."

"What did he say?"

"He got real defensive and said that wasn't very charitable coming from a so-called Catholic."

"Did Vera spend the night?"

"You'll have to ask her. Floyd's clammed up about the whole thing."

Wenda was shocked when I told her I'd handed in my notice.

"It won't be the same here without you, Danny."

"No, I expect it will be better–at least for you!"

I slept until late afternoon, then drove to Delia's. The van was gone from the driveway.

"Hello, Danny," she said, cantilevering Brynn off her hip. He was sucking avidly on a binky. "I've got my garage back!"

"Glad to hear it, dear."

"Oh, I've got something for you."

She handed me an envelope; it was thinner than expected.

"I hope you don't mind, Danny. The sale was for so much less than I expected. So I cut your commission to ten percent."

"Not a problem," I said, shocked.

"I have all these expenses and I have no idea when Lizzie's insurance settlement is coming through."

"I understand, dear. You've been through so much, and I'm sure returning to work is the farthest thing from your mind."

"It's not easy being a single mother, Danny. Would you like to make a contribution to little Brynn's educational fund?"

"Of course," I heard myself say.

Delia took back her envelope.

"We'll put this in the bank for Brynn, Danny. It will make a wonderful start for him."

I smiled in numb stupefaction.

You had to admire her finesse in executing the bonusec-tomy. She extracted the entire bundle with not even a whimper from the victim.

This poem I found written in a nearly illegible hand on the back of a fake million-dollar bill:

Hard Times Are Here Again

Money is there and then it's not.
Yet daily your belly insists
On something tasty and hot.
Plus, one clamors for trysts

Which seldom get dished out gratis
As certain standards must be met.
One must exude a certain status,
If hook-ups one hopes to abet.

And sleeping under a bush–
Although dandy for a Scout–
Can be taxing to one's tush,
And the lice can be a gross out.

Nor is nudity accommodated
When your clothing fund departs.
Prudes may be discombobulated
By your dangling and jiggling parts.

They didn't call it the Great Depression
Because people were feeling blue.
It was an era of dispossession
'Cause the economy was in the loo.

Nobody had a dime, the folding
Green was a fading memory.
Now I'm again beholding
A dive into 1930s penury.

Twenty/DAMN WENT HE

Obviously, I need to expand my stable of therapines. I renewed my Craigslist ad, which shockingly had been allowed to lapse.

Delia, I've decided, is a luxury I can no longer afford. Who had been buying those take-out dinners expecting to be reimbursed? I'm sorry she got shot, but she has a nice house and plenty of art to sell if the wolf is at the door. All I have is Dennis's handcrafted walnut humidor, which I listed on Craigslist for $350. My headline: "Perfect Holiday Gift for the Cigar Lover!!!" His cigars I'm keeping as a salutary break from destitution.

When I returned to work, I suggested to Mr. Park as politely as possible that I no longer wished to quit my job.

"Too late, Danny!" he said. "I already hired Hwan's uncle! He not a drunk! He wears clean shirts!"

"How's his English?" I asked.

"Very great, Danny! Almost as good as mine. This your last night! You sell many lottery tickets or you fired!"

I didn't point out the absurdity of that statement. Since it was my final night as a mini-mart clerk, I decided to go out with a bang. I filled the green decaf coffee pot with the extra-caffeinated brew. All the other pots got straight decaf. I turned the hotdog roller grill up to HIGH, sizzling those dogs black as they spun like tops. I told customers wishing to buy lottery tickets that the machine was down. Two patrons paying with Benjamins I stiffed for the full $80 in change. Cigarette buyers got two packs for the price of one. Gals in hot pants, fishnet stockings, and platform shoes were undercharged severely for their purchases.

I was prepared to give Olivia a free carton of wine coolers

in the flavor of her choice, but she never showed. More proof of the fickleness of the hearts of young girls.

Abby breezed in at 1:15 a.m. looking even more beautiful than usual. Somehow she had heard on the grapevine of my employment change.

"How will I cope without you, Danny?" she asked.

"A constant lament of so many lovely women," I affirmed. "How bitterly do they reproach themselves. What's your pleasure tonight, darling?"

Abby eyed the shelves of inviting pint and quart bottles arrayed behind me.

"What else, Danny? A pint of Widow Jane."

"Such an appropriate choice, sweetheart," I replied, slipping her bourbon into a sack.

"And one for yourself as well, Danny."

"Too generous by far, darling!" I exclaimed, taking a bottle for myself.

"I hope that's not a cigar sticking out of your shirt pocket, Danny."

"Only for show! Not to be smoked, dear one!"

"Glad to hear it."

I rang up her purchase and gave her an extra $5 bill with her change.

"I get off at eight, darling," I said. "How about we go out for breakfast and then retire to my place for light calisthenics followed by a hearty siesta?"

"Sorry, Danny, I've got an important dye job scheduled tomorrow."

"A friend of Mrs. Bizal?"

"Yes. Ninety-two and thinking of altering her will."

"Keep me in mind for legal work."

"I'll do that, Danny."

Wenda arrived at her usual hour with no pink boxes.

"Where are our donuts?" I demanded. "I was counting on a fresh one for my celebratory post-employment breakfast."

"No donuts today, Danny. Floyd's taking the week off."

"What!"

"He and that Vera girl left on a road trip in his van. I hope they're not headed to Vegas to get married."

"What makes you think they could be?"

"I know for a fact Floyd packed along his best sports jacket."

"I'm beyond flabbergasted, dear."

"Yeah, our customers are screaming bloody murder. I hope we don't go bankrupt just so my brother can have sex. I blame you, of course."

"You should be happy for your brother, Wenda. Everyone deserves someone to love."

"And what about me, Danny? Who have I got?"

"You've got Jesus, dear. Not to mention Father Thomas and your cats."

Looks like I'm down one therapine. Another blow to my finances. Oh well, perhaps Vera will write me a favorable Yelp review.

Mrs. Park arrived with her husband. She had prepared my final paycheck and handed it to me without comment. I thanked her anyway, and said I would continue to favor their store with my patronage.

"You sold no lottery tickets!" exclaimed her husband, aghast.

"Sorry, Mr. Park. I guess no one was feeling lucky last night. I do have that effect on people."

* * *

Delia called me later to invite me to dinner. I was skeptical.

"Do you intend this to be another meal of take-out cuisine?" I asked.

"Not at all, Danny. I've been to the market. I'm cooking dinner. Brynn misses you."

"What makes you say that? Has he expressed that sentiment in his vocabulary of zero words?"

"He's quite talkative, Danny. I understand what he's expressing. He's happiest when you're here. It's very plain to see."

"OK, Delia. Should I bring anything?"

"Nothing, Danny. We can open one of Dennis's wines if you want."

There's been one positive development. I sold the cigar humidor. An older gal talked me down to three Benjamins. She was buying it as a Christmas gift for her father-in-law, a gent with two interests in life: cigars and golf. This year she had run out of golf novelties to buy. I lugged the humidor down to her car (a fancy Mercedes) and wished it a reluctant farewell. Cedar-lined humidors are one of those things striving guys aspire to, like glamorous wives, swanky cars, rippling abs, lavish wine cellars, and low golf handicaps. The humidor was out of my league and had to go.

Delia made a stir fry with exotic ingredients such as fennel root, jerusalem artichokes, parsnips, bitter melon, etc. All organic and fresh from the farmers' market. It was the worst stir fry ever, but I shoveled it in without complaint.

She told me about her work as an art consultant. Most of her clients are tech millionaires and corporations. Once in a while she advises someone from the Old Money crowd. She told me this story:

Last year she got hired by a bank to buy art for their new branch. It was a large space with high ceilings in a new building. She bought eight large, modern paintings in a strictly abstract style from an up-and-coming Oakland artist. Boldly colorful, but not at all offensive. The bank spent a fortune framing the art under glass, which is not usually done for such works. Bank hosts a gala reception for the artist. Everyone very pleased.

Five months later a bigger bank buys the bank. That branch is deemed superfluous. Bankers depart with their adding machines and cash drawers, but the art is left behind. Building manager arrives and orders janitor to heave paintings into dumpster. Instead, the janitor calls the Salvation Army, which hauls art away and advertises it on Craigslist for $500 a pop. Friend of artist sees ad. Artist goes to Salvation Army, makes an offer, and hauls home all eight paintings for a flat $2,000. Artist calls Delia. She sells three paintings to collectors, who remove glass from frames. Other five she places in offices of San Francisco tech start-up. They retain glass in frames because their employees are known to have food fights.

"So you sold the work twice?" I asked.

"Sure did, Danny. And got a commission both times. The artist got paid twice too, less her $2,000. The Salvation Army made a tidy sum. The janitor felt good about not being a philistine. Everyone won except the bankers, who couldn't care less. That's the art world for you."

"How do you get a job like that?"

"You major in art history in college and then network like crazy. It helps to be lucky."

"And beautiful," I added. "I expect that helps too."

She smiled and flashed me a look, the import of which was unmistakable. But here's the rub: did a woman whose late husband tried to kill her need me as the next man in her life? I wasn't enough of a scumbag to answer in the affirmative. So I did the dishes, spooned some strained pears into her son, gave her a warm hug, and made ready to leave.

"I like you, Danny," she said.

"I like you too, Delia."

"You don't have to go you know."

"I better, dear. It's getting late."

"Can I ask you a question? Is it because you're put off by my injuries?"

"Not at all, dear. Far from it. I think you're a highly desirable woman."

"Then why, Danny?"

"Uh, I'm not quite over the last one," I lied.

"Really? Lizzie implied that you were unattached."

"I'm working on it. Not quite there yet."

"Oh, I understand. Take your time, Danny."

"Right. See you soon, dear."

"I hope so, honey."

* * *

Loud pounding on my door late that night.

This time it wasn't a cop. It was Tim the fugitive in a deputy sheriff's uniform.

"Tim!" I exclaimed. "You're back!"

"Can I use your computer, Danny?"

"Uh, sure."

I fired up my laptop and asked him why he was wearing the legal-eagle uniform and blue latex gloves.

"It's a long story," he replied, typing away.

"Jesus, Tim. Why are you Googling 'abandoned cemetery West Hartley, California?'"

"I'm looking for a grave."

"Whose grave?"

"Mine."

"What?"

Tim grabbed a piece of paper off my desk and noted some street names displayed on a map on the screen. He closed out the browser and continued typing.

"What's happening, Tim?" I asked. "Talk to me, dude. Why aren't you in Mexico?"

"I wasn't in Mexico, Danny. I never left town. An old girl-friend's been hiding me in her garage. She brought me one meal a day: frozen dinners that she microwaved. I had a ratty sofa, a nine-inch black and white TV, and a bucket to crap in. At night I took ice cold showers from a garden hose behind the garage."

"That sounds grim. How come the eats were so poor?"

"Like many ex-girlfriends Carol wanted me to live, but also to suffer."

"Grizzoffski said you were in Mexico."

"I talked to some day laborers in front of Home Depot. One kid said he was on his way back to Mexico. So I gave him my phone and told him to call his mama regularly."

"Why would he accept a cellphone from some stranger?"

Tim had finished typing, but my hard drive continued to whirl away.

"Because, Danny, he thought I was a crazy rich Gringo. I need your help for a few hours."

"Sure. When?"

"Right now. I need to move a body."

"What! Whose?"

"Whose do you think?"

"You shot Grizzoffski!!"

"I didn't shoot him. But he's dead. It was him or me, Danny. He tracked me down to the garage. Don't ask me how. He had me cuffed and was taking me to 'a place of torture and execution.' His exact words."

"He might have been kidding."

"He wasn't kidding. He told me where I was going to die: in a forgotten Gold-Rush-era cemetery in West Hartley. A place buried deep in the woods. He said he had already dug a grave for me there. He said nobody would find it or know about it."

"Jesus, how did you get away?"

"Booby trap. I figured he'd show up eventually. I had plenty of time to work it out. I booby-trapped the door knob. I had a switch concealed on the sofa. Thing is, he wanted me to go out first. He had his gun on me, of course."

"What did you do?"

"I said I couldn't open the door with the cuffs on. So he did it. I had hung some aluminum screening down from the rafters. Aluminum is a good conductor of electricity. He brushed aside the screening with one hand and grabbed the doorknob with the other. That completed the circuit. Stopped his heart immediately with no blood. The guy was toast–literally."

"Actually, figuratively."

"Whatever."

"Where is he now?"

"In a body bag in the garage. He had stowed a body bag and a shovel in the trunk of his patrol car. The guy intended to murder me, Danny. It was self-defense."

"You could explain all that to the cops."

"Right, Danny. I killed one of their own. And clearly premeditated. I'd spend the rest of my life doing hard time at San Quentin."

"How come you're wearing his uniform? It's a very bad fit."

"I had to drive his cruiser to get here. I figured I should dress for the part."

"What do you want me to do, Tim?"

"I plan to put Grizzoffski in the pit he intended for me. I need your help. The guy must weigh 250 pounds at least."

I gasped. "I can't do that, Tim. I'd be an accessory to murder!"

"I talked to Maeve, Danny. She told me you were meeting people for some reason in my condo. So one night I sneaked out and checked things there. If you don't help me, I'm going to make a call to the state. I expect they like their psychotherapists to be fully licensed and get annoyed if they're not."

"That's blackmail, Tim!"

"I'm a desperate man, Danny. So be a pal and help me out. Grab your car keys and let's go."

Grizzoffski's patrol car was parked out back next to my Cordoba.

"You follow me, Danny," said Tim. "I know a place to ditch the cruiser."

"Those cars have GPS trackers," I pointed out.

"I already checked. The wire was disconnected. I don't think Grizzoffski wanted anyone following his movements tonight. His body radio I drowned in my bucket of piss."

"The dispatchers will be wondering why he's not answering calls."

"They'll give him some slack. A guy with his reputation, they'll assume he's taking a nap or banging some bimbo. Hell, we don't even know if he's on duty tonight."

I followed Tim to an unlit alley several miles away. He parked and opened the cruiser's trunk. He stripped off the uniform and folded it neatly in the trunk, where he had stashed his clothes. He put Grizzoffski's gun and other gear on top of the pile, then dressed hurriedly.

"Damn, Tim, you're as skinny as a rail."

"Nothing but bad rations and daytime TV, Danny. I was ready to die."

"I like daytime TV."

"Yeah, you would. No sex either. I tried, but Carol said no dice. It was 24 hours a day of garage hell boredom. I almost was glad when Grizzoffski showed up."

"He might have shot you right there."

"Too much mess, Danny. He wanted to commit the perfect crime. The guy was too crafty for his own good." Tim shut the trunk lid. "OK, let's go."

"If you left one hair on that uniform, they'll have your DNA."

"Are you suggesting I torch the cruiser?"

"Not at all, Tim."

"Then don't make provocative statements."

He took my keys and drove the Cordoba. The hideaway garage was in Martinez, overlooking the Carquinez Strait. I could see the lights of Benicia twinkling across the wide black void of the river. Tim backed the Cordoba up the driveway to the garage and popped the trunk lid.

"I hope my trunk is big enough," I whispered.

"Yeah, me too."

"Do you have any more of those gloves?"

"Inside the garage. Don't touch anything until you put them on."

"Don't worry about that!"

The black vinyl body bag looked enormous.

"You want to open the big door?" I asked, donning gloves.

"Nah, we'll drag him through the side door. You grab one end, I'll take the other."

We tugged, the bag moaned, I dropped my end.

"Jesus, Tim! He's still alive!"

"Not possible, Danny. He's been in there for nearly an hour with no air. These bags are air- and watertight. It's just a corpse passing gas. Let's go."

It was all we could do to lift the bag up into my trunk. It just fit. Guess those Chrysler engineers figured they'd sell a certain number of Cordobas to Mafia types. The shovel from the cruiser we stashed in my back seat.

"Where the hell is West Hartley?" I asked as Tim headed east on Highway 4. Hardly any cars on the road this time of night.

"Inland from Antioch according to the map. I never heard of the place."

"What if we can't find the grave?"

"Then we'll dig a new one. We got nearly four hours until it's light. How's your love life, Danny?"

"Rotten."

"Maeve says you've got some beauty on the go."

"Abby? Just a tease in a winsome package. Out of our league, Tim."

"Nobody's out of my league, Danny."

"Yeah. And we're proving it right now. What if he's not dead, and we're burying him alive?"

"He's dead, Danny. You can't live with a heart that's not beating."

"They used to have trouble with Old Sparky, Tim. Guys would take forever to die in the electric chair."

"They didn't have me doing the wiring. OK, I confess: he didn't die right away. He buzzed up and down a bit. I only had 110 volts to work with."

"Jesus, Tim. That's awful."

"He had worse planned for me!"

"Yeah, I guess so."

We discussed my efforts to cope with unemployment after our county jobs were terminated.

"I hope to have that bastard Darnel Petersen in my next body bag," said Tim.

"Jesus, Tim. Don't even joke about that. One murder is more than enough."

"I don't know, Danny. I think I'm starting to get the hang of it. Guys may learn it's dangerous to cross me."

We exited the highway and went down a series of deserted rural roads.

"I think around here is where they grow your fresh corn-on-the-cob," said Tim.

"Perhaps we'll come to a farmer's stand and you can ask for directions."

"I know where I'm going, Danny."

"I just hope it's not Death Row with me as your cell mate."

Tim pulled over beside a fallow field. The half moon illuminated some distant woods.

"This looks like the place, Danny. The cemetery should be somewhere in those woods over there."

"That's a long way to drag a body, Tim."

"Next time we'll bring a wheelbarrow. Or a pack mule. Let's go," said Tim, releasing the trunk lid.

We got out of the car and looked around. There were no houses within view; not a light could be seen.

"We're benefitting from Grizzoffski's thoroughness, Danny. I wonder how long he searched before he found the perfect place to ditch a body?"

"What if some car comes along, Tim?"

"We haven't seen a car in a half hour. The bars closed a while ago. Come on."

"I wish I'd thought to put on a jock strap, Tim. I can't believe how much that guy weighs."

"Six donuts a night, Danny. It packs on the pounds."

The bag made a sickening thud on the asphalt when we rolled it out of the trunk. More moans from the interior.

"Tim! I tell you! The guy's alive!"

"Shut up and drag, Danny."

It was a chilly night, but we were both panting and sweating by the time we reached the trees.

"OK, Danny, you go back and get the shovel. I'll poke around in the woods and see what I can find."

Another moan from the bag; Tim kicked the end containing the head.

When I returned with the shovel, I could see the light from Tim's flashlight flickering in the distance.

"Find anything?" I called.

"I see some old headstones. But I haven't found a hole yet."

I heard a cry, a loud thump, and a violent curse.

"Help me, Danny," yelled Tim. "Over here!"

I snaked my way through the dark tangle of trees toward

his voice; Tim had the only flashlight. I found him standing in a deep pit next to a mound of freshly dug earth.

"Help me out of here, Danny."

I extended the handle of the shovel for him to grab and tugged him up.

"That's one deep grave," I said, staring into the black abyss. "Do you think Grizzoffski dug this all by himself?"

"He must have, Danny. I don't think he wanted any accomplices on this job."

"How do we get his body past all these trees?"

"We muscle it. I don't know about you, but I got enough adrenalin flowing to heft a Humvee."

Tim did most of the tugging and pulling. It was a slow slog because the bag kept snagging on the undergrowth. I suggested we remove the body from the bag.

"No way, Danny. I don't want to see the guy again. As far as I'm concerned, we're just burying a sack of discards."

Eventually, we got the bag beside the pit.

"OK, Danny. On the count of three we roll it in."

"You want to say some words over him, Tim?"

"All right. Sorry you had to end this way, Grizzoffski. Next time you should try to raise a daughter who's not a tease and a slut. She was a great lay, but caused us all a lot of bother–you especially. Better luck next time. Amen. OK, Danny, let's roll him."

The bag thudded into the pit. No moans or screams were heard. Tim did the honors with the shovel. When the dirt got high enough, I jumped in and tamped it down as Tim shoveled away. In less than 40 minutes we had the hole filled in.

"It looks like a very fresh grave," I observed.

"You're right, Danny. Let's find branches and forest shit to cover it."

That took another 15 minutes. We were both dog tired and scratched up as we hurried toward the car.

"What do we do with the shovel?" I asked.

"We leave it on a residential street. Some amateur gardener will nab it."

Tim managed to start the Cordoba without flooding it. He did a U-turn at a wide point in the road and headed back the way we came.

"What are you going to do now?" I asked.

"Hole up in the garage until the excitement dies down. Then I'll show up and deny any knowledge of the affair. The guy was in the sheriff's department a long time. I'm sure he had other enemies besides me."

"I hope he had lots of them."

"He was a first-class prick, Danny. I'm sure he collected them by the gross. I don't know about you, but I'm feeling a sense of accomplishment here."

"Really?"

"We took care of business, guy. You and me together. We're still the best damn team the county ever saw."

"We did rise to the occasion, Tim."

"You just have to keep your lip buttoned, Danny. You can't say anything to the cops. You spill one word and I'll have to take you out too."

"I'm not saying anything, Tim. Jesus, I never realized you were this homicidal."

"Pushed up against a wall, Danny, we're all killers. It's the way guys are made. It's because our genitals are exposed and vulnerable. I'm just protecting my *cojones* here, Danny boy."

I always knew he was a Lothario and a thief. I never realized he was a nut case as well.

Tim smiled. "The forecast calls for rain by morning."

"Why is that good?"

"Rain will wash away our tracks across that field and compact the grave."

"In that case I hope it pours."

Tim switched the radio to a hard-rock station. I thought of Grizzoffski lying alone at the bottom of that pit. I hoped to hell he was deceased. I also hoped he wouldn't haunt me for the rest of my life. It's at times like this when a guy wishes he was a sociopath.

"I just had a thought," I said. "We're depriving his kiddies of their father at Christmas time."

"And what about me, Danny? He was planning to do the same to my daughter."

This poem I found wedged behind a plastic crucifix in a junked Cadillac hearse:

The Body in a Bag

Black vinyl shrouds human forms:
That lump is a foot, flopped sideways.
That shape to a face conforms.
A contour there its sex conveys.

Death sealed against oozing:
Packaged for disposal
In a place of your choosing.
A sunny plot on Rose Hill?

Or is your budget tighter?
There's a pit in the woods
To swallow the poor blighter.
A dump for unwanted goods

That will molder there,
Overlooked by the living.
To be recalled in a nightmare
Of wretchedness unforgiving.

Twenty-one/NERVOUS ANYONE?

My circadian clock has gone haywire. My body doesn't have a clue when it's supposed to sleep. It just knows I haven't been getting enough of it. I never went to bed. I drove in the rain to Tim's condo and somehow (mostly) stayed awake through sessions with Gene and Luke. Neither is making any progress that I can discern, but at this point that is the least of my worries.

I discovered my laptop isn't working. Tim must have reformatted my hard drive, wiping out the operating system and all my files. What was up with that? If I were attempting to be a writer, I'd be distraught over all the work he erased.

Later while attempting a nap I was shanghaied by Mrs. Goodsolm to erect her artificial Christmas tree. She asked me why I was once again visited by the cops–this time in the dead of night.

"Another robbery at the mini mart, Mrs. G," I yawned. "Boxes of Pampers have been disappearing mysteriously off the shelves."

"Probably some welfare mother with 10 kids and another in the oven. All with different deadbeat dads. Those women don't know the meaning of the word restraint. Did you hear about that deputy sheriff who disappeared?"

"Yeah, I heard about it on the radio."

"There's speculation it was an alien abduction. I understand all of his clothes were left behind."

"Were they scorched by some mysterious force?" I asked.

"I hadn't heard about that, Danny. I expect they're being tested in the lab right now."

"Why do you have a Christmas tree, Mrs. G? I thought you were Jewish."

"I am, Danny. This tree has no religious significance for me.

I install it in my front window to help make the street more festive. The so-called Christians on this block are too lazy to do it themselves."

"What a lovely rain," I said, looking out her big picture window.

"It's cold and dreary, Danny. What's lovely about it?"

"It's a good excuse to have some brandy."

"Only when we're finished here. You need to start stringing on those lights. How'd you get all those scratches on your hands?"

"I was helping Wenda at her cat rescue place. They had a wild one get loose in the store."

"Throw those cats in the bay is what I say, Danny. I thought you broke up with her."

"I did. I figured out I couldn't compete with those felines."

That evening Olivia dropped by my attic hovel to inquire about the missing deputy.

"Wasn't he the mean dude who accosted us that time in the restaurant?" she asked, flopping uninvited on my sofa. "The one who threatened to take you down?"

"Possibly, darling. I don't remember. You didn't visit me at the store on my last night. I was planning to give you a carton of wine coolers–for free!"

"I've given up alcohol, Danny. Jin doesn't like me to drink."

"Better you give up that guy and take up gin."

"I'm sure you remember that deputy, Danny. He was very nasty and threatening. He was planning to chop off some guy's head. You told him we were part of your prayer group."

"Oh, right. Officer Grizzoffski. I'm sure he'll turn up."

"Jin thinks he might have been kidnapped by someone to protest all those cops shooting unarmed black people."

"It's possible I suppose."

"You didn't kill him did you?"

"Certainly not. What do you take me for?"

"Just kidding, Danny. I'm kind of a mess. All I can think about is making it with Jin. Do you think he'll be up for it?"

"One can usually rely on the hormones of the teenage male. Make him use protection."

"Of course, I know that. Clare says sex is a big waste of time."

"You should try it and decide for yourself," I sighed.

"My body didn't do much for you."

"On the contrary, dear. I found it delightful in every respect."

"My boobs could be bigger."

"They also could be smaller. Be happy with what you've got."

"Shall I tell you about it after it happens?"

"OK, dear one. If you must."

"You're the only person I can really talk to, Danny."

"Well, dearest, you know where to find me."

* * *

The next day I was visited by Deputy Dudek, a guy I knew vaguely. He asked me if I'd seen Tim Chapben lately.

"Not for months, Ken. Last I heard he was down in Mexico."

"I understand he fled the country when Grizzoffski threatened his life."

"More like threatened to kick his butt is what I heard. Do they know what happened to Grizzoffski?"

"Not a clue apparently. If the detectives know anything, they're not sharing it with the team. Has Chapben called or emailed you?"

"No contact at all, Ken. Why would he? We don't work together anymore."

"I thought you two were buddies."

"Just coworkers. We didn't see each other outside the office. Do they think Tim is connected to this?"

"Just running down all the possibilities. If you hear from him, tell him to contact the department. We have some questions for him."

"Will do, Ken. I hope you find Grizzoffski."

"I couldn't care less about that, Nixon. The guy's a royal pain in the keister. I hope he's AWOL on a bender and they fire his fat ass when he shows up."

"Any results from searching his patrol car?"

"They found three joints under the front seat. Probably Griz-zoffski's. Ten million prints around the back seat, but that's to be expected. The rest of the car turned up zip."

"Have they tested his clothes?"

"Found a few stray hairs. Probably his. Be a few days for the DNA results."

"Oh, right."

Possibly dire news. Damn, we should have torched that car.

"How many deputies do they have looking for him?" I asked.

"Every spare man. I think the big brass suspect foul play. One more thing, Nixon. Where were you two nights ago?"

"Right here in bed."

"Were you with anyone who can vouch for that?"

"Unfortunately not. I just broke up with my girlfriend."

"The one who filed a TRO against you?"

"No. I had another one after that."

"The hairstyle's new," said Ken, pointing to my head. "How's that working out for attracting chicks?"

"It's helping," I lied.

"Is that a comb-over?"

For being in law enforcement, Ken Dudek always was clue-less.

"No, Ken. It's a toupee."

"Damn, you could have fooled me."

I certainly hope so.

No call from Vera cancelling her appointment. I should do the professional thing and charge her anyway. And no calls from potential therapines. Christmas is only ten days away. I thought everyone got depressed over the holidays. I'm always reliably suicidal this time of year. Neurotics should be clamor-ing for help to ease them over December's psychic minefields. At least I've cured my parents of ever expecting a gift from me. My continued absence is the most they can hope for. And even that is imperiled if my finances don't improve. Living with your parents at age 38? A celibate life in bleak Modesto? A crushing blow from which my sex life may never recover. On Christmas Day I may need to fall on my knees and accept the sacrament of Tim's booby-trapped doorknob.

* * *

Early Friday morning Ken Dudek came back. This time he had another deputy with him.

"They want to talk to you down at the station, Danny."

"Why?"

"Just routine."

"Let me grab a fast shower first. You got me out of bed."

"You're fine, Danny. Just put on your pants and let's go."

"What's this about?" I asked.

"I hear they want to show you a video. OK, let's move it."

"I need to tape on my hairpiece, Ken."

"You can skip that, Danny. No chicks to impress where we're going."

They didn't want to stop for coffee on the way or tell me anything more. They escorted me to an interview room and left. I could hear the door lock automatically behind them. A long way down that corridor was the office where I used to slave. I needed a cigarette in the worst way.

A few minutes later two detectives entered. I had seen them around, but didn't know them. The shorter one was in charge of the show. He introduced himself as Luis Sanchez. His taciturn partner was Tom O'Brien. Bad acne scars testified to a youth spent in front of a mirror obsessively squeezing.

"Danny Nixon, we missed you around here," said Sanchez, opening up a battered laptop.

"I doubt that," I said.

"No, Darnel Petersen was talking about you just the other day. He's not thrilled by the work those J.C. students are doing. He says every print job comes back looking like a flyer for a punk nightclub."

"Really? He said that?"

Had they dragged me down here to offer me my old job back?

"His exact words, Danny. Lots of misspellings too. So have you heard that one of our deputies has gone missing?"

217

"Yeah, it's all over the news."

"Deputy Grizzoffski. Did you know him?"

"I saw him around."

"Talk to him lately?"

"Not that I can recall."

"We got a video that might interest you, Danny. From a security camera on an auto parts store near where we found Grizzoffski's car."

Sanchez pressed a few keys on the laptop. The screen showed a grainy B&W video of a street at night. Grizzoffski's Crown Vic passed by, followed by my Cordoba–its spinning wheel spinners shining brightly. Duct tape on its roof flapped in the breeze. The view showed the passenger side of the cars. Thankfully, the faces of the drivers were too dim to make out.

Sanchez backed up the video and paused it on my car. "Recognize this distinctive automobile, Danny?"

"Yeah, that could be my Cordoba."

My next car is going to be the most anonymous-looking Toyota I can find.

"Yet you told Deputy Dudek you were home in bed that night."

"I forgot. I went out for some groceries."

"You forgot a lot of things about that night, Danny. We talked to your landlady. She looked out her bedroom window and saw you conversing with a deputy beside his cruiser. This transpired just a few minutes before the time recorded on our video."

I really needed a cigarette now. I cranked up my brain to maximum overdrive, yet its sluggish gears were processing mostly desperate pleas for nicotine, alcohol, and caffeine.

"OK," I said. "Grizzoffski visited me. I didn't say anything about it because he asked me not to."

"Now we're getting somewhere," said Sanchez. "Let's hear your story from the beginning, Danny."

"Could I get a cup of coffee and an ashtray?" I asked.

"No smoking in the building," said O'Brien, his stale breath reeking of cigarettes.

Sanchez pushed a button under the table. Dudek poked his head in from the corridor.

"A cup of coffee for our guest," said Sanchez.

It was the same miserable vending machine coffee I used to drink by the gallon.

"OK," I said. "Grizzoffski showed up at my door that night. I was surprised to see him. I barely knew the guy. He asked me to do him a favor."

"What kind of favor?" asked Sanchez.

"He said he needed a ride. He said he'd had some business dealings with guys that had gone sour. He needed to leave town for a while. He needed a ride in a car that they wouldn't recognize."

"So why did he come to you?" asked Sanchez.

"I asked him the same thing. He said I was the one guy he could think of that had no real connection to the sheriff's department. And he figured I'd be home alone."

"Why did you agree to help him?" asked Sanchez.

"You know Grizzoffski. He can be very intimidating. I couldn't see any way to refuse him. He said if I told anyone about it, he would come back and hurt me bad."

"He threatened your life?" asked O'Brien.

"It sure felt like it to me. And I knew how he'd been menacing Tim Chapben."

"For screwing his daughter?" said Sanchez.

"Right."

"So you followed him in your car to where he parked his cruiser," said Sanchez.

"Right. I stayed in my car while he changed his clothes."

"So now what was he wearing?" asked Sanchez.

"I don't know. Dark pants, dark shirt. Denim jacket maybe. I wasn't paying attention. Civilian clothes."

"Did he have anything with him? Like a suitcase?"

"More like a gym bag. Not that big."

"So where did you go after that?"

"He had me drive out Highway 4 toward Antioch. We got off at an exit. He got out of the car and that was the last I saw of him. Then I drove home and went back to bed. End of story."

It was the best I could come up with. I knew I had to divulge our drive out Highway 4 in case they came up with any more videos from security cameras along that route.

"You drove him all the way to Antioch?" said Sanchez. "That's a long way. What did you talk about?"

"We didn't talk."

"Why not?"

"He seemed preoccupied and I was scared."

"Why were you scared?"

"Because it was the middle of the night. Because I was with a guy who frightened me."

"Did he say he was meeting someone?"

"He didn't say anything about that. He just said he needed a ride to that location. He was being very vague and secretive. And I didn't want to know the details."

"Why not? Weren't you curious?"

"I didn't want to get mixed up in his business. I was most relieved when he got out of the car."

"What did he say at that point?"

"He said to go home and keep my damn mouth shut."

"Did he walk away? Did he get in another car?"

"I don't think so. I don't know. I beat it out of there. I didn't watch him in my mirrors. Can I go home now?"

Fat chance of that. They had me repeat my story. Endlessly. At every point in the tale they had questions and more questions. They left the room for a time, then came back with more questions. A lot of them were about me. They asked me about the scratches on my hands. They wanted to know what I'd been doing since I was fired by the county. How I was making a living? Did I deal drugs out of the mini mart? Was I paying off Grizzoffski? Fantasy questions that assumed I was some big-time hoodlum. Lunchtime came and went; I hadn't eaten all day. I could sense my blood sugar plummeting in my veins. If it got any lower, I'd pass out in the chair. My head ached and I was beginning to shake.

"Why are your hands shaking?" asked Sanchez.

"Because I need a drink."

"Why do you need a drink?"

"Because I'm an alcoholic."

"Since when, Danny?"

"Since I was 17."

"Why would Grizzoffski recruit an alcoholic to drive him to Antioch?"

"You'll have to ask him that."

"I can believe you're a drunk" commented O'Brien. "Your whole story sounds like one big hallucination."

They told me they had impounded my car and obtained a warrant to search my apartment.

"Why?" I asked. "You won't find anything. You know everything that I know about Grizzoffski. All I did was give him a ride. I'm just an unemployed mini-mart clerk. Would I be living in that dump of an apartment if I was a drug dealer?"

"Explain the pimp car, Danny," said Sanchez. "What's that all about? Your landlady says you have teenage girls coming and going at all hours of the night. Were you paying protection to Grizzoffski? Did he welch on the deal, so you had him snuffed?"

"None of the above. The only girl visiting me was my ex-girl-friend, and she's 29. My landlady is ancient. Every chick under 40 looks like a teenager to her."

It was like the worst nightmare of my life. Except it was really happening. I knew it wasn't going to stop either. I was the only link they had to Grizzoffski's disappearance. They were the rabid terriers and I was the only bone they had. No way they were going to let go of me. They were going to chew on me until I went stark raving mad.

The only good news: clearly, they weren't much interested in Grizzoffski's feud with Tim Chapben. Fine with me. I may have been going nuts, but I was blowing a thick, dark smoke-screen over that part of the story.

The detectives left again. They didn't tell me where they were going. Dudek escorted me to the men's room, then let me buy a sandwich and a candy bar from the vending machines. He wouldn't let me grab a smoke outside. Too bad I hadn't had time to pack my cellphone flask and my nicotine gum. My old boss Gladys passed by and pretended she didn't know me. I ate my lunch alone in the interview room. They hadn't confiscated my belt and shoelaces, so I could have offed myself. I decided not to give them the satisfaction. Several hours passed, and then Sanchez and O'Brien returned with some fresh evidence against me.

"Tell us about these checks, Danny," said Sanchez, laying out a couple of my undeposited therapy payments. Evidently they'd been out ransacking my apartment.

"It's perfectly clear," said O'Brien, whose breath now smelled of cigarettes and beer. (I was envious of his lifestyle.) "These are checks from johns paying for your prostitutes."

"Not at all," I replied. "I do counseling. Informally, on the side."

"Counseling on what?" asked Sanchez.

"Oh, minor personality and domestic issues. I'm a good listener. Troubled people come to me for help."

"I know Gene Crosley of Crosley Towing," said Sanchez. "The only thing that troubles that guy is missing a car to tow."

"You'd be surprised. I can assure you these checks represent entirely legitimate income."

"Don't you have to be licensed to do counseling?" asked Sanchez.

"Not if you're doing it in a religious capacity," I said.

"Oh, so now you're claiming to be a minister?"

"I'm a layperson with a spiritual bent," I lied. "I'm part of a long tradition of helping others."

"Helping others get their rocks off," scoffed O'Brien. "With minors! At $125 a pop!"

It was now clear that he was the designated bad cop of this duo.

"Get real," I said. "Nobody pays for a prostitute with a check. You'd have to be a moron to do that. And half my clients are women. You can check the deposits I've made."

"They're paying you $125 to bang them?" asked O'Brien, incredulous.

"Don't be absurd. You guys are really off the track here. I say arrest me for something or let me go."

"Calm down, Danny," said Sanchez, playing the good cop. "We're just trying to get to the bottom of things. You have to admit your story is pretty improbable."

"I've explained everything a dozen times. I've told you everything I know. In the immortal words of the original Richard Nixon: I am not a crook."

"Could be," said Sanchez. "Except he turned out to be a lying asshole."

"Like father like son," added his partner.

"My father is a retired roofing salesman in Modesto."

"We took a clear set of Grizzoffski's prints off the front passenger window of your car," said O'Brien.

That actually was good news. The dead deputy must have been snooping around my car at some point. Good thing I never wash my vehicles.

"Proving what?" I asked. "I already told you I drove him to Antioch. The prints confirm my story."

"Do they, Luis?" asked O'Brien.

"They don't prove jack shit. How come you erased your laptop memory, Danny? What were you trying to hide?"

"Uh, I was drunk one night and hit the wrong keys."

"That was certainly convenient," said O'Brien. "For you!"

"Normally the contents of a hard drive can be recovered," added Sanchez. "Except in your drunken state, you thought to record random gibberish over every sector."

Tim always was good with computers. Thank God he'd been on the ball that night. We don't need the cops poking around any "abandoned cemeteries in West Hartley."

And it's not like extinguishing a lifetime of my literary efforts was any great loss.

Insert poem here.

Not bloody likely. No poet in history ever produced a work on the theme of the day I just experienced.

Twenty-two/END IN VIEW

It was dark by the time they finally let me go. I power-smoked two Chesterfields, then made a beeline for a liquor store down the block. I bought a pint of their cheapest rye whiskey and guzzled it out of the brown bag on the bus ride home.

When I got there, Mrs. Goodsolm was on the warpath.

"Cops have been in and out of here all day, Danny. They towed your car. What's going on?"

"Nothing criminal, Mrs. G. I foolishly made the mistake of doing a favor for that deputy who's been in the news. I knew him from my county job. They were thinking I might know something about his disappearance—which I don't. It's all a big misunderstanding."

"I'm sorry, Danny. I can't have my tenant mixed up in police business. At my age I require a placid life. I want you out of here tomorrow."

"But, Mrs. G, none of this is my fault. I'm the innocent party!"

"Too much smoking and drinking and partying with teenagers, Danny. Your lifestyle is out of control. My mistake for renting to a bachelor. I know for a fact you smoke in bed. And do God knows what else there. You could burn the house down at any time. No, you're out of here tomorrow."

"How can I leave, Mrs. G? They towed my car!"

"That's your problem. Be out by noon. That's the time I'm having the locks changed on your door."

Damn. You help a friend move a body, and your entire life tumbles down around you.

My attic hovel was in total disarray. That's its usual state, of course. Only a critical eye could discern the extra disruption caused by Sanchez and his henchmen. All my drawers had been rifled. My laptop was gone, also my bank records, tax files, and undeposited checks. Someone had drunk the two beers in my fridge (probably O'Brien). Quite a few of Dennis's cigars were missing, including all the Cubans. (They had left behind the cheaper brands.) My dirty-clothes basket had been dumped out on my unmade bed. And where the fuck was the foam head with my toupee?

I was working on a bottle of tequila and a bad case of despair when I must have passed out.

The next morning I phoned Delia. She drove over and helped me load my stuff in her Subaru wagon. The ratty furniture I left as my gift to the next occupant.

"What happened, Danny?" she asked, when we were underway. "You weren't very coherent on the phone."

"My landlady has dementia. Going downhill fast. Last night she decided I was the Antichrist. She gave me until noon to vacate the premises."

"That's awful, Danny. Frankly, I'm surprised you were living in such a place."

"It's not usually so unkempt. She went a bit berserk last night."

"Well, it's all for the best. You're welcome to stay with me, Danny."

"I'm not quite who you think I am, Delia. I'm a few units short of my master's degree. I've been practicing without a license."

"That sounds like just a technicality, Danny. I'm sure you're helping your patients."

"I've been doing my best. One of my clients couldn't get a date. Now she's away on her honeymoon."

"That's wonderful, Danny. I'm sure you did her a world of good. Our talks have been helping me. No question about that. And where is your car?"

"Apparently stolen. It disappeared from Safeway's lot when I was buying a cantaloupe."

"That's terrible. And where is your nice new humidor? I didn't see it in your apartment."

"Still in the trunk of my car," I lied. "I just pray it's there if my car is recovered. The cops suspect teenage joy-riders, so I may get it back."

"Let's hope so. What a string of bad luck, Danny."

She doesn't know the half of it.

"And what happened to your nice toupee?"

"Torn asunder by my landlady in a fit of religious fervor. I think it was my sudden manifestation of hair that sent her around the bend."

"That's awful. Doesn't she have any family? You could demand compensation from them."

"That's a thought, but I don't want to add to her burdens."

"You're so selfless, Danny. Really, you're like a saint."

Except for the art on the walls, Delia's guest room was quite nice. This must be the room where she consigns art acquisitions that didn't quite work out. I did my laundry in her gleaming machines and folded everything away neatly in drawers. No point abusing her hospitality by being a slob. I also phoned Culver to cancel today's appointment.

"I'm suspending my practice until further notice," I told her.

"I was worried you were going to do that, Dr. Nixon. Was it something I said?"

"Not at all. You've been a model patient. How did things go with you this week?"

"Not too bad. I've been repeating your mantra about things getting better and better. I drop the needle on that thought whenever I start to worry."

"That's the ideal record for you, Culver. You should play it as much as possible."

"I visualize a jukebox keypad, Dr. Nixon. I press A-12 for that thought. All my worries are under the B listings. I try not to play them."

"Very good."

"Please let me know, Dr. Nixon, if you start up your practice again. I'd love to meet with you some more."

"I'll do that, Culver."

"Have a wonderful holiday, Dr. Nixon."

"You too, dear."

I also left a message on Luke's phone. He called me back sounding distraught.

"You can't be suspending your practice, Dr. Nixon. My sessions with you are the only part of my life that feel real."

"Face it, Luke. We weren't making much progress. You're not willing to change."

"I want to change, Dr. Nixon. I do!"

"Luke, you say you want to be an actor. You won't get anywhere hiding out here in the burbs. You need to quit your job and move to New York or Los Angeles."

"Really? You think so?"

"That's where the action is, Luke. Plus, you'd get away from your toxic roommate."

"But I love Tina."

"Get a clue, guy. She doesn't love you and never will. She's playing you for a sucker. She enjoys tormenting you!"

"Are therapists allowed to say such things?"

"I'm not your therapist any more, Luke. Take my advice: leave town. The sooner the better. Your life will feel real when you start living it. When you start working toward what you want. I gotta go. Have a nice life."

I hung up on the guy. I hope some of what I said sunk in.

Delia made lunch while I spooned some strained peas into Brynn. When we sat down to eat, she said she had a proposition for me.

"I need childcare, Danny, and a general dogsbody. Someone to run errands, answer the phone, go to the store, etc. If you're interested, I could pay you $200 a week, plus room and board. Perhaps a bit more when my work picks up again."

"Sounds fine to me, Delia."

"One thing, Danny. Since you'd be my employee, I don't think we should add sex to the mix."

"Right, I understand."

"It might be too confusing to Brynn. And to us."

"Very true. I couldn't agree more."

If there's one concept I understood, it was celibacy.

"And no smoking in the house, even when I'm not here. We have to think of Brynn's pristine little lungs."

"Certainly, dear. Not a problem."

"And you might think about joining AA. They meet in that church down on the corner. It would be very convenient."

"Right. I'll think about that."

"Good, Danny. I think this is going to work out splendidly."

"I hope so, dear."

I decided it would be churlish to point out that she will be getting 16 weeks of my services for the price of my confiscated sales commission. And here I'd been thinking I might be one of those houseguests of indefinite duration in the grand tradition of Kato Kaelin of O.J. Simpson fame. No such luck.

* * *

Detective Sanchez called me a few days later.

"We checked your phone records, Danny. You weren't making or receiving any calls from Grizzoffski."

"That's what I told you."

"So it doesn't look like you were doing business with him."

"I wasn't."

"We checked Grizzoffski's bank records. There are a few deposits his wife can't explain. So he may have been bent like you implied."

"He told me there were guys after him."

"So it seems. I wish he had given you a hint where he was going."

"He's in law enforcement. He knows the score. A smart guy wouldn't have told me as much as he did."

"Anyway, thanks for your cooperation, Danny."

"I want my car back, Sanchez. Also my laptop, my bank records, my checks, my cigars, and my toupee."

"You can get your car back from Crosley Towing. I think you know where that is. The rest you can pick up here at the front desk. I don't know anything about missing cigars or wigs."

"If I see Tim Chapben, do you still want to talk to him?"

"Only if he wants to talk to me. I've got plenty on my plate as it is."

"Dudek said you were testing some hairs from Grizzoffski's uniform."

"Two from Grizzoffski and three from his rottweiler. Another dead end. You living in the same place?"

"Hardly. You guys scared the hell out of my landlady. It cost me my apartment. I'm staying with a friend."

"Sorry, Danny. We did what we had to do. You take care."

"Yeah, you too."

Delia dropped me off at the Crosley Towing yard. The gal behind the counter said I owed $378 for towing and storage. I asked to speak to her boss Gene. He invited me into his office. Pretty fancy, with deluxe hardwood desk, swanky leather executive chair, shelves displaying colorful scale-model cars, and the big wide sofa.

"Have a seat, Nixon. Or do you want to work out payment right now on my couch?"

"What?"

"Just kidding. Apparently you're not a real therapist. What's that about?"

"I'm a real therapist, Gene. I'm just not fully licensed."

"Not licensed at all is what I heard. You were some sort of low-level serf for the county until you got fired. Makes a fellow feel like he's been used."

"Sorry, Gene. I was sincerely trying to help you."

"Where's your pricey wig? I'm getting a bad glare off your scalp."

"It disappeared. I'm looking for it now."

"I could beat the shit out of you, Nixon. I got a tire iron right here under my desk. I could knock off those glasses and rearrange your face. I could put a few more dings in that naked skull of yours."

"That wouldn't solve anybody's problems, Gene."

"Might make me feel better though."

"We both had some bad days, Gene. Can I get my car back?"

"You think I should stop with the stealing?"

"You have a lot to lose if you get caught. You know that. All those shakers stored in your garage are a burden on your psyche. Did you steal these model cars?"

"Most of them I bought. Are you going to spill to anyone about me?"

"Certainly not."

"OK, Nixon," he said, tearing up the paperwork and tossing over my keys. "Take your car and go. Why do you drive such a piece of shit?"

"It's just a thing I have. I like stuff from the year of my birth."

"Oh, yeah? Maybe you should see a therapist about that."

"Yeah, I probably should."

The interior of my Cordoba was trashed. Not a surprise. I drove to the courthouse for the rest of my stuff. No foam head or accompanying toupee. Looks like my brief fling with a full head of hair is over. Oh well, that double-sided tape was starting to itch. After that I went to Bottle Chalet and the post office, where I filed a change of address card. God forbid my credit card bill should go astray. The bottles I plan to keep in the trunk of my car. I'll take a toot behind Delia's garage when I grab a smoke.

* * *

On Christmas Eve I got a call from Tim. He's out of his hideaway and back in his condo. We spoke in generalities in case anyone was listening in.

"Thanks for being such a pal, Danny."

"Don't mention it."

"I got my old job back."

"What!"

"Yeah. Got a call from Darnel Petersen himself. Those clueless students were driving him batty. I'm back and so's the photocopier. Right next door to Gladys now, since the sheriff grabbed our old office."

"How come they didn't call me?"

"I don't think Darnel's your biggest fan, Danny. I really need this job. I missed some mortgage payments. Plus I'm in arrears on my child support. Looks like I'll be cranking up my eBay business too."

"Yeah, I expect you'll have to. What about your court case?"

"I've been discussing that with Mrs. Grizzoffski. She's more sympathetic than her husband. I may be headed to the altar with her sex-kitten daughter."

"Really?"

"She says she's running wild in the streets. She thinks marriage to me could be a stabilizing influence."

"You want to marry that girl?"

"Better her than jail, Danny."

"Keep me posted, Tim. I'll send you a wedding gift."

"We'll need lots of stuff, since you sold off most of my worldly goods."

"Just trying to help."

"Good thing I got my old job back. Only 25 more years till I collect my pension."

"I envy you, Tim. Did Mrs. Grizzoffski say anything about her missing husband?"

"She thinks he ran off with some babe. Apparently, he had a long history of fooling around. Kind of hypocritical of him if you ask me. I don't think she's missing the guy that much. So how's your love life, Danny?"

"I'm living with a gal now. Former homecoming queen, if you can believe that."

"Glad to hear it. I hope she's orifice-accommodating."

"So far so good," I lied.

"That reminds me, Danny, these framed items of yours, do you want them back?"

"Nah, you can heave them."

"I may keep the frames. They're pretty nice. Might use 'em for the new wedding photos."

"My gift to you, Tim. How's your neighbor Maeve?"

"In Nevada, Danny. She ran off this week to marry that scarred-up guy. What's his name?"

"Owen."

"Yeah, Owen. Not a face I'd want to wake up to, but as we all know, chicks are different."

"That they are, Tim. That they are."

The next day we opened presents around the Christmas tree. Delia gave me two nice shirts and a camera for taking videos of Brynn. Parents figure they'll be watching those kiddy antics 20 years down the road, but I have my doubts. I gave her a $25 gift card to Outback Steakhouse. I figure she'd like a break from the stove sometimes. Brynn made out like a bandit, but he's still too young to revel in the joys of materialism.

After lunch I called home. I talked to my mother, which wasn't too bad. She said they really appreciated my card.

I received a couple of cards, including one from Olivia. Inside she wrote: "It was better than I expected. Love, O." I'd send a card to Abby if I had her address.

I'm watching Brynn while Delia takes a nap. I think she's been overdoing it a bit. So I've been initiated into the full baby-care regimen. I'm now vice president in charge of wiping the kid's ass.

Ever wonder why birthrates fall precipitously in richer countries? It's because people with alternatives in life simply refuse to deal with diapers.

But after 38 years on this planet I've learned that life hands you shit by the carload. It's just something you have to deal with. Too bad the baby variety is such a messy stink fest. Now I see why people get permanently warped by parents pushing that premature toilet-training. I'm so ready to run out and get a potty chair for Brynn. Or a cork at the least. Let the neuroses chips fall where they may.

Speaking of which, I strolled down to that church last Friday to check out the meeting. My first visit ever with that crew. A bigger crowd than usual because of the holidays. Best coffee I've had in a while. Some of the sober chicks smiled in a friendly way, suggesting I didn't make their skin crawl. I may be back.

This poem I found stuck under the last diaper in a jumbo box of Pampers:

Endings

The final word is nigh.
No more of this tale be told.
Some lives and lies and then a sigh.
A wink of time, a trail gone cold.

And what of this childishness?
Phantoms conjured out of fluff.
A scribbler's relief from idleness:
A laugh for you and that's enough.

The spotlight dims, the pen runs dry,
Yet he lingers on this last page.
In vain he makes a final try
To dance upon his empty stage.